Event Board

A private reception for the President and First Lady will be held in the courtyard this evening. Please note that admission is by invitation only, and the courtyard will be closed to resort guests until tomorrow morning. We apologize for any inconvenience.

The Clubhouse will be open from 8:00 a.m. today.

Golf, tennis, swimming and the health spa are available for your enjoyment. Refreshments are available at the juice bar. Horseback riding can be arranged from the Bride's Bay stable.

GUEST REGISTER

The President and
First Lady of the United States

Mr. Arthur Rumbaugh

General and Mrs. Burkhoff

Adam Hopewell

Madeline Hopewell

Connie Bennett

MARRIED TO A STRANGER

Harlequin Books

TORONTO • NEW YORK • LONDON
AMSTERDAM • PARIS • SYDNEY • HAMBURG
STOCKHOLM • ATHENS • TOKYO • MILAN
MADRID • WARSAW • BUDAPEST • AUCKLAND

This one is for Jacqui,
a new friend who seems more like an old one

ISBN 0-373-70695-2

MARRIED TO A STRANGER

Copyright © 1996 by Harlequin Books S.A.

ABOUT THE AUTHOR

Missouri author Connie Bennett is no stranger to
Superromance readers. *Married to a Stranger* is her tenth
Superromance novel. Her ninth, *Single...With Children,*
was a RITA finalist last year. But whether or not you're
familiar with Connie's earlier books, you're in for a real
treat when you read *Married to a Stranger!*

Books by Connie Bennett

HARLEQUIN SUPERROMANCE

HARLEQUIN INTRIGUE

HARLEQUIN AMERICAN ROMANCE

Dear Reader,

Welcome back to Bride's Bay, where excitement and intrigue are on the menu this month as the staff of the luxury resort prepares for a very important guest. The President of the United States is coming to spend his vacation here. Unfortunately, an infamous assassin, known as the Raven, is also planning to visit the resort. The only person who may be able to foil the plot to kill the president is a lovely amnesia victim who finds herself *Married to a Stranger* on her second honeymoon at Bride's Bay.

Writing about Bride's Bay allowed me the opportunity to do some really exciting on-site research on historic plantations throughout the south. My only regret is that Bride's Bay is purely fictional. I'd love to spend a week or so there myself...after the Raven is captured, of course.

If you enjoy *Married to a Stranger*, I'd love to know. Please drop me a line at P.O. Box 14, Dexter, MO 63841. If you'll include an SASE, I'll reply as quickly as I can.

All my best,

Connie Bennett

PROLOGUE

HE LOOKED like a hospital janitor. He wore the appropriate khaki coveralls, and his clip-on badge seemed completely authentic. He had a rag mop, a rolling bucket of tepid water and a yellow plastic board that read: Caution Wet Floor! The name he had invented for himself had even been placed into the hospital's computer so that if anyone challenged his presence he would seem perfectly legitimate.

But he wasn't a janitor.

Using the mop handle for leverage, he rolled the bucket forward, moving a few feet closer to the nurses' station. It was time for the shift change, and the head nurse was giving her report to the nurses clustered behind the desk. None of them noticed the man with the mop, and none of them would be able to identify him later if they were called on to describe him. Disguises were his specialty. Even without props like the mop and bucket he could assume a hundred different personas, project a hundred false images. Tonight he was an anonymous, aging Hispanic janitor. Tomorrow, if he had to return to the hospital he might become a muscular blond doctor of Swedish descent or a plump, sweet-faced nurse. Whatever it took to get the job done.

He edged farther down the hall with the mop, surreptitiously darting glances around the counter of the nurses' station until he could see the cop. The good one was on duty tonight—the one who stood his guard by the door, instead of sitting lazily in a chair across the hall; who never allowed himself to be distracted by the nurses and meticulously questioned anyone who lingered too long near the room of the woman he was guarding.

He didn't allow himself to be disappointed by the presence of the diligent guard, instead of the lazy one who shared the boring duty. If it became necessary to eliminate the woman tonight, the good cop wouldn't be hard to dispose of—not for a professional assassin like the Raven. He had killed heads of state, corporate magnates and cabinet ministers. One underpaid uniformed policeman wouldn't be a problem.

The assassin kept playing his role, completely ignoring the policeman now, and listening intently to the patient progress reports until he heard the one he wanted.

"Four-seventeen," the head nurse finally said, referring to the patients by room number, instead of name. "Her condition is stable, but we're to continue regular monitoring of the EEG. Dr. Manion has ordered another MRI scan first thing tomorrow, so have her ready to be taken downstairs before shift change in the morning."

"How's she doing?" another of the nurses asked.

"She's stronger and growing more frustrated, but other than that, there's been no significant change."

"She had nightmares last night, but couldn't remember them when she woke up," the nurse informed her superior.

"That's typical, given the kind of blunt trauma she suffered. Just keep a close eye on her tonight," the head nurse replied, then went on to other patients.

The assassin's face remained immobile, but inside he smiled. The woman's condition hadn't changed. There was no reason to rush the job. She wasn't going anywhere and for the time being she couldn't do him any harm. He had plenty of time to plan her termination carefully.

Of course there was no question that the woman had to be killed. Not only could she identify him, she knew when and where he would make his next kill. Loose ends like the woman in four-seventeen were dangerous. The Raven couldn't allow her to live.

His first attempt to eliminate her had been made hastily, and it hadn't been successful. This time, though, he would take more care and do it right. He had never failed before, and he'd spent too many months setting this plan in motion to even consider the possibility of failure now. He was being paid well to assassinate the President of the United States, and he wouldn't allow anyone to come between him and the biggest kill of his career.

Very soon the only person in the world who had enough information to stop him would be dead.

And the President would be next.

CHAPTER ONE

SHE LOOKED so fragile. The starched, white hospital linens emphasized her deathly paleness, and the machines around her bed made her seem delicate and defenseless. At the moment Madeline Hopewell looked nothing at all like the picture Adam kept of her in his mind. That woman was vibrant and vigorous, colorful, and so beautiful it almost hurt to look at her. The woman in the hospital bed was still beautiful, of course, but now there was a vulnerable quality that hadn't been there before.

Adam stood outside the room watching Maddy through the observation window, trying to decide what he should be feeling. His wife was lying here in a South Carolina hospital bed. He should've been distressed, overwrought. Frightened, even. But for now, there was nothing but an empty space where his emotions should have been.

She stirred, just a slight flutter of movement, and then was still again. Adam couldn't blame her for not wanting to wake up. After what she'd been through and what she was facing, it wouldn't be surprising if her subconscious kept her asleep for a very long time.

"She's going to be all right, Mr. Hopewell."

Adam forced his attention away from the hospital bed and looked at the white-coated physician beside him. "Are you sure of that, Dr. Manion?"

The doctor gave him a reassuring smile. "I know this must seem very new and alarming since you've only just arrived, but we've had her under observation for five days now. She was unconscious for the first forty-eight hours, but she's responded beautifully to treatment. There are no broken bones and the intercranial pressure that resulted from the concussion is gone. Medically speaking, she's out of danger."

"But what about..." Adam stumbled over the words because he couldn't bring himself to believe the diagnosis. "What about the amnesia?"

"Temporary," the doctor reassured him. "Most amnesia is."

"She doesn't remember anything?" Adam asked incredulously.

"No. Nothing about herself, at least. But her language skills are intact and she seems to have a good grasp of the world around her." When Adam frowned in confusion, Manion explained, "She not only remembers most words, she knows their meanings and how to apply them. Some amnesiacs have to relearn simple functions, like tying their shoes. Some don't even remember what shoes are. But your wife's memory loss isn't that total. That's why I'm confident it will return in time—probably in small increments. There is always the possibility that it will come back all at once, of course."

Adam shook his head. It was just so hard to accept. "How did this happen? How *could* it happen?"

"The human brain is a very delicate instrument, Mr. Hopewell. A blow like the one your wife received can do a lot of damage. We're lucky it wasn't much worse." Manion hesitated a moment before continuing, "But there's also another possibility to be considered. Concussive amnesia is the most likely diagnosis, but considering the circumstances, this could also be a case of hysterical amnesia."

Adam shook his head. "Maddy isn't the type," he said forcefully. "She's never been afraid to face anything."

Manion's eyebrows shot up. "Even attempted murder?"

Adam's gaze slid automatically to the uniformed policeman at Maddy's door. Just minutes ago, the officer had questioned him intensely, insisting that he provide proper identification to prove that Madeline Hopewell was really his wife. He had produced enough documentation to satisfy the policeman, but Adam wasn't ready to consider the significance of the officer's presence yet.

Instead, he told Manion, "You don't know Maddy, or you wouldn't ask that. She's a very strong woman. She can handle just about anything."

"I hope you're right, because these next few weeks are going to be difficult. For both of you," he added gravely. "As you can imagine, she's very frustrated right now. She keeps straining to remember, but nothing is coming to her. Her life's a blank slate, and it's going to be your job to help her fill in those blanks."

"Of course I will," Adam said with a touch of impatience. "I'll do anything it takes to help her remember." He looked through the observation window again and his shoulders stiffened. The head of Madeline's bed was elevated. "She's awake. I want to see her," he said, making a sudden move toward the door, but Manion scrambled to block his path.

"Not just yet, Mr. Hopewell. Please don't be hasty."

Adam stood several inches taller than the physician, and he used his superior height to its fullest effect. "Hasty? My wife is alone and confused. I want to see her. Comfort her."

Manion didn't back down. "Naturally. But at the moment you have to consider what's best for her."

Adam's scowl deepened. "Are you saying that a visit from me could be detrimental to her recovery?"

"At this very instant? Frankly, yes." The doctor sighed and adopted a more conciliatory tone—one filled with genuine sympathy. "Mr. Hopewell, I don't think you've had time to grasp the full impact of what I've told you regarding your wife's condition. She doesn't remember *anything* about her life, and the identification she had on her at the time of her injury told us almost nothing about her except her name." He paused a second. "Not only will Madeline not remember you specifically, she doesn't even know she *has* a husband. Realizing she's forgotten a relationship that intimate is going to be a great emotional shock. She has to be prepared for it. You can't just walk in there and say 'Hi, honey, I'm home.'"

Adam didn't like relinquishing control of any situation, but in this instance he had to do things Manion's way. "All right," he conceded, backing away from the door. "How do you suggest we proceed?"

Manion nodded in approval. "Let me speak with her first and prepare her. It will be better for both of you if she has a chance to absorb the shock before she meets you."

Adam nodded. "Whatever you think best."

"And when you do see her, it's important that you not push," Manion added. "Let Madeline set the tone of the meeting. Answer her questions, but don't try to elicit emotions from her that she simply isn't capable of feeling yet. You're going to have to be very patient with her."

"I understand."

"I hope so." The doctor gave him an encouraging smile. "Now, why don't you have a seat in the waiting room around the corner while I talk to her? I'll come get you as soon as she's ready. It won't be long, Mr. Hopewell. I promise."

Adam glanced at the observation window again, but his movement toward the door had removed Maddy's bed from his line of sight. It wasn't easy to fight the urge to return to the window for another look at her, to stand there watching as Manion told her she had a husband. Adam needed to see her reaction to the news—to see if it shocked her into remembering who she was and how she came to be in this Charleston hospital.

As if he'd read Adam's mind, Dr. Manion stepped between him and the window, gesturing toward the waiting room. "Please, Mr. Hopewell. For your wife's sake, let me do this my way."

Adam had to concede. There was no other choice. He had to do what was best for Maddy.

With great reluctance, he nodded and allowed Manion to escort him around the corner. He took a seat and waited.

As always, the panic hit her the moment she woke up. It didn't matter if it was the middle of the night or after a morning nap, the result was always the same. As soon as consciousness dawned, the unsettling sense of not knowing where she was washed over her, making her feel disoriented and out of control. She lay very still, fighting for calm. Then, opening her eyes and turning her head, she recognized her hospital surroundings.

That was when the real panic hit. That was when her adrenaline soared and her hands began to tremble, when her breathing became harsh and irregular. That was when she wanted to scream or cry, wanted to run and run until she left this waking nightmare behind.

That was when she was engulfed by the deep black hole where her memories should have been, and she had to fight the horror of not knowing *who* she was. She started by controlling her breathing. She forced her hands to be still. She reminded herself that she couldn't run because there was no place to run *to*. As she had for the past three days, she gained control over her fear by distancing herself from it. She enforced a sense of calm detachment on her psyche, and though it was entirely artificial, so far it had kept her from going insane.

Focusing on her physical condition sometimes helped, too. She had learned yesterday afternoon that if she moved very slowly her body didn't scream with pain and her head didn't throb as fiercely, so now she inclined her bed a few inches at a time, then eased up the rest of the way on her own until she was sitting on the edge of the bed.

Except for the IV tube that pierced her hand, the machines that had been monitoring her recovery had all been disconnected when she was taken downstairs for an MRI scan earlier this morning. No one had come to hook them up again, and she was grateful.

Being free of the machines made her feel a little less vulnerable.

It was one small step, not much of an improvement certainly, but anything was better than the feeling of total helplessness she'd had since awakening three days ago with a blinding pain in her head and a thousand questions she couldn't even begin to answer. Everyone was calling her Madeline Hopewell, but nothing inside of her embraced that identity or told her anything about this Hopewell woman.

Still moving slowly, she turned her head toward the wall mirror that hung over the lavatory. The woman who stared back at her had a dark bruise on her temple that spilled out under the edges of the thick bandage taped to her forehead. Her tousled hair was dark and straight, almost long enough to touch her shoulders. Her eyes were an odd shade of gray, her nose was a little too thin and her lips a little too full. With a bit of color in her cheeks and some carefully applied makeup, her face would probably be considered an attractive one.

But it was a stranger's face—as alien as her name, and the emptiness she felt was terrifying.

Nothing made sense. The police said that someone had tried to kill her, but they didn't know who or why. She'd been here five days, yet no one had filed a missing-persons report on her. The police had conducted an intensive media campaign, displaying her photograph on every TV station and newspaper in the city, asking anyone who recognized her to come forward, but no one had.

It was as if she didn't exist.

Out of the corner of her eye, she saw the door move and she froze, fighting the urge to grab something for protection. She knew there was a policeman outside, but that didn't comfort her. Somehow she knew she couldn't—and *shouldn't*—count on him to keep her safe.

Unfortunately, though, there was nothing handy to use as a weapon, and before she could think clearly enough to improvise, Dr. Manion stepped through the door. She relaxed. She was safe for the moment.

"Good morning, Madeline."

There it was again—the name that didn't fit the unfamiliar face in the mirror. "Hello, Dr. Manion," she said with a cheerfulness that was all a facade. She suspected the doctor knew it. "Have you come to hook me back up to your instruments of torture?" she asked with a glance at the silent machines around the bed.

"No." Manion smiled and held up the chart he was carrying. "The new MRI scan indicates that the swelling is completely gone. I think we can dispense with continuous monitoring."

Madeline held up the hand that contained her IV line. "And this?"

Manion approached the bed and laid the chart on the adjustable table at the foot. "That depends. Your color is a little better, but how's the headache?" he asked as he took a penlight from his coat pocket.

"It's gone," she replied.

Manion made a little harrumphing sound as he shined the light into her eyes, checking the reaction of her pupils. He looked at the stitches under her bandage and gently replaced the tape. He took her wrist in his hand and checked her pulse.

"See?" Madeline said. "All better now."

The doctor grinned at her. "Liar. Your head is pounding ferociously. You just don't want to admit it."

"I just don't want to be hooked up to your machines," she countered, trying to keep her voice as amiable as the doctor's because she liked him. He was the only person in this strange, threatening environment who made her feel even remotely safe. "I need to be mobile, doctor."

Manion's smile faded as his eyes met hers. "So you can be ready to run?"

"Run where? Since I don't know who I am, I certainly don't know where I should be," she quipped, even though the doctor was right. She did want to run—or at least she wanted to be *ready* to run when it became necessary.

Manion gave her his best sympathetic smile. "I think I may finally be able to help you with that, Madeline."

A sliver of excitement crept in alongside the darker emotions she was feeling. "You finally tracked down someone who knows me?"

"Actually he tracked you down when he realized you were missing."

He? she wondered. "Who? My father? My employer?"

Manion hesitated a moment. "Your husband."

Madeline frowned as the black hole where her memories should have been expanded, growing wider and even darker than it had been a few seconds earlier. "Husband?" she asked incredulously. "No. That's not possible. I don't *have* a husband."

The doctor nodded. "Yes, you do, Madeline. His name is Adam. Adam Hopewell."

Madeline looked into the mirror again. A face she didn't recognize. A name she'd barely grown accustomed to responding to. And now a husband. Someone who presumably loved her. Someone she had sworn to love, honor and cherish. In sickness and in health.

No. It wasn't possible. She didn't remember ever having said those words. She couldn't even *imagine* saying them. From the moment she'd awakened three days ago, alone, frightened and unable to recall something as simple as her name, she'd been certain of only two things about herself. One was that she wasn't accustomed to being frightened. She was used to controlling fear, instead of having it control her as it did now. Being afraid was alien to her.

But being *alone*—that was something else entirely. Being alone in the world felt familiar, and though Dr. Manion and the police had been trying hard to find out where Madeline Hopewell belonged, she'd never really expected someone to step forward and claim her.

Now someone had. Madeline shook her head and glanced down at her left hand. There was no ring on it, and the even flesh tones of her skin showed no evidence that one had ever been there.

She looked at Manion again. "If this Adam Hopewell is really my husband, what took him so long to realize that his wife was missing?"

"It's a rather complicated story," the doctor replied. "I think your husband could explain it better than I."

"Then by all means, let him explain it. Where is he?"

"Down the hall in the waiting room."

"Get him in here," she ordered.

Manion looked concerned. "Are you sure you're ready for that, Madeline? I know this is a shock—"

"I'm ready, Dr. Manion," she insisted, "*more* than ready. I've been in the dark for three days. If this man can shed some light on who I am and how I got here, I want to meet him. Now."

"All right," he conceded. "But don't demand too much of yourself."

Madeline considered the weight he put behind the words. "You mean I shouldn't expect to remember anything just because I *want* to remember?"

"That's right."

"Believe me, Dr. Manion, I already know that. If desire counted for anything, I'd already know exactly who I am."

"Nevertheless, I want you to take it easy. Ask all the questions you want, but don't get frustrated if your husband's answers don't open a floodgate of memories."

Madeline frowned. "You don't consider that a possibility?"

"Of course it's possible," Manion replied quickly. "But just don't count on it. Go easy on yourself."

Madeline couldn't deny feeling a stab of disappointment. She needed to remember so desperately that she was grabbing at any possibility like a drowning woman reaching for a life preserver. She wanted a lightning bolt to strike and sear the lock off the dark room where her memories were hiding.

No matter what Dr. Manion said, surely a husband who appeared out of the blue qualified as a lightning bolt. Seeing him would make her remember; and if not, then the things he could tell her about herself would bring the memories scurrying out of the darkness. It had to happen that way. She wouldn't accept anything less.

"I want to see him, Doctor."

"All right," Manion conceded. "But I want you back in bed first."

Her eyes widened and she grinned mischievously. "Doctor, please! Haven't you heard? I'm a married woman."

Manion chuckled but refused to relent. "You know what I mean. Back in bed."

She patted the rumpled sheet she was sitting on. "I *am* in bed."

He shook his head and wiped the smile off his face. "All the way in," he replied sternly. "You can keep your head elevated if you like, but I don't want you taxing your strength. And the next time you want to sit up, ring for a nurse to help you. You're not as strong physically as you like to pretend. Now, come on." He pulled back the fleece blanket and helped his protesting patient lift her legs onto the bed. She took the blanket from him and settled it around her waist.

"Happy now?" she asked sardonically.

"Deliriously. Is there anything else I can do for you?"

She started to retort that the only thing she wanted was to see her so-called husband, but she curbed her tongue when a second thought struck her. "My bag," she told him, pointing to the table beside the bed. "I think the nurse put it in the drawer."

The request surprised Manion. He hadn't known that any of her belongings had been returned to her. But when he circled the bed and looked in the table, there was a small cosmetic bag right where she indicated. "Did Detective Hogan bring this to you?"

She nodded. "Yesterday. He said they would probably release the rest of my things today or tomorrow."

"Did any of the contents look familiar to you?" Manion asked as he handed her the bag.

"Did you hear me shouting hosannas from the rooftop yesterday?" she retorted dryly.

Manion smiled. He liked his patient's wry sense of humor, but it concerned him that she used it to cover up the emotional torment she was suffering. Instead of shedding tears or throwing tantrums to vent her fears and frustration, Madeline cracked jokes.

"Sorry," he said apologetically. "That was a silly question."

Madeline nodded again. "It ranks right up there with the ever-popular 'And how are you feeling today?'" Her faint smile faded. "Now, may I see my alleged husband?"

"All right." He patted her hand. "I'll be on this floor for a while longer. If you need me, just ring the nurse and tell her."

"I'll be fine," she assured him, unconsciously tightening her grip on the bag. "Just bring on my better half."

"As you wish."

Maddy forced herself to remain still until he was gone, but the moment she was alone, she unzipped the makeup bag and began digging through the contents she had studied yesterday.

Prettying up her face was the last thought on her mind, though. She ignored the tube of lipstick and the other cosmetics, searching, instead, for the small nail file that had a sturdy plastic handle, a coarse metal blade and a tip that had been honed to almost stiletto sharpness.

It was an innocent-looking instrument, but Madeline felt better the moment it was in her hand. Finally she had something to use as a weapon.

Turning gingerly, she put the bag on top of the bedside table and slipped the nail file under the covers where she could reach it in an instant if she needed it.

When the door slid open, she was ready to meet the man who *claimed* to be her husband.

CHAPTER TWO

HE WAS TALL and lean, with the broad-shouldered, well-muscled build of an athlete. Not brawny like a football player, though. More like a skier. And he had the healthy complexion of an outdoorsman. It showed not only in his tanned face but also in his light brown hair, with its attractive streaks of sun-kissed blond.

He was an undeniably handsome man, and the analytical part of Madeline's mind said that if he really was her husband, she'd done quite well for herself. He had straight, dark brows over dark, deep-set eyes, and the deeply carved lines bracketing his mouth indicated he probably had dimples when he smiled.

But he wasn't smiling. He stood just inside the room, entering only far enough to let the door slide closed behind him. He stared at her intently as though drinking in the sight of her—and allowing her to study him, as well. Madeline had the impression that if she gave him the slightest encouragement he would cross the room and gather her into his arms.

Though she found the notion oddly comforting, she didn't offer the encouragement. Handsome or not—*husband* or not—this man was a complete stranger to her. Just like all the other strangers around her. Without memories, Madeline had nothing but instinct to rely on, and at the moment it was screaming for her not to trust anyone.

"Hello, Maddy."

He had a deep voice, very smooth and mellow despite the tentative tone, which suggested he didn't have a clue how to deal with this situation. She could hardly blame him, since she had no idea how handle it, either. "Hello, Adam."

Those lines around his mouth deepened into dimples as he smiled with relief. "Yes," he said, stepping eagerly toward her. "Maddy, I knew you'd remember."

Guilt pierced her as she held up her hand. "No. I don't. I'm sorry. Dr. Manion told me your name."

Adam came to a halt and his smile vanished. "Oh. Of course." He closed his eyes and put his hand to his forehead, as though rubbing it would help him decide what to do next. "I'm sorry, Maddy. I feel like an idiot. Dr. Manion said not to expect anything... not to push you. I don't know how to behave."

"That's all right. I don't seem to recall how to behave, either. What's the protocol for greeting a husband you don't remember?" she asked wryly.

Madeline wondered if it was pain she glimpsed on his face before he glanced down quickly. She was suddenly ashamed of her flippance.

"Sorry," she muttered. "I'm finding this all difficult to take in. I suppose Manion told you I had no idea I had a husband until a few minutes ago."

"Yes." Adam moved toward her, and panic sent Madeline's fingers slipping toward the nail file under the covers. Apparently he read the tension in her and stopped again, a few feet away from the bed. "The doctor said you're confused and frustrated now, but your memory will return eventually." He was trying to reassure himself as much as her, she thought.

"It can't be soon enough to suit me," Madeline replied.

His nod seemed to agree with her. "How are you feeling otherwise?"

"Bruised and battered. With a vicious headache." She mustered a smile. "I guess that's to be expected when you go head-to-head with a moving vehicle."

She was trying to inject a little humor, but Adam didn't respond to it. Just the opposite, in fact. His reserved facade cracked and in an agonized voice he asked, "Maddy, how did this happen?"

"You're asking me? Haven't you talked to the police? They have more answers than I do."

"I spoke to someone on the phone briefly last night. He would only tell me that there'd been an attempt on your life. When I found out you were in the hospital, I got here as quickly as I could. Maddy, who tried to kill you?"

"I have no idea," she told him. "As for what happened, all I know is what the witnesses reported and the police were able to reconstruct. I had just arrived on a plane from New York and was in the parking garage at the Charleston airport when someone tried to run me down with his car. Apparently I tried to dive out of his way, but the bumper clipped me and threw me headfirst into the rear window of a parked car."

"Oh, God," Adam murmured, closing his eyes.

"I landed between two cars, and my attacker backed up—apparently to finish me off—but one of the witnesses came running toward us, shouting." Maddy hesitated. This was the worst part of the whole ugly mess. "I don't think my good Samaritan knew the man in the car had a gun."

"The guy was shot?" Adam asked, horrified.

Maddy nodded. "The driver of the car clipped off two rounds and hit the other man in the chest, killing him instantly."

Maddy closed her eyes against a sudden and surprising surge of tears. She hadn't cried once through this whole ordeal and she didn't want to start now. But the tears wouldn't retreat and her throat had constricted painfully. It took a moment to collect herself enough to be able to tell Adam, "He saved my life, you know. The police found me *under* the car I'd hit. I guess I was conscious enough to try and protect myself. My good Samaritan probably distracted the gunman just long enough for me to crawl under the car."

Maddy brushed at the tears in her eyes and cleared her throat. "Anyway, by that time, witnesses were screaming and a security guard was driving up. My would-be assassin didn't have time to get out of his car and finish what he'd started."

"And you don't remember any of it?"

"No."

"Maddy…" The distance between them seemed too much for Adam to bear. He stepped to the bed and probably would have put his arms around her if she hadn't pinned him with a cold, hard glare that warned him to keep his distance.

"It's your turn," she told him brusquely. "I answered your questions, now you answer mine. What was I doing at the Charleston airport? I had a small overnight bag with me, but no other luggage. Why am I here?"

"I don't know, Maddy. This wasn't what we'd planned at all. When I realized yesterday that you'd disappeared, I started making phone calls—"

"Yesterday?" she interrupted him. "I've been here five days and you didn't notice I was missing until yesterday?"

"That's right. And when you didn't show up in New York as—"

"We live in New York?"

Adam frowned at the interruption. "No."

"Charleston?"

"No, we—"

"Then where do we live?" she demanded. A floodgate of questions had been opened, and she was so impatient for answers she couldn't wait for lengthy explanations. "My driver's license has a New York address, but the police said no one there had ever heard of me. Why is that?"

"Because we haven't lived in New York for years," he replied with a touch of frustration. "Maybe I should just start at the beginning, Maddy."

He was right. She needed the whole picture, and if this man really was her husband, he could give it to her. "All right. I'll be a good girl and stop interrupting," she promised.

He smiled again, this time like a loving husband sharing a private joke with his wife. "Patience has never been your strongest virtue."

His smile was so appealingly intimate that Maddy didn't dare return it. "Save the character analysis for later," she said lightly, trying to deflect the way that smile made her feel. "Let's deal with the facts first."

The smile disappeared. "Okay. Where do you want me to start?"

"At the beginning—as you suggested. Who am I?"

Adam stepped to the foot of the bed and faced her with the adjustable table between them. "Your name is Madeline Lambert Hopewell. You're thirty-four years old, and you and I have been married for almost ten years.''

His warm brown eyes were filled with pain, but Maddy ignored the haunting sadness in them as she voiced a thought that had just occurred to her. "Do we have children? Have I forgotten my children, too?'' she asked as panic rose in her throat.

"No,'' he said gently. "We hadn't started our family yet.''

Something in his tone suggested it was an issue they'd been seriously considering, though. Maddy didn't want to think about the implications of sharing that kind of intimacy with this man.

"What about my parents?'' she asked, channeling their conversation onto safer ground.

"Your parents were Irene and Paul Lambert. They were killed in a plane crash when you were fifteen.''

Maddy searched for the emotion that should accompany such a devastating loss, but found only emptiness. "So I was raised by relatives after that?''

Adam shook his head. "No. There were no relatives. No close ones, anyway. You were in a boarding school in New England at the time, and you stayed on there until you started college.''

A young girl living alone at an impersonal boarding school. That would explain why isolation and loneliness felt so familiar to her. She gave Adam a nod, indicating that he should continue. He did, explaining how she'd dropped out of college after three years of studying archaeology and anthropology. Using the money from the substantial trust fund her parents had left her, she'd toured Europe and the Middle East, working on archaeological digs when the mood suited her and playing on the Riviera when it didn't.

Using only broad brush strokes, Adam painted a picture of a wealthy, rootless young woman with too much money, too much time on her hands and too few goals.

Madeline didn't like the picture. Nothing in her rebelled against it exactly, but it just didn't feel right somehow.

"So where do you come in?" she asked him. The ancient past could be explored later.

"We met a little over ten years ago at the film festival in Cannes."

"You're in the movie business?"

Adam shook his head. "I'm an antiquities broker."

"So we met, fell in love and got married," she said succinctly.

"In a nutshell."

"And lived happily ever after until just a few days ago?"

"More or less," he replied softly.

Maddy ignored the tenderness in his tone. "Where did we live?"

"Most recently in Paris, but we travel a great deal."

"Because of your business?"

"*Our* business," Adam corrected her. "We're partners now. Your specialty is Egyptian and Middle Eastern artifacts."

Madeline searched her memory for any knowledge of exactly what an antiquities "broker" did. "We accept commissions to find specific pieces for our clients' collections?"

"Basically," he confirmed. "And sometimes we function as an intermediary between galleries or museums and certain private collectors who wish to remain anonymous."

"I see." Madeline digested the information, but none of it sounded even remotely familiar to her.

"We also had a successful gallery in Paris on the Rue des Jardins."

The Rue des Jardins. Street of Gardens. The translation came so easily to her that Maddy was startled. Learning that she spoke French wasn't surprising, particularly if she'd been living in Paris, but she couldn't help feeling excited. Something finally seemed familiar to her. "Speak to me in French," she commanded.

Adam looked at her blankly for a moment, then replied in flawlessly accented French, "*Tu t'appelles* Madeline Hopewell."

"Your name is Madeline Hopewell," she translated, giving him a look of disgust. "Something a bit harder please."

"*Tu as trente-quatre ans.*"

"You're thirty-four years old," she recited.

"*Tu es ma femme . . .*"

"You are my wife . . ."

"*Et je t'aime.*"

"And I love you." Madeline's breath caught in her throat, and she found it impossible to look away from Adam's dark eyes. The raw emotion she saw made his words even more potent, more moving, and suddenly, she felt it herself—a sliver of the pain he was feeling. It wasn't a memory of loving him, though. It was just a deep, aching sadness for the loss she couldn't remember or even feel. For the first time it seemed possible that Adam really *was* her husband.

"I'm sorry, Adam," she whispered. "I wish..."

He nodded. "I know. It's okay. You'll remember soon."

"I hope so," she said, then determinedly pulled herself away from the emotions Adam's declaration had evoked. She couldn't afford to get mired in sentiment. "You were going to explain how a wife can be missing for nearly a week without her husband knowing it."

Adam opened his mouth, but before he could reply a voice from the door said gruffly, "I'd like to know the answer to that, too."

Adam spun around. "Who are you?" he demanded, placing himself between the intruder and Maddy.

But it was Maddy who answered him. "Adam, this is Detective Hogan of the Charleston police. He's in charge of my case."

The short, brawny detective moved toward the bed, never taking his eyes off Adam. "Now, who are *you?*" Hogan asked.

Adam didn't offer his hand to the suspicious detective. "I'm Maddy's husband. Adam Hopewell."

Hogan looked at Maddy. "Is that right, Ms. Hopewell? Do you remember him?"

She shook her head regretfully. "No. I don't remember him."

The detective looked at Adam again. "Then how about showing me a little identification?"

Adam sighed impatiently as he reached into the pocket of his suit coat. "I've already been through this with the officer outside."

"Go through it again," Hogan growled.

As she watched Adam hand over his wallet, Maddy silently berated herself for not thinking of this herself. The detective went through the wallet thoroughly, apparently satisfying himself that the visitor was who he claimed to be, but when Hogan passed the wallet back to Adam, Maddy held out her hand. "May I see it, too?"

Adam looked hurt, but Maddy was more concerned with protecting herself than worrying about the feelings of this man who said he was her husband. Adam's tenderness and solicitude had made her forget that for a moment, but she wasn't about to make the same mistake again.

Without asking for approval from Adam, Hogan gave the wallet to Maddy.

"Oh, for God's sake," Adam snapped. "Why would I claim to be her husband if I wasn't?"

Hogan looked at Adam unapologetically. "If I was a killer who wanted to finish what I started, I'd need a creative way to get past the guard at the door."

"I didn't try to kill Maddy! I wasn't even in the country at the time!"

Hogan's shaggy eyebrows lifted skeptically. "Oh? Can you prove that?"

Adam's jaw stiffened. "Not at the moment. My passport is in my suitcase in the car. Do you want me to go out to the parking garage and get it for you?"

"Eventually," Hogan replied with a nod. "But for now, I'll settle for an answer to the question Ms. Hopewell asked when I came in. What took you so long to realize she was missing?"

Maddy had been listening to their exchange with half an ear as she studied the contents of Adam's wal-

let. His American driver's license had the same inval-
id New York address as hers, and the rest of his
identification proved his contention that he'd been
living in France. But the most convincing evidence was
the small, candid photograph of her that was encased
in a protective plastic pocket alongside his credit cards.

This man really was her husband.

She replaced the contents of the wallet and returned her full attention to Adam as he answered the
detective's question.

"As I was telling Maddy, we'd decided to leave Paris
and return to New York to live," Adam began, turning to Maddy and virtually ignoring Hogan. "We've
been in the process of moving for the past two
months—packing, wrapping up business details and
closing down our gallery on the Rue des Jardins. In
the middle of all that mayhem, one of our best clients
decided to sell his entire collection of pre-Columbian
artifacts. He asked us to quickly and quietly find
buyers for the pieces."

"I take it you're an antique dealer," Hogan said.

Maddy couldn't help but grin when Adam shot the
detective a look of disgust. "An antiquities broker."

"Oh, excuse me," Hogan said in a la-di-da tone.

Again Adam ignored him and turned to Maddy.
"Anyway, the commission was too good to pass up, so
we agreed that you would finish closing our Paris
apartment while I made the person-to-person contacts needed to sell the collection. We planned to ren-
dezvous in New York on the twenty-sixth. Yesterday."

"So you had no contact with your wife during that
time?" Hogan asked.

Adam reluctantly swung his gaze to the detective.
"On the contrary. I spoke to her several times. The last

time we talked, she said she was ready to put our belongings in storage, and the landlord had already found new tenants for the apartment.''

"She gave you no indication that anything was wrong or that she planned to leave Paris ahead of schedule?"

"No. She even joked that she wasn't going to let Monsieur Rennart evict her before she was ready to leave."

"Which was?"

"She had reservations on the Concord for the twenty-sixth."

"Will you two please stop talking about me as though I'm not here?" Maddy asked sharply.

Adam turned to her instantly. "I'm sorry, darling," he said, reaching down to caress her hand.

Maddy tensed but didn't pull away from his light touch. "When was the last time we spoke?" she asked.

His brow furrowed in thought. "Ten days ago, I think. Or possibly eleven. I tried to call you a couple of days later, but the phone had been disconnected. I'd been expecting that eventually, and I knew you had my itinerary, so I didn't try to leave a message for you with any of our friends."

"Did she leave a message for you anywhere?" Hogan asked.

"No," Adam replied. "But I've been in four hotels on three different continents this past week, so I suppose it's possible that a message could have been sent that I missed."

"And you don't have any idea why I came to Charleston?" Maddy asked him.

"No."

"If you didn't expect Mrs. Hopewell to be in Charleston, how did you find her here?" Hogan asked. "Did you contact the New York police and file a missing-persons report?"

"I tried," Adam told him, "but from their perspective she hadn't been missing twenty-four hours yet, so they wouldn't take a report."

"What do you mean, 'from their perspective'?" Hogan asked.

"Maddy was supposed to meet me at the hotel in New York yesterday afternoon, and the police insisted that I give her at least a day to show up before I filed a report," he explained. "They wouldn't listen to me when I tried to tell them that she'd already been missing for several days."

"How did you know that?" Hogan inquired.

"When she didn't show up at the hotel, I checked with the airline and discovered that she wasn't on the flight she had planned to take yesterday. That's when I started calling friends in Paris and learned that no one had heard from her for at least a week. Our former landlord said she vacated the apartment on Saturday, the nineteenth."

Hogan made the calculations. "That would've been a couple of days after you talked to her last and a full week before you were supposed to meet in New York?"

"Yes. But since I'd been out of contact with Maddy during that week, the New York police refused to believe she'd been missing that long."

"Well, if the police didn't run a check and discover that we had put her in the FBI computer, how did you find her in Charleston?"

"After I had exhausted all possibilities with the police in New York and Paris, as well as all our friends in Europe, I played a hunch out of pure desperation."

Hogan's craggy face registered disbelief. "What kind of hunch? Are you sure you didn't just stick a pin in a map and call the police station there?"

Adam regarded him with annoyance. "No, of course not. But Maddy and I had made plans to come to Charleston next month. We have reservations at Bride's Bay."

Maddy frowned. "Bride's Bay?"

"It's a ritzy resort on Jermain Island," Hogan said, "just off the coast from Charleston."

"It's also where Maddy and I spent our honeymoon," Adam informed him. "We were going to celebrate our tenth wedding anniversary there." Again Maddy saw the sadness in his eyes. "Anyway, I thought perhaps you'd decided to skip New York and head for the resort early, so I called them. They hadn't heard from you, but I spoke to the manager to explain that you were missing and request that I be notified if they did hear from you. Then Ms. Jermain, the manager, remembered seeing a story on the evening news about the police trying to locate family or friends of a woman who was attacked at the airport, but she couldn't recall her name."

"So you called the police station."

Adam nodded. "I was told Maddy was in the hospital. I caught the next plane to Charleston, rented a car at the airport and drove straight here." Adam squared his shoulders. "Now that I've answered your questions, I have a few of my own, Detective Hogan.

Like what you're doing to catch the man who attacked Maddy."

"We're doing everything we can, Mr. Hopewell, but I'm afraid we don't have much to go on. No one got a good look at him or the license plate of his car," Hogan replied. "Can you think of any reason someone would want to kill your wife? Do either of you have any enemies?"

"No. On both counts," Adam replied.

"Okay." Hogan gave a noncommittal nod. "Can you think of any reason the Drug Enforcement Administration would be interested in your wife?"

"What?!" Maddy exclaimed, sitting up so quickly it made her head throb. "The DEA has been asking questions about me?"

Hogan nodded. "Day before yesterday two agents showed up at the station asking questions about you and your assailant."

Adam was scowling at the detective. "How did the DEA even know about the attack?"

"When your wife couldn't give us any information about herself, we put her description into the FBI computer to try and match her with missing persons around the country. The DEA agents said she matched the description of a woman known to be acting as a courier for a Colombian drug cartel."

"Why didn't you tell me that?" Maddy demanded.

"After they went through your belongings, they came here to interrogate you, but you were asleep. Once they got a look at you, they said you weren't the woman they were looking for and left."

Maddy was relieved but not mollified. "That still doesn't explain why you didn't tell me about it."

"Dr. Manion asked me not to," Hogan explained. "He didn't want you upset."

"Then why mention it now?" Adam confronted the detective. "Obviously she was cleared of any implications of wrongdoing. Why upset her for no reason?"

"Because there was something fishy about those two agents. Their credentials checked out and I can't put my finger on what bugged me about them, but I know when I'm being lied to—and those two agents were lying. I just don't know why. Yet."

"Detective Hogan? What's going on here?" Dr. Manion demanded as he entered the room.

"Just trying to get some answers, Doc," the detective replied.

"Well, get them some other time." Manion hurried to Maddy's bed. "Are you both blind? Can't you see what you're doing to this patient?"

"I'm fine, Dr. Manion," Maddy assured him.

"No, you're not, Maddy," Adam argued, his face lined with concern. "The doctor's right. We've exhausted you."

Maddy started to argue with him, but she found she didn't have the strength. Her headache had grown a hundred times worse in the past few minutes, and she felt as though someone had siphoned off every bit of her meager supply of energy.

"I want both of you out of here now," Manion ordered.

"All right," Adam said, stepping closer to the head

of Maddy's bed. "I'll come back later this afternoon."

"No, you'll come back tomorrow," Manion countered. "She's had enough visitors for one day."

Adam frowned at him. "But—"

"I'm in charge here, Mr. Hopewell," the doctor reminded him sternly. "You can see your wife again tomorrow morning."

With her husband and her doctor glaring at each
other over her bed, Maddy felt like a fraying rope in a
game of tug-of-war. "He's right, Adam," she said
gently. Her husband shifted his gaze down to her, and
the harsh lines of his face melted into a look of tenderness that Maddy could very easily become ad-
dicted to. "I need a chance to assimilate everything
you've told me. I still have a thousand questions, but
they can wait till tomorrow."

"All right, Maddy," Adam said, taking her hand.
"I'll settle into a hotel somewhere close by and let the
nurses know where I am in case you need to reach
me."

"Good."

As he looked down at her, his face filled with uncertainty. "Then I guess I'll go now," he said reluctantly.

"I'll see you tomorrow."

"Tomorrow." He nodded. Then, as if he couldn't
help himself, he leaned down and pressed his lips to
hers.

It wasn't a passionate kiss, or even an insistent one.
Just a simple brush of his lips against hers, but it
caught Maddy completely by surprise. Not because he

did it, but because of the way she responded. That warm, simple contact made her want more.

But Adam didn't linger. He straightened and gently touched her face, smoothing back a wisp of hair from her cheek. "Get some rest, darling," he whispered, his voice hoarse with emotion. "I love you."

Maddy felt tears stinging her eyes as, with obvious reluctance, he released her hand and turned toward the door.

Maddy's hand still felt warm from his touch, and the sensation reminded her of something that had puzzled her earlier.

"Adam?"

He stopped and turned to her expectantly. "Yes?"

"Why don't I have a wedding ring?"

He gave her a sweet, loving smile. "You have one, Maddy. You just don't wear it."

"Why not?"

"Because you're stubborn and independent, and you don't believe in antiquated chauvinistic rituals. When we got married, you said you wouldn't let anyone brand you like a heifer."

Her gaze dropped to Adam's left hand. "You're wearing a ring."

Adam shrugged. "I don't mind being branded—as long as it's *your* brand I'm wearing."

"Oh," she said, suddenly speechless.

"I'll see you tomorrow," he told her, then left with Detective Hogan right on his heels.

"Are you all right, Madeline?" Dr. Manion asked solicitously.

It was a moment before Maddy could drag her gaze from the door. "I'm just tired, Doctor," she finally replied.

"And still confused?"

Maddy looked up at him with a little shake of her head. "You have no idea how much."

CHAPTER THREE

DESPITE THE ACHE in her left leg, Maddy paced her room with a determined stride, stretching the throbbing limb and exploring the limits of her strength and endurance. She was free of the IV line; Dr. Manion had ordered it removed shortly after that first surprising and disturbing visit from Adam four days ago. She could move about as she pleased now—but only within the confines of this room.

Maddy chafed against the restrictions, but she knew she wasn't ready to face the outside world yet. Detective Hogan was convinced that the hit-and-run attack on her was deliberate, so there was an excellent possibility that her assailant was out there somewhere waiting to finish what he started.

Just knowing that someone wanted her dead was terrifying enough; not knowing *why* only added to the torment. But instinct told Maddy that Hogan was right—her life was in danger. She also knew she had to be ready for anything, so to keep fit she paced the floor of her room and did modified push-ups with her hands against the wall. She did sit-ups in bed, despite the pain they caused her.

The exercise routine, which she performed covertly as many times a day as her limited stamina would allow, was the only outlet Maddy had for the emotional confusion she was suffering. Her frustration at not being able to remember anything was growing so quickly that sometimes it was all she could do to keep from screaming.

Adam visited her several times a day, valiantly trying to keep her spirits up and patiently answering her endless questions, gradually filling in the missing pieces of her life. But it wasn't enough. Nothing Adam told her brought back any memories, but the picture he painted didn't feel *real* to her. When he talked about their life together, he might just as well have been telling her an inventive bedtime story.

He was keeping her sane, though. As much as Maddy hated to admit it, she had come to depend on Adam. Except for her doctor, the overworked nurses and increasingly infrequent visits from Detective Hogan, Adam was Maddy's only connection with the outside world. She didn't want to depend on him— didn't want to *need* him—but she couldn't deny that he exuded a kind of strength she found compelling.

She finally concluded that was probably the reason she had fallen in love with him ten years ago. Aside from his obvious physical attributes—the handsome face and sleek, athletic body—he exuded a confidence that told Maddy this was a man who, when he wanted something, took action and made it happen.

The increased security for her room was a perfect example. When he decided that Hogan's single police officer wasn't enough protection, Adam had brought in his own private security force of six guards who worked in teams of three on twelve-hour shifts. He'd sworn he'd protect her, and he was living up to that promise.

When she reached one hundred paces, Maddy stopped and moved to the lavatory to splash water on her face. Adam was late this morning and she didn't want him to walk in while she was so obviously over-exerted. In fact, she wouldn't have started the routine in the first place if she hadn't been impatient for Adam to arrive.

She toweled off, then glanced at the clock over the lavatory and discovered it was after ten. Where on earth was he? The past three mornings he'd arrived early, usually in time to share a cup of weak coffee and listen to her complaints about the horrible hospital food. Yesterday he'd even taken pity on her and snuck in a cup of real coffee and a croissant from a deli down the street.

But today he hadn't arrived in time to save her from a tray of runny scrambled eggs and rubbery strips of bacon. Where was he? What could be keeping him?

As if in answer, Maddy heard the click of the latch as the door started to open. Out of reflex, she reached for the nail file she now kept tucked in the pocket of her flimsy hospital robe, but as soon as she saw Adam, she dropped the file back into the pocket.

"Well, look what the cat dragged in," she said, noting as the door closed behind him that he wasn't arriving empty-handed. With an overnight bag hanging from one shoulder, a box under the other arm and bulging shopping bags in both hands, he looked like a slender, beardless Santa Claus. "And look what he dragged in with him. What's all this?"

Adam grinned at her as he crossed to the bed. "I'm sorry I'm late, but I had some errands to take care of this morning. When you complained yesterday about being as sick of hospital gowns as you were of hospital food, I realized I should've thought of this days ago."

"You mean you brought me clothes? *Real* clothes?" Maddy asked gleefully, moving to the bed with him.

"Real honest-to-goodness store-bought clothes," he confirmed, dropping his parcels onto the bed. "Plus the few things of your own you had with you when you arrived in Charleston." Adam held out the plain brown tweed overnight bag to her. "I went by the police station this morning and Detective Hogan released it to me."

Elated at the thought of having something that might spark a memory, Maddy grabbed the bag eagerly and found room on the bed to sit. "What about my purse?"

"It's in the bag," he told her. "How are you today?"

"Oh, peachy," she replied as she dumped the contents of the bag in front of her. "I'm caged like a wild animal at the zoo, I can't remember who I am, and I've got three oversize gorillas camped on my doorstep. How the hell do you think I am?"

Adam chuckled. "At least you're in a better mood than yesterday."

Maddy stopped rooting through her belongings and looked at him. "Is that a polite, husbandly way of telling me I'm being a grouch?"

"You've earned the right to be grouchy, Maddy," he said.

"Yeah. I just wish we knew *how* I earned it."

"True." Adam nodded sympathetically, then pointed at the tangle of clothing in front of her. "Does anything look familiar?"

She held up a flimsy scrap of ecru silk and lace. "I recognize this as a being a teddy, but I don't remember ever having worn it."

"I do." He grinned again, showing the dimples that Maddy was beginning to find irresistibly sexy.

"I suppose you remember this, too," she replied dryly, holding up a blue nightgown.

"Vividly."

Maddy realized she had just led them into dangerous territory, and she regretted it. Adam Hopewell had enough sex appeal to knock any woman off balance. Maddy had seen that in the way the nurses responded to him, and she had certainly felt it herself. That was why she'd been careful to avoid asking any questions that might lead to the topic of the more intimate aspects of their marriage. She was far from ready to dive into those waters.

Trying to cover her discomfort, she tucked the teddy and nightgown back into the overnight bag, along with several other bits of lingerie, then began inspecting the remaining items—a pair of serviceable tan slacks, a beige blouse and a light brown jacket. The three made a reasonable outfit, but certainly not one designed to make her stand out in a crowd. And not one that jogged any memories.

Since Detective Hogan had returned her makeup and toiletries to her days ago, there was nothing else in the overnight bag, so Maddy turned her attention to the large black leather purse. A small wallet with her driver's license, two credit cards and several hundred dollars in cash—but no photo of Adam similar to the one he carried of her. And no French currency or anything else that indicated she'd recently arrived from Paris.

Maddy thought back to the items she'd seen in Adam's wallet. "Where's my national driving license, Adam? And my insurance green card, like the one you had? My French identification? My passport?"

"I don't know, Maddy. I can only assume you left them wherever you left the rest of your luggage."

"What makes you think I had more luggage?"

Adam laughed shortly. "Maddy, my darling, in the ten years we've been together, I've never made a trip with you where we didn't have to pay for at least one extra suitcase. And the bags we *were* allowed were usually overweight."

"So I like clothes?"

He nodded. "Beautiful ones."

Maddy thought of the plain brown suit she'd just returned to the overnight bag. If she was such a clotheshorse, why had she chosen to travel with only one drab outfit?

She sighed and returned to the contents of the purse. Besides her wallet, the purse contained a half-empty pack of gum, a magazine and a cosmetic bag, which held a tube of lipstick, a compact, a small hairbrush and another nail file like the one in her pocket.

Not one thing was familiar.

She couldn't help being disappointed.

"Maddy?" Adam said.

She shook her head and looked up at him plaintively. "Nothing. Not a damned thing." She scooped up the bits and pieces of her life and held them up to Adam. "Damn it, why don't these make me remember something? I want to remember, Adam!"

"I know, I know," he said soothingly, gently taking the items from her and dropping them back into her bag before she could hurl them across the room in frustration. "You'll remember eventually, Maddy. Just give yourself some time."

"How much time, Adam? A week? A month? A *year?*" She felt the control she maintained over her fear slipping. "How much time do you think my friend with the itchy trigger finger is going to give me before he comes back to finish what he started?"

Adam sat on the bed, facing her. "Maddy, I've told you that I won't let him get near you. I promise, he'll never hurt you again."

"How can you promise that? We don't know who he is—or even what he looks like!"

"We'll find out who he is and why he wanted you dead."

"How?" she demanded, furious with herself and the circumstances. "How are you going to do that, Adam? Look into a crystal ball?"

"I've hired a private detective, Maddy. One of the best."

Maddy was stunned. "You did? When?"

"Two days ago."

"Why didn't you tell me?"

"Because there was nothing to report. He's trying to reconstruct your trip and figure out what you did during the thirty-six hours you were in New York before you caught the plane to Charleston."

She frowned. "Thirty-six hours? How do you know I was in New York for a day and a half?"

Adam sighed patiently, the way he always did when Maddy's questions interrupted the flow of what he was saying. "That's what I haven't had a chance to tell you about yet. I finally heard from Immigration yesterday afternoon. According to their records, you came through customs in New York at 7:15 p.m. on Sunday, the twentieth."

"From Paris?"

"Yes. I've given the flight number to the detective, and he's sent one of his men to Paris to question our friends. Meanwhile he's in New York trying to figure out what happened in those thirty-six hours that prompted you to come to Charleston."

Maddy pushed herself off the bed. "I want to go to New York, too," she said adamantly. "As soon as Manion releases me."

"Absolutely not," Adam said just as adamantly. "You're in no condition to play sleuth. You have to recuperate. And besides that, it would be nearly impossible to protect you in the middle of Manhattan."

"But—"

"No buts, Maddy. This isn't even open to discussion."

She couldn't believe what she was hearing. "Who the hell died and made you dictator? If this is any indication of the kind of marriage we had, we should've been divorced years ago!"

"Well, we're not divorced," Adam said hotly, "and I am not a dictator! But I'm not going to stand by and let you get yourself killed on some wild-goose chase! I almost lost you, damn it..." His words seemed to catch up with him, and his voice became choked with emotion and frustration. "I *have* lost you, Maddy," he said softly. "But I've got to believe that you'll come back to me someday."

Maddy was ashamed of the way she'd blown up at him. "I'm sorry, Adam. I keep forgetting how hard this is on you."

"I just want to keep you safe, Maddy." He reached out, placing his hands on her shoulders as though he meant to gather her into his arms, but Maddy stepped back out of his reach.

It was an action she instantly regretted. These past few days, Adam had gotten better at covering up how saddened he was by the distance she maintained between them, but this time she could see she'd hurt him, and that was the last thing she wanted to do.

"I'm sorry, Adam," she said quickly, but it was too late. He'd already buried his feelings as though they hadn't existed and waved her apology off.

"It's all right, Maddy. Don't worry about it."

"But I keep hurting you without intending to."

Almost tentatively he moved one hand toward her face, and when she didn't shy away, he brushed the back of his hand against her cheek. "It's okay, Maddy. I'm a big boy. I can handle it. Just promise me you won't do anything stupid—like try to run off to New York by yourself."

Clearly he wanted to let the incident pass, so Maddy did. She raised one eyebrow. "How could I possibly run off with your three trained gorillas watching my every move?"

Instinct told her, however, that she could easily evade Adam's guards if she wanted to. But she didn't want to. Not yet, anyway. She was impatient and frustrated, but she wasn't stupid. She didn't have the physical strength to protect herself yet, and until she did, she was going to have to rely on Adam and his hired guards.

Apparently Adam wasn't fooled by her apparent compliance with his edict. "Maddy, please. You have to trust me."

Trust. He'd hit the nail squarely on the head. At moments, she could imagine having loved Adam Hopewell, could envision their having had a very passionate relationship. She could even, sometimes, imagine having been married to him.

But she couldn't imagine trusting him. Couldn't imagine trusting anyone, in fact, and deep in her soul, she knew she never had. Distrust was almost as intrinsic to her life as loneliness.

But telling him so would only hurt him, and Maddy had done enough of that for one day. "I promise you, Adam, I won't ditch your gorillas. I won't go running off to New York to sleuth without giving you proper warning."

She wasn't sure she would keep those promises, but she made them, anyway, without compunction. Apparently lying was quite comfortable to her. And so were diversion tactics.

"But there are a couple of things we need to consider, Adam. You can't hire round-the-clock security for me forever, nor can I stay in this hospital room indefinitely. Dr. Manion expects to release me in three or four days. What are we going to do then?" she asked as she returned to the bed and sat.

Adam sat down facing her. "I've already talked to Dr. Manion about that. He was at the nurses' station when I came in a few minutes ago, and he approved of the plan I presented to him."

"What plan?" Maddy asked, trying not to show her displeasure that Adam had obviously made an important decision about her welfare without bothering to consult her.

"Well, you know that Manion thinks it's important for you to go someplace familiar when you leave here so that it'll stimulate the return of your memory."

Maddy nodded. She, Adam and the doctor had discussed this yesterday. "Right. But he doesn't want me to fly anywhere because of the changes in air pressure, so going back to Paris is out of the question, and you've summarily ruled out New York. What's left that's within driving distance?"

"Bride's Bay," he answered.

Maddy frowned. "The resort where we spent our honeymoon?"

"That's right. You loved it, Maddy. That's why you wanted to go back and celebrate our anniversary there," he told her with a loving smile. "It's the perfect solution to our problem. Not only is it someplace familiar, it's very exclusive."

"Exclusive?"

Adam nodded. "It's a high-security resort on a private island. Diplomats hold international conferences there. Heads of state come year round to play golf. I've even heard a rumor that the President of the United States is vacationing there this year."

"And we can afford to stay at a place like that until I'm able to fly or my assailant is caught?"

"Absolutely."

Maddy was astonished. "Are we rich?"

"Well..." He paused a moment. "We're not exactly the Rockefellers, but between your trust fund, the inheritance my father left me, our gallery and the hefty brokerage commissions we've earned these last ten years, we could very easily take a two- or three-year vacation and do anything we wanted without worrying about our finances."

"Wow."

"So money is not a problem," he assured her, then returned to his original subject. "And the beauty of going to Bride's Bay is that you wouldn't feel like a prisoner there. The security isn't impenetrable, but with proper precautions, we could have the run of the island. We can do all the things we did on our honeymoon, and eventually something is bound to jog your memory."

Maddy wanted to ask if "all the things" included the activities of their wedding night, but she thought it best not to bring that subject up again.

Instead, she concentrated on the important issues. Like regaining her strength and her memory—in that order, because she readily acknowledged that until her memory returned, her strength was the only weapon she had against the man who wanted her dead. Since she didn't have either at the moment, she really had to depend on Adam to keep her safe.

And he obviously believed Bride's Bay was the best place to do that.

"All right, Adam. As soon as Dr. Manion releases me, we'll go to Bride's Bay."

"Good," he said, smiling happily. "You'll be safe there, Maddy. I promise." He turned and reached for one of the shopping bags he'd brought. "Now, would you like to see what I bought for you?"

"Sure," she replied. "Let's see what the well-dressed amnesiac wears to an exclusive resort on her second honeymoon."

THE JANITOR ROLLED his bucket into the small maintenance closet, clicked his mop into the brackets on the wall mounting, closed the door behind him and turned the lock.

This charade was over. After today, he would no longer need to return to the hospital. He had the information he needed. Just minutes ago he'd heard the nurses gossiping about how lucky the Hopewell woman was to be going to Bride's Bay to recuperate.

The news was almost too good to be true. It was perfect, in fact. He had delayed too long in making his move at the hospital, giving the woman's husband time to triple the guard at her door. The increased security decreased the Raven's odds of killing the woman and making a clean escape. He'd hung around only to learn what the husband had planned for when the woman left the hospital.

And now he knew. She was going to Bride's Bay, where the security was excellent—but where he'd have a much better chance to kill her because he already had a carefully crafted plan to infiltrate the resort. He'd spent months cultivating contacts there and making the necessary preparations. When the time was right, he would blend into the fabric of the resort so completely that no one would ever question his right to be there.

He would have to be careful, of course. He couldn't afford to do anything that might disrupt the detailed plan already in place for the biggest contract hit of his career. But with a little luck, he could kill two birds with one stone—first Madeline Hopewell, then the President.

Whistling merrily, the Raven took off his janitor garb, donned a new costume and slipped out of the closet.

No one paid the slightest attention to the fair-haired young intern who went bustling through the emergency room doors into the parking lot ten minutes later.

CHAPTER FOUR

THE BLOOD WAS EVERYWHERE. *It stained her hands, her clothes, the dirty tile floor around her. The smell of it was worse than the sight, and the sight was something out of a nightmare.*

Some of the blood was hers. She could taste the acrid bite of it on her tongue, but most of the scarlet flood was his—the man whose face she couldn't quite see, whose words she couldn't quite hear. His voice was garbled, and no matter how hard she strained to listen, she couldn't bring the dying man's message into focus. He pressed something into her hand and babbled more unintelligible words, and then he was gone. Dead. No more words, but blood everywhere and the shrieks of voices like cawing crows.

Dark, faceless shapes converged on her, pointing accusing fingers in her direction, screaming words she couldn't understand. She was terrified. It was clear that they blamed her for the blood. The terrible guilt she felt told her that they were right. The blood was her fault, and the screaming demons wanted her to pay for what she'd done. But she couldn't remember what that was. She didn't know why the man had died in her arms.

The demons didn't care about that; they only cared about retribution. Their dark shapes closed in on her, cutting off her escape when she tried to run. They pinned her into a suffocating space that grew smaller and smaller as they grew closer and closer, until they congealed into one shape, a giant shadow that spread its dark, evil wings and streaked toward her. The black wings enfolded her and the demon laughed at her as she fought desperately against the wings . . . the terror . . . the certainty that she was about to die.

GASPING FOR BREATH, Maddy awoke in the pitch-black hospital room, fighting for air and sanity as the nightmare slithered back into the darkness from which it had emerged. This wasn't the first time she'd had the dream, and instinct told her it wouldn't be the last. It had just been a little more vivid this time, which was probably understandable. She was leaving the hospital tomorrow, walking away from the only world she knew into a vast unknown where someone was waiting to kill her.

She was frightened by that—who wouldn't be? But that didn't mean she was weak, did it? No matter how hard she tried she couldn't escape her fear—or the inexplicable guilt she was left with every time she had the dream. The blood was so vivid that even when she was awake she could sometimes see it, smell it, feel it.

More than a little nauseated, Maddy rubbed her hands together, trying to make that hot, sticky warmth go away. When that didn't work, she rubbed her hands on the blanket. Finally she got up, padded across the dark room to the lavatory and scrubbed them with hot soapy water.

Nothing worked. And the thought that somewhere outside this room a man was dead because of her remained.

"Or maybe it is just a stupid dream," she muttered in disgust as she fumbled in the dark for the towel beside the basin. "Didn't a famous psychiatrist once say, 'Sometimes a cigar is just a cigar'?"

She moved to the bed and crawled between the rumpled sheets. "Well, this dream is just a dream, nothing more. You didn't kill anyone, Madeline. Someone tried to kill *you*. You're the victim, not the assassin," she said vehemently. "Now stop talking to yourself and go to sleep."

But it was a long time before she did.

"THERE IT IS. Jermain Island, dead ahead," the pilot said pointing. "We'll be coming in over Smuggler's Cove, which will give you a really good view of the fourth and fifth holes of the golf course."

"Oh, goodie," Maddy murmured dryly. She didn't mean to be sarcastic to the charming helicopter pilot who'd picked them up at the hospital helipad fifteen minutes ago, but the roar of the helicopter was making her head pound, and her stomach heaved precariously every time she glanced out the window on her right.

"Are you okay?" Adam asked in concern as he adjusted the microphone of the headset that matched hers and the pilot's.

Maddy attempted a reassuring smile. "Of course. Don't I look okay?"

Adam shook his head. "Sorry, but no. You look a little green around the gills—not that green isn't an attractive color on you," he added quickly.

Maddy chuckled. "We've been flying so low over the water it's made me a little nauseated, I guess," she told him, not bothering to mention that lack of sleep might be a contributing factor. She was already too dependent on Adam; she had no intention of increasing that dependency by running to him with every little problem. Besides, what could he possibly do about her nightmare?

"Why didn't you warn me that I get airsick?" she asked him, instead.

"Because you don't. In fact, you're a better flier—not to mention sailor—than I am. This is obviously just another of the side effects from that nasty bump on your head."

"Mmm. Let's hope it's more short-term than some of the other side effects."

"Amen."

The chopper—and Maddy's stomach—gave a small lurch when they hit a strong updraft of air. Solid earth was below them now, and as the helicopter slowed, she closed her eyes and took deep breaths until she felt the craft settle onto its pad.

Almost instantly her stomach settled, too, leaving nothing but acute embarrassment when she looked up and realized that the handsome, forty-something pilot was studying her.

He had removed his headset and Maddy did likewise in time to hear him say, "Sorry about the rough ride, Mrs. Hopewell. Blame it on your doctor. His last instruction to me before we took off was to keep to a low altitude so that you wouldn't be subjected to too many changes in air pressure."

Now that she was feeling better it was easy to forgive him. "I understand, Mr. Masterson. But if you don't mind, I think I'll take the ferry back to Charleston when I leave."

He flashed a roguish grin. "I won't object—on one condition."

"What's that?"

"You have to call me Duke."

"All right, Duke," she acquiesced, returning his friendly smile.

"I didn't mean to interrupt, *Duke*," Adam said, "but could you let us out of this tin can? My wife needs to get to her room so she can rest."

"Certainly," the pilot replied amiably, completely unfazed by Adam's brusque tone. Maddy got the distinct impression that Duke flirted with all the female guests, married or single. If he kept it up, Maddy suspected she'd find out whether her husband was the jealous type.

The passenger door behind Maddy's seat opened, and the heliport attendant deployed the retractable stairway. Adam offered Maddy a steadying hand, but as soon as she climbed out of the helicopter and the warm, sea breeze brushed her skin, she felt a renewal of her strength.

Taking in a deep breath, she closed her eyes and let her head fall back so she could relish the feel of the sun on her face.

Adam gestured toward the white Bride's Bay mini-van across the tarmac. "Why don't you get us a seat while I check the luggage?"

The minivan was parked beside a small, cottagelike building that apparently served as the heliport office. Duke Masterson was standing beside the open passenger door of the van as she approached.

"All aboard!" he called out merrily. "Next stop, Bride's Bay, main hotel."

"You're the pilot *and* the chauffeur?" she asked as she approached.

"Only when I have passengers as beautiful as you—" he grinned mischievously "—or when I have business at the hotel."

As he held out a hand to assist her into the van, she asked, "Have you worked here long, Duke?"

"Almost two years."

"It must be a good job, then."

"One of the best I've ever had," he replied, leaning against the door. "Sun, sand, elegant surroundings, a steady paycheck, and best of all, I meet some of the most beautiful women in the world on a daily basis."

He made the statement with just the right look and enough emphasis to let Maddy know he included her in that final job perk. She chuckled. "Tell me, Duke, are all the Bride's Bay employees such outrageous flirts?"

"Absolutely. It's part of the job."

"Really?" She glanced over her shoulder to the rear of the van where Adam was tipping the attendant who'd just loaded their luggage into the back. Thinking of the way he'd snapped at the flirtatious pilot, Maddy murmured, "Well, that ought to make this honeymoon more interesting."

"You're on your honeymoon?" Duke asked.

The implication of what she'd said hit Maddy like a ton of bricks and she felt her cheeks turn bright red. "No! Absolutely not. This is not a honeymoon," she said hastily. "Our trip to Bride's Bay was originally supposed to be a *second* honeymoon, but our anniversary plans were scuttled by my accident," she explained.

Adam slid into the seat next to Maddy just in time to hear those last few words, and his eyebrows shot up at her choice of the word "accident," but Maddy didn't retract it. Dr. Manion hadn't explained the full nature of her head injury to the helicopter pilot, and Maddy didn't want to spend the next few days explaining that she had amnesia to everyone she met.

Duke slid the passenger door closed, and as he circled the van, Adam's curious expression turned to one of concern as he looked at Maddy. "Are you all right? You look flushed."

He raised his hand to her forehead to check her temperature, but Maddy waved him off. "I'm just a little tired, I guess."

As soon as they were underway, Duke asked, "So, what anniversary will you two be celebrating?"

"Our tenth," Adam replied.

"When, exactly?"

Maddy knew Adam wasn't thrilled by the pilot's questions, but he answered, anyway. "A week from Wednesday. Why? Are you planning on giving us a party?"

Duke shot a quick glance over his shoulder. "Yes, actually. That was pretty much what I had in mind. The manager of Bride's Bay takes great pride in providing personalized service to all our guests. I'm sure Ms. Jermain will want to do something special to help you celebrate."

"That's not necessary," Maddy said quickly. She had no desire to celebrate the anniversary of a wedding she couldn't remember, and she was determined to avoid anything that even hinted at romanticism.

Adam might not have shared her feelings, but clearly he understood them. "No, it's not necessary at all," he said. "My wife and I are planning a very quiet celebration."

"No problem," Duke replied. "I'm certain Ms. Jermain will take that into consideration. Surely even a quiet celebration could make use of a complimentary bottle of champagne."

Maddy darted a nervous glance at her husband. "I suppose that'd be all right. Please . . . just don't let anyone make a fuss."

"All right. No fuss," Duke promised.

They fell silent, and Maddy shook off her discomfort by studying the impeccably manicured grounds of the island resort, looking for anything that seemed familiar. They were following the shoreline of a wide cove dotted with sailboats and pleasure craft of every description. A small village and marina lay directly ahead, and across the bay Maddy could see the twin spires of a large, two-story structure.

"What's that building to the south?" she asked. "The one with the flags on top of what appear to be turrets."

"That's the clubhouse, where you'll find the golf pro shop, the health spa, indoor pool, racquetball and tennis courts and a juice bar. Its facilities are open to all guests and island residents," Duke explained. "Are you a golfer, Mrs. Hopewell?"

Maddy felt a small stab of panic and she looked at Adam. He came to her rescue immediately. "No, my wife isn't much of a golfer," Adam told Duke. "It's a little too slow for her taste. She prefers tennis."

If Duke noticed that Maddy didn't answer for herself, he didn't comment on it. "What about horseback riding?"

Again Maddy looked to Adam, but this time he just

gave her an emphatic nod. "Yes, I enjoy riding very much," she told Duke.

"Then you're in luck. The Bride's Bay stable is one of the best in the state, and the riding trails through the wilderness area are beautiful at this time of year."

Adam was right, she obviously did like horses, because she found the idea of a ride very appealing. Before she could say so, though, Adam was telling Duke, "Yes, I remember all the wildflowers that were in bloom on the trails the last time we were here. We'll have to check with Dr. Manion to see how long it'll be before Maddy is able to ride."

"You've been to Bride's Bay before?" Duke asked.

"On our honeymoon," Adam replied.

"Well, welcome back."

Duke didn't seem puzzled by the fact that she hadn't recognized a building she'd have seen on her honeymoon, Maddy thought. He probably hadn't caught the inconsistency, she decided.

Duke went on to tell Adam about some of the changes that had been made in the resort in the last ten years, but Maddy listened with only half an ear to the conversation about beach cabanas and new security surveillance cameras. Her full attention shifted back to her surroundings as she searched for something familiar among the moss-draped live oaks, towering magnolia trees, palmettos and the parklike lawn trimmed with banks of sculpted azalea bushes. At last a magnificent antebellum mansion appeared at the end of the road, like a pot of gold at the end of a rainbow.

It was an imposing structure, two stories with a veranda on both levels and a couple of sprawling additions. Maddy fell in love with it instantly—but unfortunately, nothing seemed even remotely familiar.

About the time Maddy realized that all conversation in the van had ceased she also felt Adam's eyes on her, searching for a glimmer of recognition on her face. She couldn't bring herself to look at him. Her own disappointment was keen; she didn't need to feel the weight of his, as well.

Duke stopped the van and Adam didn't wait for him to come around to open the sliding door. He did it himself and climbed out, then turned and gave Maddy a hand out.

"Well?" he asked anxiously as soon as she was on her feet.

Maddy looked up at the lovely hotel and shook her head. "I recognize the architectural style of the building, but that's all. I'm sorry, Adam," she added with genuine regret.

He shook his head. "Quit saying that, Maddy. None of this is your fault. Come on. Let's get checked in." He moved up the stairs, past the doorman into an elegant entry hall, and Maddy followed, noting every detail of the magnificent room, from the sweeping central staircase to the shops that lined the hall on her left. Still nothing triggered her memory. They crossed to the front desk and Maddy waited patiently as Adam signed an old-fashioned guest register while the clerk behind the counter punched their names into a computer.

The door to the manager's office behind the front desk opened, and an attractive, smartly dressed woman carrying a portfolio and a sheath of computer printouts emerged.

"Ms. Jermain?" Adam asked, raising his voice slightly.

The woman turned toward him and stepped to the

desk with a perfect may-I-help-you smile in place. "Yes?"

"I'm Adam Hopewell. We spoke on the phone."

Liz Jermain's smile broadened appreciably. "Of course, Mr. Hopewell. Welcome to Bride's Bay." Her look encompassed both Adam and Maddy. It was clear she knew who they were, but she tactfully refrained from mentioning their unusual circumstances. "If there's anything I can do to make your stay more enjoyable, I hope you'll let me know."

"Thank you," Adam said. "In fact I wondered if I might meet with you later this morning, if you have a few minutes free."

"Certainly. I have a staff luncheon at noon, but any time before that you'll find me here in my office."

"Thank you."

Liz Jermain turned her attention to assisting the desk clerk, Moira Petty, handing over two room keys as Adam signed the computer copy of their registration slip. She gestured across the lobby to a white-haired man in his mid-sixties, who came over immediately. "This is Shadroe Teach, our bell captain and resident historian," Liz explained. "Shad's great-great-great-grandfather was one of the island's first settlers, so if there's anything you'd like to know about Jermain Island or Bride's Bay, he's the man to ask."

"It's a pleasure to meet you, Mr. Teach," Maddy told him. "Are you any relation to Blackbeard the Pirate?"

"Yes, indeed, ma'am. And proud of it," the bell captain replied. "Every family should have at least one black sheep."

"Shad, Mr. and Mrs. Hopewell are in room 215," Liz said.

Maddy looked around. "But where's our luggage?"

"It's already upstairs in your suite, Mrs. Hopewell. If you'd care to follow me..." Teach gestured toward the curving staircase.

Liz Jermain watched the threesome cross the lobby. Her efficient but noncommittal hotel-manager smile stayed firmly in place until the guests reached the stairs, but as soon as she was certain they were out of earshot, her smile disappeared.

"Where's Tom?" she demanded without looking at the clerk beside her. "Is he in the security office?"

"I don't think so," Moira replied. "I saw him leave the Fortress about twenty minutes ago."

"Well, if he's not there, he could be anywhere," Liz noted. "Page him for me and tell him I want him in my office immediately."

"Yes, ma'am."

Liz cast one last glance at the staircase just as Shad led the new guests across the second-floor landing into the central corridor. Her hotel had a new security chief operating from an office appropriately known as the Fortress, an upgraded surveillance system and employees who were being trained in security measures. If what she'd been told about Madeline Hopewell was true, Bride's Bay was going to need all of that—and more—to keep its newest guest alive.

Refusing to give in to the apprehension gnawing at her, Liz turned on her heel and disappeared back into her office to wait for her chief of security.

CHAPTER FIVE

THE SUITE the bell captain led Maddy and Adam to was magnificent, no question about it. The sitting room was late Victorian in style, its furnishings a combination of authentic antiques and excellent reproductions, with a richly hued Turkish carpet occupying the center of the hardwood floor.

Shadroe Teach pointed out the fully stocked bar standing in one corner and the Hepplewhite secretary in the other. When he reached the French windows, which were framed by hunter green velvet drapes, he pulled back the sheers and threw open the doors to the balcony.

"As you can see, this is a corner suite, and it offers a little more privacy than some of our other rooms," Teach said as he stepped onto the balcony. Maddy followed him with Adam right behind her and discovered a long, wide, shady veranda that did, in fact, offer considerable privacy. A jungle of tropical palms and ferns formed a seemingly impenetrable wall to the left, separating Maddy and Adam's balcony from the one next door.

When she stepped around the corner to the right Maddy discovered another bank of plants that almost but not quite camouflaged the blank wall that marked the junction between the north wing and the main house. The centerpiece of the balcony was a pair of cushioned fan-backed chairs and a glass-topped table of wrought iron that matched the iron railing.

Impressed, Maddy stepped to the railing and discovered a magnificent garden spread out below her. A formal rose garden flowed into a labyrinthine maze. A fountain stood in the center of the rose garden, and here and there was a stone bench.

"Oh, this is wonderful. I've never seen anything so beautiful," she breathed.

The bell captain heard the compliment. "Thank you, Mrs. Hopewell," he said. "The Judge prides himself on having the most beautiful gardens in the Carolinas year round, but he's particularly proud of them at this time of year, what with the roses at their peak."

Maddy turned to him. "The Judge?"

"Judge Cameron Bradshaw," Teach expounded. "He's the husband of Miz Elizabeth, the owner of Bride's Bay. The Judge retired over ten years ago, but you wouldn't know it by how hard he works in the gardens. He doesn't allow anyone to touch his roses."

Maddy couldn't quite cover her surprise. "The hotel manager we met downstairs is married to a retired judge?"

"No, Maddy," Adam replied. "Liz Jermain is the granddaughter of the resort's owner, Elizabeth Jermain."

"That's right," Teach said as he turned and unlocked a second set of French doors. "If you'd care to move on now, I'll show you the rest of the suite. This is the master bedroom, of course." He threw open the double doors and stepped inside.

Adam was politely waiting for Maddy to precede him, so she tore herself away from the magnificent view of the gardens and followed the bell captain into the bedroom.

Like everything else she'd seen at Bride's Bay, the room was picture perfect, with a ceiling fan, planted palms, two more fan-backed chairs and a king-size bed draped in mosquito netting. It was very old-fashioned, decidedly tropical—and unabashedly romantic.

That impression was dramatically highlighted when Maddy realized that all their suitcases—both Adam's and her own—were sitting at the foot of the bed, making a bold statement about an intimacy Maddy had been doing her best to avoid even thinking about.

"Adam—" she began, but he was already one step ahead of her.

"I believe there's been a mistake, Mr. Teach," he said. "I asked for a two-bedroom suite."

If the bell captain had an opinion about married couples sleeping in separate rooms he was too experienced to show it. "Yes, sir. The second room is through here, on the other side of the dressing room," Teach said, throwing open the door on the far wall.

Breathing a sigh of relief, Maddy followed the bell captain across the room, eager to leave the luxurious tropical bedroom and its implications behind.

Unfortunately her imagination wasn't being cooperative. Unable to stop herself, she paused to take one last look at the romantic room and saw a sudden flash of it under other circumstances: the bedclothes thrown back and hopelessly rumpled; her clothes and Adam's strewn across the room as though they'd been shed in a great hurry; she and Adam on that rumpled bed, locked in a heated embrace.

The image was so vivid that for a moment Maddy felt certain it was a memory, but despite the flush of heat that swept through her, there were no other memories or emotions accompanying it.

The graphic vision of Adam making love to her wasn't a memory; it was a fantasy.

Her disappointment at that realization was profound—but only because it meant her memory wasn't returning. At least, that was what she tried to tell herself. It had absolutely nothing to do with the fact that remembering how much she'd loved Adam would lower all the barriers she'd erected against falling in love with him now.

Turning away from the room and those thoughts, Maddy hurried after Adam and Teach, moving through a spacious dressing room and past the door to the bathroom to emerge into the second bedroom. Though Maddy was undeniably relieved that there *was* a second room, she wasn't impressed with the decor. It was pretty but unimaginative, very feminine in tone, with lots of frills and lace and pink roses. That might not have been so bad if there'd been windows to let in natural light and carry the almost oppressive rose theme outside to the garden, but that wasn't the case. There was only the door that connected the rose room to the master bedroom and another that sat around a corner, presumably leading back to the sitting room.

"Is this satisfactory, sir?" the bell captain asked once Adam and Maddy had both had a chance to view the room.

"It's perfect," Adam declared. "Thank you."

"If you'll tell me which luggage you'd like moved into this room, I'll—"

Adam shook his head, cutting him off. "That won't be necessary, Mr. Teach. I'll take care of it myself."

"Very well, sir." Teach stepped around the corner and opened the other door. Maddy followed him and found herself in a tiny corridor with the door to the master bedroom directly opposite. A tall archway to the left led them back into the sitting room, completing a big circle—and their tour.

While Adam thanked the bell captain verbally and monetarily, Maddy moved toward the French doors. By the time she reached them, Teach was gone, and Maddy was finally alone with her husband. There was no Dr. Manion to intervene, no nurses to interrupt, no guards waiting just outside the door.

Just Maddy and Adam.

Alone.

Maddy suddenly felt as nervous as a bride on her wedding night. Remnants of her bedroom fantasy still sizzled inside her, and she had to sternly remind herself that this wasn't a honeymoon. Adam had already proved that he had no intention of pressing her for intimacy until she was ready, and Maddy was absolutely, one-hundred-percent certain that she was *not* ready. Being attracted to Adam didn't mean she trusted him enough to share a bed with him.

"Well, do you like the suite?" Adam asked her.

When Maddy turned and found that he had stayed on the other side of the room, she wondered if he, too, was nervous. "It's beautiful, Adam. Thank you for bringing me."

"It was your idea—originally," he reminded her.

Maddy nodded. "I guess that's true, but a considerable amount of water has passed under the bridge since then."

He quirked one eyebrow. "That's one way of putting it."

"Adam . . . ?" Her question hung suspended in the air while Maddy debated whether or not to ask.

"What?" he prompted.

"Did we . . . Was this the room where we spent our honeymoon?"

"No. Our room was downstairs. Why? Have you seen something familiar?" he asked hopefully.

Maddy shook her head. "No. Absolutely not."

Adam frowned at her vehemence, but didn't question it. Instead, he cleared his throat and stepped toward the archway that provided access to both bedrooms. "Listen, why don't I put your things into the rose room and you can lie down and get—"

"Whoa, there! Wait a minute, big fella," Maddy said, moving around the sofa toward him. "Who decided you get the gorgeous tropical paradise with the sunset exposure and a view of the garden while I get the windowless dungeon?" she demanded to know even though she wasn't really sure she wanted the bedroom that had already evoked such a sexy image of her and Adam together. But on the other hand, she was getting tired of the way Adam made decisions without bothering to consult her. It was time to make a stand.

"Maddy, the smaller bedroom is hardly a dungeon," Adam argued. "And the reason you should take it is obvious."

"Not to me," she countered. "Please elaborate."

"All right," he said, his tone deadly earnest. "The rose room has no exterior access to the balcony, which means that if someone wants to get to you, they'll have to go through me to do it. And I promise you, Maddy, *no one* will get past me." He turned and disappeared through the archway.

Maddy just stood there, stunned. He was absolutely serious. She was certain of it. The protection her husband had promised wasn't limited to bodyguards and high-security hotels. He was more than willing to put his own life on the line to keep her safe, and there was no bravado in his promise. He believed he could do it—and instinct told Maddy that she should believe it, too. Her husband was a dangerous man.

But where did an antiquities broker acquire such macho confidence? As she listened to the sound of Adam moving her luggage from the master bedroom, through the dressing room and into the smaller one, Maddy realized just how much she still didn't know about her husband.

"Maddy, I feel certain that if Dr. Manion was here he'd tell you it's time for you to rest," Adam said as he came back through the arch, this time from the direction of the rose room. "This is the most activity you've had in quite a long time."

Like Dr. Manion, Adam didn't know about the exercise regimen Maddy had prescribed for herself, but he was right in one respect. Her strength wasn't anywhere near normal—whatever that might be—and she was already exhausted even though the day wasn't half over yet.

Though she hated being told what to do, arguing with Adam just for the sake of arguing would have been pointless. Instead, she decided to barter. "If I take a nap like a good girl, can we explore the island this afternoon? There has to be *something* around here that'll jog my memory."

"I'm anxious to test that, too," he answered. "You get some rest and we'll start with a short walking tour after lunch."

Maddy cocked her head to one side. "And in the meantime, you'll go downstairs and meet with the hotel manager?"

"Yes."

"Would you care to tell me why?"

He didn't look as though he wanted to answer, but he did. "I have some security considerations I want to discuss with her."

"Such as?"

"Nothing you need to worry about."

His answer was tantamount to waving a red cape in front of a bull. "I beg your pardon?" she gasped. "Look, mister, I don't know what our marriage was like before, but I'm not going to play 'the little woman' for you or any other man. I refuse to be dismissed with a pat on the head, a smile and a condescending—" she lowered her voice dramatically and propped her hands on her hips "—'don't worry your pretty little head, honey, this is man's work'!"

Adam bit back a smile. "That's not what I'm doing, Maddy, I promise you. I'm sorry if it appeared that way. But I swore I'd make sure you're safe and I'm just trying to keep that promise. Do you want to go downstairs to Ms. Jermain's office with me?"

The stubborn, independent part of Maddy wanted to say, "Yes, definitely," but the part that was still recovering from an attempt on her life was demanding somewhat insistently that she get some rest. She'd already seen enough of the resort's security precautions to know she was safe for the moment. There would be plenty of time later to check out the details for herself.

"No, you go on alone," she said after a moment. "I'll lock up the balcony doors and get some rest."

Adam smiled at her. "You rest. I'll lock up."

She started to tell him she was perfectly capable of locking a couple of doors, but she suddenly felt too drained to assert her independence. "All right," she acquiesced, heading for the rose room. "Will you wake me about one?"

"Of course. And I'll have lunch waiting for you on our balcony when you get up. If that meets with your approval," he added with exaggerated deference.

"That would be lovely."

"Rest well, darling."

"I will." She slipped through the hall and closed the door to her room, throwing it into shadows because the only light source came from the other bedroom. She switched on the lamp on the night table, then folded back the bedclothes on the old-fashioned four-poster and lay down without bothering to remove her dress.

She turned off the light, but despite her exhaustion, she forced herself to remain alert, listening to the sounds of Adam moving about until she finally heard him leave the suite. Then she got out of bed and returned to the sitting room. She checked the French doors to be certain they were locked, then performed the same ritual in Adam's bedroom. Once she was certain she was secure, she returned to her bed in the rose room, removed her trusty nail file from the pocket of her sundress and slipped it under her pillow.

"I've gotta get a better weapon," she murmured as she drifted off to sleep with the stiletto-tipped file clutched in her hand. Macho husband or not, Maddy was a long way from trusting anyone.

THOMAS GRAVES took the front stairs two at a time and hurried through the hotel lobby. Nothing about the message he'd just received summoning him to Liz Jermain's office indicated that there was an emergency, but the fifty-one-year-old security specialist had been running at maximum speed since the day he'd taken this job, and it didn't appear he was going to be able to slow down anytime soon.

He was spending every waking moment solving the problems he'd inherited from his predecessor, whipping the staff into shape, installing new equipment and instituting new security measures. And in his spare time, he was taking care of little details like preparing for a presidential visit and providing added security for a woman being stalked by a killer.

He didn't have time to waste even a minute, but his new boss wouldn't have demanded his presence if it wasn't important. She was a tough, fair-minded woman who'd earned his respect early on by making some difficult decisions and sticking to them even though it meant opposing her grandmother, Elizabeth Jermain. The old woman hadn't seen the need for some of the high-tech security measures Tom had recommended, but Liz had stood up to the iron-willed dowager and eventually won.

Tom had been here long enough to know that anyone who could stand toe-to-toe with Miz Elizabeth deserved lots of respect, and Liz Jermain had his.

When he slipped behind the reservation desk and saw that Liz's door was ajar he rapped twice before sticking his head in. "You wanted to see me, Boss Lady?"

Despite her concern, Liz had to smile at the nickname for her that seemed to have cropped up recently. "Yes, I did, Tom. Come in, shut the door and have a seat," she said, laying aside a stack of photographs she hadn't been able to concentrate on. Selecting pictures for a new set of Bride's Bay postcards wasn't high on her priority list today. Her smile faded as Tom dropped into one of the two chairs on the other side of her desk. "The Hopewells just arrived, Tom. I hope you've got all your ducks in a row on this one."

"I'm as ready as I can be, Liz," he replied with a shrug. "The added security is going to cost Mr. Hopewell a small fortune, but I've provided everything he asked for—including two bodyguards."

"Good. Because he made it clear that money is no object," she reminded him. "Have you told Dan Luther about Mrs. Hopewell yet?"

Tom shook his head. "Nope."

"He's not going to be happy."

Tom made a sound that was somewhere between a laugh and a grunt. "That doesn't begin to cover it. Our friendly, neighborhood Secret Service agent wants this place locked down tighter than a drum before the President arrives, and he's only got two weeks to do it."

Liz glanced down at her desk calendar, ignoring the bright red slashes that crossed off the last two weeks. "Actually it's more like ten days—" she consulted her watch "—twenty-one hours and fourteen minutes."

Tom chuckled. "Don't worry, Liz. We'll survive this."

"Which one? Madeline Hopewell or the President of the United States?"

"Both," he replied.

"This Hopewell thing is just such bad timing," Liz moaned. "Luther has been turning this place upside down for weeks now, driving everyone crazy. We didn't need even more pressure."

"But Luther's security measures are going to work to our benefit with the Hopewell woman. Between my security details and Luther's, it should be nearly impossible for any unauthorized persons to step foot on Jermain Island."

"What about *authorized* people, like guests?" Liz asked.

"I've taken care of that, too, Liz," he assured her. "The Secret Service has already done security checks on everyone whose reservations coincide with the President's visit, and I'm doing computer background checks on everyone who's made a reservation since you booked Adam Hopewell. Logically current guests and those who made reservations *before* Hopewell shouldn't pose any threat, since no one could've known that he planned to bring his wife here. That eliminates ninety percent of the hotel's guests as a potential threat."

Liz was impressed. Tom did, indeed, sound as though he had things under control. "That's excellent, Tom."

"As my mother always said, 'An ounce of prevention is worth a pound of cure,'" he quoted with a smile.

Liz smiled, too. "I wish you'd been around to remind me of that when the White House called to ask if the Presidential Suite was available the last two weeks in June. I could have prevented a lot of major headaches with a simple, 'No, sorry.'"

He chuckled. "You don't mean that."

"In my rational moments, I don't mean it. If everything goes smoothly, the prestige and publicity we stand to gain will be worth a headache of any size, but on days like this I start to wish that the President had elected to spend his vacation down at Hilton Head."

"Well, that's not going to happen this year. You can't create one of the most challenging golf courses in the U.S. and expect the world's most famous golf fanatic to pass it up."

Liz rolled her eyes. "I might be more inclined to accept that rationale if the President was a decent golfer. Even with the help of his famous lucky towel he hasn't played a par game since he took office."

Tom chuckled. "Don't worry, Boss Lady, this will all be over in a few weeks and things can get back to normal."

"I certainly hope so."

He frowned as a new thought occurred to him. "Liz, this business with the Hopewells doesn't have anything to do with your reasons for canceling your weekend trip, does it?"

The question clearly caught her off guard. "No, of course not. I just have too much to do to go away at a time like this."

Tom knew she was a busy woman, but he wasn't sure he believed her excuse. She'd seemed a little distracted these past few days, and Tom wondered if it had anything to do with the love affair she was supposedly having with some mystery man on the mainland. Tom wasn't convinced that he believed the rumor, which had been circulating even before he'd arrived at Bride's Bay, but he did find it a little strange that Liz always refused to talk about where she'd been on her days off. Duke Masterson, who usually flew Liz off the island when she made these trips, had apparently been sworn to silence, because he refused to comment whenever anyone asked him where he took her.

Now, though, Liz had canceled a trip, and despite her outward efficiency, Tom could tell that something was bothering her. He had to wonder if it was her mystery lover.

"Are you sure it's just business, Liz?" he asked her. "Because if there's anything else wrong you know you can always talk to me."

For just a second Tom thought he saw a crack in Liz's cool facade, but she sealed it quickly. "I'm fine, Tom, really. I just need a vacation, and I'm going to take one as soon as the President—"

Liz's intercom buzzed and Tom got the distinct impression she was relieved by the interruption. He started to rise as though to leave, but Liz waved him back into his seat. "No. I think I know what this is. You stay," she ordered. "Yes?" she said into the phone.

"Mr. Hopewell is here to see you, Liz," the desk clerk informed her.

"Send him right in." Liz replaced the receiver and moved around her desk toward the door as she told Tom, "It's Adam Hopewell. When he checked in this morning he asked for a meeting with me, and based on the phone conversations I've had with him, I'm certain he's going to want to speak to you, as well. That's one of the reasons I sent for you."

Displaying impeccable timing, Liz opened the door just as Adam reached it. "Please, come in, Mr. Hopewell," she said, extending her hand for a brief but firm handshake that ushered him through the door. "I hope your wife got settled in comfortably."

"Yes, she did. Thank you."

"Good." Liz gestured to Tom, who rose to meet the guest. "This is our chief of security, Thomas Graves."

"Mr. Graves. I'm glad you're here." Adam shook the man's hand. "I assume you both know what I want to discuss."

"I believe so," Liz replied, moving behind her desk. When she was seated, the men took the chairs opposite hers. "You've expressed your concerns regarding security to me, and I've passed them along to Mr. Graves."

"And I've passed them on to my staff," Tom told Adam. "I believe we have everything in place, Mr. Hopewell. Your wife will be safe here."

The security chief's confidence didn't seem to impress Adam at all. In fact, Liz noted that Hopewell's sharp, handsome features were a mask that held not one trace of warmth or friendliness. His manner went beyond businesslike; it was coldly confrontational as he replied, "Frankly, Graves, that doesn't reassure me as much as it might have twenty-four hours ago. I made the decision to bring my wife here based on the reputation Bride's Bay has for privacy and security. Unfortunately the private detective I hired to verify that reputation discovered a number of serious security breaches within the past six months that have me deeply concerned."

Liz stiffened, but Tom's calm demeanor didn't change. "If your detective was thorough, you know that most of those security breaches happened under my predecessor," he told Adam.

"True enough," Adam said, "but one man does not constitute a security system or a security *staff*. Within the last six months, this resort has had a baby abandoned on the concierge's doorstep, the disgruntled ex-husband of one of the employees hold a diplomat at gunpoint, and a convicted traitor hiding out on the island for weeks. And those are only the minor breaches! Would you care to talk about the murder that took place in room 207? Or the attempted murder of a juror who was—"

"Mr. Hopewell, there were extenuating circumstances surrounding all of those incidents," Liz told him firmly, her face flaming with embarrassment.

"Oh, really? Tell that to the woman who died in room 207," Adam retorted.

Words failed Liz, but not Tom Graves. "What would be the point, Mr. Hopewell? My predecessor was a nice guy who got sloppy, but I was hired to change that, and I believe I have."

"Prove it," Adam challenged him.

"Gladly. If you'll come with me we'll take a tour of the facility and I'll show you everything I've done to improve security. You can meet the men I've assigned to protect your wife, and I'll go over every detail of the special arrangements I've made for Mrs. Hopewell. If that still doesn't satisfy you, we'll talk about what else we can reasonably do to assure your wife's safety."

"All right, let's do that," Adam said, coming to his feet. "Show me what you're going to do to keep my wife alive."

Tom rose, as well, and met the guest's stern gaze without flinching. "We're going to do everything we can, Mr. Hopewell."

"You'd better, Graves, because if anything happens to Maddy I'm going to hold you personally responsible. Now, let's get started on that tour." Adam turned on his heel and stalked out.

Tom looked at Liz. "If you're not going to take the weekend off, can I?" he asked forlornly, then headed out the door without waiting for an answer.

MAGIC CRYSTAL

For a while, Charley knew it and so
pushed. Maddy, I'm giving in until you obey my response how I've appreciated in this line." John
running on his breath and stared out.

"I suppose so." "...Don't want to go to table th
week day off..." ... we said..." ... fountain itself
off the door with anything no power

CHAPTER SIX

"WELL? WHAT LOOKS GOOD to you?"

"Everything. Since you let me sleep all afternoon I'm so hungry I could eat the menu itself," Maddy replied. She closed the embossed leather folder and handed it across the table to Adam. "But I'll settle for the lobster."

"Oops," he said, handing the menu right back to her. "Bad choice. You love shellfish, but if you eat it I'll be visiting you in the hospital tomorrow."

"I'm allergic?"

"You've been known to break into hives if a waiter carries a lobster past our table. You don't want to find out what happens when you ingest it."

Maddy groaned and opened the menu again. "Great. Back to the drawing board." The rumble of her stomach and the delicious smells all around her gave her the incentive to choose quickly. She opted for the veal and Adam signaled the waiter.

"What else am I allergic to?" she asked as soon as he'd placed their order.

"Nothing. Just shellfish."

Maddy tilted her head to one side. "What about you? Any allergies I should be aware of?"

Adam seemed a little surprised by the question, and Maddy realized it was one of the first she'd ever asked about him personally. It was about time, she decided.

"No allergies," he told her. "And no major health problems of any kind."

"What do you do for exercise?"

"I try to run several mornings a week, and we had a rowing machine in our apartment that I used at night before bed."

"Did we ever jog together?" Maddy asked him.

He made a seesaw motion with his hand. "Oh...sometimes, but not often."

Maddy sensed a story behind his answer and she leaned forward, resting her forearms on the table. "Why not?"

"Because you're too competitive," Adam said matter-of-factly. "Whenever we go out for a run you turn it into a race."

"*I'm* too competitive!" Maddy exclaimed. "Doesn't it take two to make a race?"

A sheepish smile teased Adam's lips. "Well...I suppose, maybe...just maybe I'm, uh, *almost* as competitive as you."

"Yeah, right. Almost, my eye," she grumbled. She fought back a grin as she pictured them jogging along the bank of the Seine, an early-morning mist rising from the water. They picked up speed until they were running flat out, leaving other joggers behind, and raced neck and neck, neither of them giving ground as they pounded toward the Pont des Arts. By the time they reached the footbridge that led across the river to the Louvre, they were both laughing as they gasped for air. The image was fuzzy and a little romantic, too.

But then the image sharpened so abruptly it left Maddy breathless. She could *see* the Pont des Arts. She could smell the faintly acrid scent of the river and feel the mist that brushed her face. She could hear her own pounding footsteps as she ran, and somewhere behind her she heard voices raised in an argument.

Maddy could see the whole scene as clearly as she could see Adam across the table from her, and she knew she had just reclaimed a memory.

That realization made her grab onto it, trying to bring more of the moment into focus, to feel what it meant to be Madeline Hopewell jogging in the Paris dawn, but as soon as she tried to enlarge the memory it evaporated.

"Maddy?"

She blinked twice and realized that Adam had reached across the table and was holding her hand. A smile started inside her and burst out. "I could see it, Adam. I remembered!"

He squeezed her hand, his eyes glowing with excitement. "Remembered what?"

"Jogging on the Quai d'Orsay across from the Louvre. I remember being there! The sun was barely up, and there was a couple—man and woman, joggers, I think—and they were arguing because one of them had left their apartment without the door key. They were locked out."

Adam laughed. "Maddy, that's amazing! That's wonderful! What else do you remember?"

Her smile faded. "Nothing. Just . . . that one instant." She shrugged off her melancholy as quickly as it had come. This was good news, not bad. It proved that her memories were still intact and eventually she'd get them back. She managed something that resembled a smile. "Did we ever jog together there?" she asked Adam.

"Sometimes. But I guess . . ." He hesitated. "I guess you didn't see me in the memory?"

Maddy was as disappointed as he was, but she wasn't going to let it spoil their evening. "No, but I didn't really expect to."

Adam stiffened and withdrew his hand from hers. "Why not?"

"Didn't you say our jogs always turned into races?" He nodded. "Yes."

Maddy shrugged and spread her hands wide. "Obviously I was winning."

Adam had to fight hard to keep from laughing. "Well, I suppose that's possible. I probably did let you win once or twice."

"Let me win! That will be the day Adam Hopewell!" she chided. "You're clearly not above taking advantage of my condition in order to glorify your own meager accomplishments. You ought to be ashamed."

"Oh, I am," he said much too seriously. "I am mortified. I should be horsewhipped."

"Yes, you should be," she said with mock disapproval. "I'm going to have to put you on a lie detector and find out what other fibs, misrepresentations, falsehoods, and out-and-out lies you've told me."

He snapped his fingers. "Shucks. My deceit has been unmasked. I stand guilty as charged, madam."

"Oh, ho! Then you admit that I won most of our races."

Adam nodded, but made it look like the hardest confession he'd ever made in his life.

"Anything else you'd like to tell me?" she asked with mock suspicion.

Growing suddenly covert, Adam darted quick glances around the room to be certain no one was within earshot, then leaned toward her confidentially. His manner was so exaggerated that it was everything Maddy could do to keep a straight face. "Don't tell anyone else this, darling," he whispered, "but you're a spy for the Central Intelligence Agency."

Maddy stifled a laugh and widened her eyes in mock amazement. "Really? A spy for the CIA? Wow. I guess that means you're a spy, too."

He nodded. "Actually I'm the one who recruited you."

"And together we chase bad guys the world over?"

Adam took a sip of wine. "Something like that. Although I think the CIA is more involved with collecting intelligence than capturing villains."

"Oh. Of course. I stand corrected," Maddy said with a chuckle. "Is there anything else I should know about myself?"

Adam appeared to think it over. "Nope. That's it."

"But where's my secret decoder ring?" she asked.

He reached across the table and took her left hand in his, then lightly massaged the base of her ring finger. "You refused to wear it, remember?" he said wistfully. "You really can be obstinate."

His touch left Maddy a little breathless. She yanked her hand away, wanting to shatter the intimacy of the moment. "Obstinate? Obviously you're one of those men whose egos are threatened by independent women."

"Obviously. That's why our marriage has lasted so many years."

"Touché." She conceded the point to him, but it raised another issue she'd been wondering about. "All joking aside, Adam, why has our marriage lasted ten years?"

He took the question seriously. "Because we love each other, and more importantly, we understand each other."

Maddy tilted her head to one side. "What's the most important thing you understand about me?"

"That you're the most independent, self-sufficient woman I've ever known, and you won't settle for anything less than being treated as a fifty-fifty partner in any relationship."

Her brow furrowed in thought. "Oh, really? If you understand that about me, why have you been making so many decisions about my welfare without bothering to ask my opinion?"

He grinned sheepishly. "Well... let's just say that the thing you understand best about me is that I have a tendency to be an overprotective, dictatorial chauvinist."

She quirked one eyebrow skeptically. "And our marriage has lasted in spite of that?"

Adam nodded. "Because you know that when I turn into a Neanderthal it's only because I love you more than anything in this world." His eyes twinkled merrily. "And because you've never been shy about letting me know when I've crossed the line."

A smile teased Maddy's lips, too. "Like my over-the-top reaction this morning when you told me not to worry about your meeting with the hotel manager?"

"Exactly."

The waiter appeared with their first course, and it was a moment before Maddy could ask, "How did the meeting go?"

"Fine. Her chief of security, Tom Graves, sat in on the meeting, too. He seemed very competent."

"And they satisfied your concerns?"

"Yes. Our room is one of several that has especially high security. Video surveillance cameras cover all of its access points, including the roof and balcony."

"Video on the balcony?" Maddy asked, not sure she liked the idea of having her every move scrutinized in her own quarters.

Adam read her thoughts. "No, no. Not the balcony itself. Just the exterior access points. If he tries to come across the roof and drop onto our balcony, he'll be spotted in the security room."

They both knew what "he" Adam was referring to. "What about the rest of the resort?"

Adam explained the general precautions Tom had shown him and ended with, "And you'll have two armed security men following you wherever you go. I can introduce you to them later if you'd like."

"Absolutely. Do I have to notify them before I leave the room?"

"No. They're stationed in the security room on this floor, and their only job is to monitor our quarters. Once you set foot in the corridor, they'll know it and will pick you up in the lobby—very subtly, I might add," he told her. "If they're as good as Tom thinks they are, we'll hardly know they're there."

"Good. I'd rather concentrate on regaining my memory than watching my back."

Adam gave a nod that told her he understood completely. "Would you like to meet them after dinner?"

Maddy glanced around. "Are they here now?"

Adam shook his head. "No. I saw one of them in the lobby when we came downstairs, but I imagine he went back into the Fortress when he realized that we were coming to the dining room. The staff in here has received extensive training in security measures," he explained. "If you want to meet your shadows, though, I can send for them."

Maddy thought it over. "No, I don't think so. I'd rather wait until tomorrow and see if I can pick them out myself." She grinned at him. "After all, a good spy should be able to spot a tail from a mile away."

Adam shook his head. "Sorry, Maddy, my love."

She frowned. "Sorry about what?"

He shrugged. "I said you were a spy, but I never said you were a *good* one."

AS IT TURNED OUT, Adam was wrong; Maddy decided she would have made a very good spy indeed. It took her less than five minutes the next morning to spot her security guards.

The first one was ridiculously easy. After breakfast on their balcony, Adam had taken his turn in the shower, and Maddy had decided to start exploring without him. She left a note saying she'd meet him in the rose garden near the fountain and headed downstairs. She picked out guard number one before she even reached the lobby.

He was a tall, sandy-haired fellow in his late thirties wearing light blue chinos and a matching polo shirt, with a fanny pack strapped around his waist. He was idling in a nook near the concierge's desk, and though no one else in the busy lobby seemed to notice him, he caught Maddy's eye immediately, because there was no reason for anyone to be in that out-of-the-way nook unless he was waiting for someone.

Maddy was halfway down the stairs when he caught sight of her and straightened visibly—not as sharply as a soldier coming to attention, but enough to betray his interest in Maddy and a connection to the military somewhere in his past. When she moved across the lobby toward the rear exit that led to the garden, "Sandy" came out of his nook and followed at a discreet distance.

So much for guard number one.

Pleased with herself, she breezed out the door and down the stairs. She strolled past the terrace dining area and headed for the fountain at the center of the garden. From there, she could see her own balcony, and she glanced up just in time to see Adam, dressed in the hotel's white terry bathrobe, step to the rail. He had Maddy's note clutched in one hand. When he caught sight of her, he seemed visibly relieved. Maddy waved to him and he flapped the note at her, then disappeared into his bedroom.

So much for reassuring her husband. Now to the real task of unmasking guard number two.

Maddy crossed to one of the benches that dotted the garden. This one had an outer wall of the hedge maze behind it, and when Maddy sat facing the rose garden, she had a commanding view of the back of the hotel.

"Well, drat," she muttered in disappointment. She'd been hoping that guard number two would be a challenge, but she picked him out immediately. He was by the fountain, just standing there watching her, making no attempt to hide his identity. But then, why should he? Adam had said the guards would be discreet, not invisible. They were there to protect her, not play cat-and-mouse with her, and it seemed that they were doing their job adequately so far.

This guard, who was shorter and darker complected than his partner, nodded to her, acknowledging that yes, indeed, he was one of her bodyguards, then he redirected his gaze, scanning the rest of the garden.

"Well, so much for that game," she said, slapping her hands against her thighs as she stood.

"What game would that be, my dear?"

Maddy whirled to her right. A silver-haired gardener was massaging his back as he struggled to rise from the bed of chest-high rosebushes he'd been pruning. His pale blue eyes twinkled at her as he continued, "You're a little old to be playin' hide-and-seek and too young to be talking to yourself."

Maddy laughed. "True on both counts. You must be Judge Bradshaw."

The elderly gentleman with the delightful Carolina accent removed his battered straw hat. "At your service, Miss, though I can't imagine how you deduced my identity."

"I was told that no one was allowed near this garden with a pair of pruning shears except Judge Cameron Bradshaw," she explained. "Ergo, you had to be the Judge—or an exceptionally foolhardy serial gardener."

Cameron chuckled heartily. "Serial gardener. I'll have to remember to tell that one to Elizabeth. Although I suspect she'll think that's a very fitting description of me. Which means you were right on two counts, Miss..."

"Mrs. Hopewell," she supplied. "Madeline Hopewell."

A light of recognition flared in the Judge's eyes. "Mrs. Hopewell, of course! Liz told us all about you when she was going over the weekly report with Elizabeth." He stepped out of his bed of roses and joined

Maddy on the path of crushed seashells. "I must say, you look astonishingly healthy for someone who's been through such an ordeal, my dear. The dreadful attack resulting in memory loss..." He clucked his tongue sympathetically. "Very tricky business, amnesia. You know, I sat on the bench for a number of cases that involved amnesia."

"Really? I wouldn't have thought amnesia was all that common."

"Oh, the real thing isn't common at all, but as a defense strategy...oh, my, yes," he said, lowering himself onto the stone bench. He patted the space beside him, leaving Maddy with two choices—be rude or sit and listen. Since Cameron seemed sweet and totally harmless, Maddy sat.

"You'd be astonished," the Judge continued, "at how many defendants use the temporary-insanity plea because they've conveniently lost all memory of committing the crime with which they've been charged. Actually, in all my years on the bench, I had only one amnesia case that I felt was truly genuine."

"Oh? What was it?"

"A sixteen-year-old girl murdered her entire family with a butcher knife and then blotted out everything—including her own identity."

Maddy thought about her own amnesia and the nightmare she'd had almost every night since. She also thought about the feelings of guilt she couldn't shake. "Do you really think that's possible, Judge? To kill someone and forget all about it?"

"Oh, certainly. The mind is an amazing instrument, but it can only tolerate just so much anguish. If I had murdered my family I think the only way I could live with the guilt would be to forget everything—even who I am. You see, this poor girl..."

The Judge went on with the particulars of the case, and Maddy listened to the long story without realizing that Judge Cameron Bradshaw was as wily as a fox. Before she knew it, the Judge had finished his amnesia tale and coaxed Maddy into telling him about hers!

Under his gentle prodding, she told him everything the police knew about the attack in the airport parking garage, and even explained what had prompted Adam to bring her here to recuperate.

Maddy was amazed at how easy it was to confide in the charming old gentleman. He was kind and supportive, and the concern he expressed seemed entirely genuine. By the time Maddy finally spotted Adam coming out of the hotel, she felt as though she'd made a friend.

"Oh. There's my husband now," she told Cameron.

The Judge looked at the veranda. "Is that him talking to Agent Luther?"

Maddy took note of the man who had emerged from the building with Adam. They were similar in height and build, but where Adam was dressed casually in slacks and a polo shirt, the other man was dressed in a crisp gray suit that looked much too warm for the island at this time of year. "Agent Luther?" she questioned.

"Yes. He's the Secret Service point man for the President's visit. He's bringing our security up to presidential standards."

Maddy rose and Cameron did likewise. The men had stopped at the edge of the porch and were deeply involved in conversation. "I wonder what he wants with Adam," she murmured more to herself than the Judge.

Cameron answered, anyway. "I can't say for certain, of course, but I would imagine that the threat against you is something that would be of great interest to the Secret Service. If the police are right and, God forbid, your assailant makes another attempt—"

"I suppose you're right," Maddy conceded. Then, anxious to join her husband and find out what was going on, she turned to her new friend and extended her hand.

"Judge Bradshaw, I can't tell you how nice it was to meet you," she said warmly. "It seems you have a green thumb with people, as well as roses. Thank you for letting me ramble on."

"It was my pleasure, Madeline. Thank *you* for taking the time to visit with me."

"I hope we can do it again."

"You can count on it, my dear."

The Judge watched as her bodyguards fell in behind her at a discreet distance. Then he went back to his roses, but part of his mind was now occupied by this lovely new guest. She was a thoroughly delightful young woman who clearly didn't deserve to be suffering such a terrible ordeal.

There was obviously nothing he could do to help restore the poor girl's memory, but surely there had to be something he and Elizabeth could do to make her stay more enjoyable.

If he thought about it long enough, he was sure he could come up with a good idea. And if not, Elizabeth would. That was why they made such a good team.

Yes, indeed. Somehow they'd think of something special for their lovely guest.

...ought that was why they made such a good team.

Yes, he reflected ruefully. Some kind of something...
...pered their lovely affair.

CHAPTER SEVEN

MADDY WAS BARELY halfway across the garden when Agent Luther completed whatever business he had with Adam and returned to the hotel lobby. As Adam descended the veranda stairs, Maddy could see a scowl forming on his handsome face.

"I ought to turn you over my knee, Madeline Hopewell," he said as soon as he reached her.

Maddy searched for evidence that he was joking, but she didn't find any. "Why?"

"For running out on me. Don't ever do that again."

His tone alone was enough to raise her hackles. "Don't order me around, Adam," she snapped. "And don't expect me to spend the rest of my life walking two paces behind you like a well-trained dog."

He shook his head as though trying to clear it of irritation and disbelief. "God knows I've never expected obedience from you, Maddy, but I thought you had an ounce or two of common sense. Running off by yourself like—"

"I wasn't alone," she informed him. "I have bodyguards, remember? I wanted to see if I could spot them, and once I had I knew I was as safe as I'm ever going to be until my assailant is caught."

"Not true. You're safer with me," he argued. "Those bodyguards are just backup."

Maddy's dark eyebrows arched. "Forgive me for injecting a note of reality into your macho fantasy, but what, exactly, do you plan to use to protect me in the event of an attack? A slingshot? Bow and arrow? Harsh language?"

His dimples started to deepen the way they always did just before he smiled, and all the wind left his sails. "Sorry. I guess that sounded really stupid, but it just scared me silly when I came out of the shower and you were gone."

"I'm sorry, too. I promise to be less impulsive and more considerate." She grinned at him. "Next time I want to ditch you, I'll tell you where I'm going as I tie you to a chair."

"Very funny."

"Adam, the point is, you can't stay glued to my side all the time."

"I can try, can't I?"

Maddy finally realized she wasn't going to get the last word on this subject, so she might as well stop trying. "What did the Secret Service agent want?" she asked him. "Are we in hot water with the law?"

"How did you know he was . . ."

Maddy pointed toward the other end of the garden. "I was talking to Judge Bradshaw when you and Agent Luther came out of the hotel."

"Oh. It was no big deal. The hotel security chief told him about us, and Luther was just voicing his concern over the potential threat to your life."

"Don't you mean the potential threat to the President?"

"Well, he did express the hope that we might be gone before the Chief Executive arrives," Adam admitted reluctantly.

"Will we?"

"I don't know. Our reservation extends through the end of the month, but I suppose the length of our stay depends on Detective Hogan's investigation and the state of your health."

"You mean the state of my memory," she said.

"Yes."

Maddy smiled at him. "Then let's see what we can do about that. Shall we go a-wandering?"

Adam smiled, too. "All right. One trip down memory lane coming up."

"GOOD MORNING, sir. I'm sorry for the delay. May I help you?" Liz Jermain asked the slight bespectacled gentleman, the last of the three guests who'd arrived this morning on the hotel's motor launch.

Liz's smile was so pleasant and her voice so friendly that no one would ever have guessed how harried she was. It had been a while since she'd had to handle the front office entirely alone, and before the day was out she was going to have a long talk with Tom Graves about the scheduling of his employees security-training courses. Liz understood the importance of these ongoing sessions, but they shouldn't leave her so shorthanded that one employee calling in sick could throw the entire office into chaos.

"I'm Arthur Rumbaugh," the little man told her. "I have a single on reserve for the next two weeks."

"Do you have a copy of your confirmation slip?" she asked as she prepared to key a new entry into the computer.

"I'm afraid not," he replied. "I made the reservation four days ago and the slip hadn't arrived in the mail before I left home yesterday. However—" he removed an index card from the breast pocket of his suit coat and handed it to Liz "—this is the confirmation number I was given over the phone."

"Thank you." Liz keyed in the number and up popped the name *Rumbaugh, Arthur,* along with all the information that had been taken over the phone from him four days ago.

Working quickly, Liz cleared his credit card and ran his driver's license through Tom Graves's newest toy— a scanner that automatically recorded the guest's photo and ID information in his registration file. While that was processing, she invited Rumbaugh to sign the old-fashioned guest register, which was nothing more than a charming and sentimental tradition that her grandmother, Elizabeth, refused to let go of. Rumbaugh signed the register and everything else that was required, and Liz was finally able to process the card key for his room.

"Here you go, Mr. Rumbaugh. You're in room 156, which is in the south wing." She handed him the key folder with one hand and with the other gestured toward the bellman.

"Where is that, exactly?" he inquired. "I have a terrible sense of direction."

Liz smiled at him. "The bellman will show you."

"But couldn't you . . ." He gestured toward the hotel floor plan that was lying on the counter between the check-in stations. "I'd really like to get a sense of where I am in relation to your other facilities."

"Of course." Liz placed the diagram on the counter between them and showed Rumbaugh his room, which was on the east side only two doors away from the hotel's southernmost exit.

"Mmm. Rather out of the way, isn't it?"

Oh, brother, Liz moaned inwardly. Outwardly she smiled at her picky guest. "Yes. It's a very quiet part of the hotel."

"And where is it, exactly, in relation to the suite the President will be using?"

A huge red flag began waving, and though Liz's expression didn't change, she withdrew the map. The entire staff had standing orders from Graves and Agent Luther to notify them about anyone who asked questions like this. "In the Presidential Suite," she replied, giving a nod to the bellman who was standing patiently behind the guest. "You'll find a map of the island and all the resort's facilities in your room, Mr. Rumbaugh. Please let us know if there's anything we can do to make your stay more enjoyable."

He seemed on the verge of asking another question, but instead, he muttered a thank-you and followed the bellman into the central foyer.

Liz felt almost sorry for him. It was clear that the demanding guest was going to drive her staff crazy, but he was probably harmless enough. Tom and Luther wouldn't see it that way, though. Once Liz marked Rumbaugh's computer file with a special security flag and made note of his question regarding the President's room, the poor guy would become a bug under a microscope. The security checks that had been run on him when he reserved his room were nothing compared to the surveillance machinery that would go into motion.

But Liz had her orders, and she wasn't about to defy the Secret Service. She shifted her attention to her computer monitor and keyboard.

"Good morning, Liz. You're looking exceptionally lovely today."

The familiar masculine voice came from right behind her, and Liz's hands froze over the keyboard before she'd entered a single stroke. When she turned to Duke Masterson it was all she could do to keep him from seeing how much he'd startled her. She glanced around to see who was in the vicinity and for the first time this morning was glad her office staff was elsewhere.

That didn't ease her discomfort, though. "What are you doing up here, Duke?" she demanded.

The smile on the pilot's ruggedly handsome face froze. "I didn't think I needed permission to come up to the main building."

Liz flushed. "Sorry. I didn't mean to suggest that you did. I just thought you were supposed to meet the Vandergraf party at the airport this morning."

"Not for another hour. Their flight's been delayed, so I thought I'd see if you were free for a cup of coffee." He edged a little closer and lowered his voice. "We have to talk, Liz."

"No, we don't, Duke," she said, turning back to the counter and trying to recall what she'd been doing before Duke Masterson had thrown her off track. All she could think of, though, was the ultimatum he'd delivered to her last night. "We've kept our relationship quiet for months now, and I see no reason to change that. I'm the target of too much gossip as it is."

"You're the target of too much gossip because everyone is itching to know the identity of your mystery boyfriend."

"And I want it to stay a mystery," she said sharply.

"I'm not an 'it,' Liz. And if you can't bring yourself to acknowledge—"

"Don't threaten me, Duke! I won't be bullied—"

"Liz! We're here."

Duke automatically took a step back as Moira Petty and Shane Foster, the scheduled desk clerks, hurried into the reception alcove.

"Mr. Graves said to tender his apologies for keeping us so long," Moira explained. "Shad and the others will be along shortly, too. Have you been swamped?"

Liz could barely conceal her relief. Years of painting on the appropriate managerial face helped, though. "It could've been worse, but if Mr. Graves had kept you any longer, I'd have started training Duke here on the computer."

The pilot was almost as good as Liz at covering his feelings. "Whoa, there, Boss Lady. Me and a computer? Not on your life," he said with a laugh as he stepped aside to make room for the clerks.

"Don't worry, Duke. You're safe now," Liz replied, forcing a smile for him as she, too, vacated the front desk. "We can both get back to our respective jobs. Moira, if you need me for anything, I'll be in my office."

Fortunately her office was so close that by the time she got the words out she was at the doorway. Without looking at Duke again she closed the door, making it absolutely clear she had no intention of pursuing their argument any further.

Moira cast a speculative look in Duke's direction as she assumed her station. "What gives with you and the boss? You two looked pretty tense just a minute ago."

Duke shrugged. "Haven't you heard? I figured it was all over the island by now. My contract is up next month, and the Boss Lady and I are having trouble coming to terms."

Moira grinned and lowered her voice. "Really? That surprises me. I figured you, of all people, could name your price and she'd meet it without batting an eyelash."

Duke frowned. "Why would you think that?"

"Because you know all her deep dark secrets. I'm sure if you threatened to reveal the identity of her mysterious boyfriend, she'd cave to any demand you'd care to make."

The frown on Duke's face turned to a scowl so intense that Moira wished *she* had an office to escape into. "Liz's secrets—if she has any—are her own business, Moira. I wish everyone here would remember that."

He stalked off, leaving Moira totally mystified. Duke Masterson was the most charming, carefree rogue on Jermain Island. He was a drifter who'd flown in a couple of years ago, latched onto a great job that allowed him to live a life of luxury in exchange for being on call twenty-four hours a day and had proceeded to romance every young, single woman on the island.

"What was all that about Ms. Jermain's secrets?" Shane Foster asked, leaning over from his station.

Moira pulled her attention away from Duke's retreating—not to mention perfectly proportioned—backside and looked at Bride's Bay's newest employee. "Nothing, Shane. Just a running joke between Duke and me," she fibbed. After Duke's stinging comment about Liz's right to privacy, wild horses couldn't have made Moira share any rumors with the handsome but somewhat naive desk clerk who'd started work just three days ago.

She glanced over at Shane's station where Liz had been working. "You'd better check that last transaction and make sure Liz completed it before she left," she advised the rookie. "Liz is thorough, but it never hurts to double-check an entry before you clear it."

"Hmm..." Shane studied the screen for several seconds. "I don't see anything missing. Credit-card number...photo ID...room key issued...no special requests and no security flags..." He looked at Moira. "It looks perfectly normal to me."

"Then file it and clear your screen," she advised him as she checked her watch. "If the ferry from Charleston is on time, we're going to get busy any second now."

"Yes, ma'am," Shane replied, hitting a succession of keys that cleared the name *Rumbaugh, Arthur* from the computer screen.

CHAPTER EIGHT

EXPLORING THE ISLAND proved to be a slow but enjoyable process. Adam had rented a canopied golf cart, and Maddy's bodyguards followed them in an open-top Land Rover as they took a leisurely drive along the well-tended roads. Their looping circle led them around the northern end of the island past the private estates on the east coast and through the village and marina on the west. They strolled through the marina, explored the village shops and ate lunch in a charming little deli, then they set off on the last—and longest—leg of their road trip through the vast and varied resources of Bride's Bay Resort.

Through it all, Adam told anecdotes about their honeymoon—moonlight walks on the beach, horseback rides on the unspoiled trails, a picnic lunch at the lighthouse. He described a disastrous sailing expedition when they'd gotten caught in a ferocious storm and barely made it back to the island alive; he told her about the fierce doubles tennis matches they'd played with a couple from Great Britain who had taken an almost sadistic pleasure in beating them.

Maddy listened to Adam's stories with great interest, asked lots of questions and ultimately concluded that theirs had been the perfect honeymoon. Unfortunately none of the stories, nor any of the dozens of places Adam showed her, jogged any memories at all.

"And now, madam," Adam was saying in the studied manner of a very bad tour guide, "if you will direct your attention to the left you should soon catch a glimpse of the last stop on our tour today, the lighthouse." Maddy did as he directed, peering through the dense forest of palmettos and cypress that bordered the road until she finally caught a flash of the white tower. It wasn't until the road curved, though, that she got her first good look at the lighthouse.

Standing more than a hundred feet tall, with an adorable two-story keeper's cottage attached, the whitewashed brick structure looked like something off a picture postcard.

"Oh, Adam, it's gorgeous," Maddy murmured. "How old is it?"

Still using his tour-guide voice, he told her, "The current lighthouse, which is no longer in use, is 106 years old. However, this structure is actually the third of its kind to grace Sandy Point in the last 170 years."

The little golf cart inched along until the road dead-ended about thirty yards from the tower as he concluded, "It is, of course, listed on the National Register of Historic Places."

"I love it, Adam. I want to see the view from the catwalk." Maddy swung her legs out of the cart, but Adam put his hand on her arm to stop her.

"It's getting late, Maddy, and you've had a very full day. Are you sure you're up to the climb?"

"Would I suggest it if I wasn't?"

"Yes, you would," he replied.

"Adam, I'm fine, really. In fact, I could use the exercise to work the stiffness out of my legs. Except for our stroll through the village this morning, I've spent most of the day sitting in this cart."

He grinned at her. "All right. Let's explore."

Something about the century-old building excited Maddy, and she couldn't wait to get inside. She quickened her pace until she was almost running, with Adam hurrying to keep up.

"Hey, what's the rush?" he asked, grabbing her hand.

"I don't know," she replied, half turning toward him without slowing, so that she was actually pulling him along with her. "I just have to see inside. Come on!"

They ran across the sand only to discover that the keeper's cottage was locked. Maddy peered through the windows into the empty rooms, then they circled the tower until they found the lighthouse entrance.

"I don't know about this, Maddy," Adam said hesitantly after they'd gone in and were standing in the center of the tower, craning their necks to see to the top of the corkscrew staircase. His voice echoed eerily, and the only light came from the open door behind them and the series of small windows that followed the spiraling line of the stairs. "That's a lot of steps and you've had a long day already."

"I can make it, Adam," she assured him as she started up the stairs. "Stop being so practical."

He sighed heavily and followed her. "I'm not practical, I'm protective. There's a difference."

She flashed a teasing grin over her shoulder. "Not much of one."

"Well, somebody in this family has to be sensible," he said.

"Has it always been you?"

"We try to take turns."

Maddy paused on the wide second-story landing and turned to him. "That sounds sensible."

"And practical." He grinned and pointed to a door that was set into the wall behind Maddy. "Try that and see if it will allow us to get into the cottage. Maybe I can convince you to settle for seeing it today and saving the tower for another time."

"Don't count on it." She tried the door, but it was locked tight. "Nope. Start climbing," she said, leading the way.

Adam cautioned her to hold on to the iron railing, but Maddy didn't take his advice until they were more than halfway up and the stone staircase began to narrow, the leisurely slant growing steeper as the conical tower closed in. Despite Adam's nagging, Maddy paused only once to rest before they reached the upper landing and emerged onto the catwalk on the ocean side of the tower.

The view was breathtaking, and Maddy circled the tower slowly so that she could enjoy the changing vista. To the south and east the limitless ocean was dotted with colorful sailboats; to the north the island's wilderness preserve was a dark, mysterious expanse that blocked any possible view of the resort; toward the northwest the forest gave way to a marshland teeming with life.

Maddy turned to find Adam leaning against the iron rail, watching her with his arms folded across his chest. She could tell by the look in his eyes that he liked what he saw. "This was my favorite spot on the island, wasn't it?" she asked him.

He nodded and asked hopefully, "A memory?"

She shook her head. "Just a guess. It's my favorite so far. It figures it would've been ten years ago, too."

"It was," he confirmed. "Your favorite way to spend the day was to pack a picnic lunch in our saddlebags and ride down here on horseback. We'd climb up here, eat lunch, and you'd spend hours studying the marsh or just staring out to sea."

"Was that boring for you?"

He smiled wistfully. "No. I can spend hours watching *you.*"

Maddy felt a blush creeping into her cheeks and her pulse quicken, but she didn't look away from her husband's appreciative gaze. It made her feel feminine. It made her feel wanted. "Tell me something, Adam...when we met at that floating casino in Cannes, was I swept off my feet the moment I saw you?"

The question caught him so off guard that he threw back his head and laughed. It was a moment before he could tell her, "Not hardly, my darling. As I remember it, you were distinctly unimpressed. I was the one who got knocked for a loop."

Maddy's gaze made a slow sweep of her husband from head to toe, drinking in the sight of him with as much appreciation as he'd shown her. She shook her head. "That's not possible, Adam. I had to be very impressed."

His head dipped as acknowledgment of the compliment. "Well, if you were, you never told me. As I recall, we were standing on opposite sides of a roulette table and I couldn't take my eyes off you. But you, on the other hand, acted like I wasn't even there."

Maddy had no trouble visualizing the scene. "I was probably playing hard to get."

Adam chuckled again. "Yeah. From me and about a hundred other adoring men in tuxedos. Your hair was long then—almost waist-length—and you had it lightened to an ash blond," he told her. "You were wearing a white strapless evening gown that was slit all the way up your thigh and looked as though someone had poured you into it, and you had this maddeningly aloof, slightly cynical air about you that challenged every man in the casino to do his damnedest to find the chink in the Ice Maiden's veneer."

"Ice Maiden?" Maddy pursed her lips and her brows drew together into a frown. "I'm not sure I like that description."

"You were the sexiest, most beautiful woman in the room, and you couldn't have cared less. That's what made everyone want you."

"You're either exaggerating or prejudiced—or a little of both," she accused him, and then cut him off before he could protest, asking, "If I *was* such a hot property, how did I end up with you?"

He shrugged. "When I know what I want I'm utterly relentless."

His gaze was locked with hers in a look so potent it made Maddy's heart skip a beat. "Have you ever been sorry you got me?" she asked with what little breath he hadn't stolen from her.

Maddy saw a flash of something she couldn't identify in Adam's eyes, and she sensed she'd caught him off guard again. He answered her quickly with a fervent, "Of course not," but when he turned away to look out over the ocean, Maddy knew she'd struck a nerve.

She moved along the catwalk until she was right beside him. "Not until now, you mean?" she questioned him. "Or have I given you other reasons to regret marrying me?"

Adam turned to her, and the unidentified emotion she'd glimpsed a moment ago was gone.

"I have never regretted marrying you, Maddy," he swore.

Maddy wasn't entirely certain she believed him. At the very least, he was leaving something unsaid. Part of her wanted to know what it was, but an even stronger part of her needed to believe in the idyllic picture he'd painted of their marriage. The day he'd walked into her hospital room, Adam had become her anchor in a sea of chaos. As much as she hated being dependent on him, she wasn't ready to be set adrift. His unspoken truth might do exactly that, and Maddy didn't think she could bear losing him.

It was much easier to accept his declaration at face value. She turned toward the sunset and sighed softly when Adam slipped his arms around her. It was easy to lean against him and permit herself a moment of purely hedonistic pleasure. The sea air, the sunset, the exquisite feeling of security she always experienced in Adam's arms...she soaked them all up without remorse.

Unfortunately the rigors of their long day finally caught up with her. A moment of total contentment and relaxation suddenly gave way to great weariness. Maddy thought of the long staircase she had ascended, and she groaned.

"What's wrong?" Adam asked.

"I was thinking about the stairs."

"I knew this wasn't a good idea. You're exhausted."

Maddy nodded. "It hit me all at once. You think the resort management would mind if I took a nap up here before we start down?"

"I don't know about the resort management, but *I'd* mind. It's going to be dark soon, and I don't remember seeing any lights in the tower."

Maddy chuckled. "That's clever. A lighthouse without light."

Adam took her by the shoulders and turned her toward the door. "I'm glad you see the irony. Now, let's get out of here before we can't see anything at all."

Thanks to the fading daylight, when they moved into the tower they discovered a whole new set of shadows that were deeper and much darker than the ones they'd contended with on their way up. Looking down was like staring into a dark, dizzying well, with only a splash of illumination spilling across the stone floor below—just enough to remind Maddy of what a long drop it would be if she lost her footing.

Adam, apparently, was thinking along the same lines. His concern was obvious in his voice when he suggested, "Maybe I should signal for your bodyguards. I know they're down below somewhere, and they've probably got a flashlight in their vehicle."

The idea of being "rescued" was too humiliating to even consider. "Adam, it's not *that* dark. And since the only way out is down, we can't possibly get lost." Mustering all the energy she could summon, she started down.

On the way up, the steps hadn't seemed so irregular in height or their stone surfaces so uneven, but they did now. She didn't need Adam to caution her about holding on to the rail, nor did he have to encourage her to rest. She stopped briefly several times. Adam was staying close to her so that he could catch her if she started to fall.

She wanted to tell him not be such a worrywart, but with every step she took, a tremor in her legs reminded her that she'd left the hospital less than thirty-six hours ago.

When she stumbled the first time, Adam had a hand on her arm to steady her before she fully realized that she'd almost fallen. When she lost her footing the second time, Adam's hand shot out again, but steadying her wasn't enough. Her legs collapsed, throwing Adam off balance, too, and they grabbed for the iron rail and anything else that might keep them from tumbling down the last quarter of the staircase.

Whether it was adrenaline, acrobatics or just plain luck, Maddy couldn't have said, but somehow Adam controlled their fall. They ended up sprawled on the stairs with Maddy more or less on Adam's lap, her pulse racing and her limbs tangled with his.

"Well..." The word came out as a rasp as Maddy tried to catch her breath. "I hope...you're happy. You just had to see the view from the catwalk, didn't you? Couldn't have waited a day or two. You stubborn, mule-headed—"

Adam's laughter and a sharp squeeze of his arms around her midsection cut her off. "Woman, you are insane," he said, chuckling. "Completely and totally nuts."

Maddy tilted her head back so she could look into Adam's eyes. "I know. I'm very difficult and you're a saint to indulge me with such patience and good humor." She patted his thigh. "Not to mention, you'd make a damn fine lawn chair."

He shook his head in exasperation. "Are you hurt?"

"No."

"Then get up."

"All right. All right." Maddy took hold of the rail and the boost Adam gave her helped her stand. She moved down several steps to avoid his outstretched legs, then turned to him. It took only a quick, assessing glance to know he'd gotten the worst of their spill. He didn't appear to be hurt, but his clothes were disheveled and his white slacks would never be the same.

"Are you all right, Adam?"

"I'm fine," he said, coming to his feet.

"Are you sure?"

"Certain." He straightened his shirt and dusted off the seat of his trousers. Even in the dim light, Maddy could see that he was wasting his time. The slacks were filthy.

"Your cuff is hiked up, too," she informed him, bending down automatically to assist him, but as she reached for the cuff Adam grabbed her hand.

"That's okay, Maddy. I can do it," he said.

But it was too late. Maddy had already gotten close enough to see that the pant leg had snagged on something strapped to Adam's ankle.

She straightened and looked into her husband's eyes. "A gun, Adam? You're carrying a gun?"

"I'm carrying a means of protecting you," he replied, settling the pant leg over the weapon.

Maddy remembered her gibe this morning about slingshots and harsh language. "Why didn't you tell me you had a gun?"

"Because I didn't want you to know," he replied matter-of-factly. "My job is protecting you. Yours is to get your memory back. A gun's not going to help you do that."

"Maybe not, but it would make me feel a lot safer," she said shortly. "Where did you get it?"

"Here in the U.S. About six years ago."

Maddy sighed with exasperation. "I wasn't asking where you *bought* it, Adam. I want to know how it came to be in your possession now. Didn't you tell me all of our belongings are in storage in Paris?"

"Yes, but I usually travel with this when I'm transporting artifacts," he explained. "I had it on this trip."

She held out her hand. "May I see it?"

Adam hesitated a moment before bending to unsnap the leather safety guard. He removed the gun from the holster and held it out to her.

Maddy took the slender, stainless-steel automatic. "A 9mm Smith & Wesson 669," she murmured.

It fit her hand perfectly—size, weight and balance all excellent. It felt wonderful—no, better than wonderful. It felt as though it belonged there.

Without really even thinking, Maddy slipped off the safety, popped the clip out, then slapped it back in and jacked a shell into the chamber as though she'd done it a hundred times a day, every day of her life. Without pausing, she brought the automatic over her head, arms extended in a two-handed grip, and took aim at an iron bracket on the tower wall forty feet above her.

"Maddy!"

"Don't worry, I'm not going to fire," she said, lowering the gun. "But I could hit that hook, couldn't I? Even in this light, from this angle . . . this distance, I could hit it."

Adam breathed a visible sigh of relief. "Yes. But please don't. Island security doesn't know about the gun yet and I'd rather keep it that way."

Maddy wasn't concerned about island security. "Adam, why do I know how to do this?" she asked as she cleared the chamber and slipped the safety back on. "Why does this gun feel so right in my hand?"

"Because you've got an International Marksman rating of 'expert' with both handguns and rifles."

Before she'd touched the gun, that would've surprised her. It didn't now. "Why? Why did I go that far?"

"Maddy, you've never done anything halfway in your life. When you decided you wanted to learn to shoot, you had to become the best."

The burst of adrenaline Maddy had gotten as a result of their fall was wearing off, and she turned to sit on the stairs. "But isn't that a strange hobby for a woman? Why did I want to learn in the first place?"

Adam sat next to her. "Your father was a champion marksman. He taught you to shoot when you were fairly young, and from what you've told me, he was grooming you to follow in his footsteps. You won several junior competitions, and you continued on your own after he died."

Maddy felt a wave of sadness that was even more oppressive than her exhaustion. She leaned against Adam, her shoulder pressed to his, her gaze fixed on the automatic in her hand. "Why can't I remember that? My father spent time with me, taught me…and I can't remember any of it."

"You will, Maddy," Adam assured her, taking the gun out of her hand and returning it to the ankle holster.

Maddy was struck by the ridiculous feeling that he'd just stripped her naked. "I don't suppose you have another one of those handy."

"No."

"Can you get me one?"

He looked at her sternly. "No, Maddy, I can't. I won't even be carrying this one much longer. Once the Secret Service sets up metal detectors, I won't be able to leave our suite with this thing."

"But in the meantime . . ."

"In the meantime, I'll take care of you—and the Smith & Wesson."

Maddy knew that arguing with him was pointless. Adam was never going to relinquish the gun to her. But accepting his edict didn't mean she'd lost her curiosity about just how good she was with a gun. "There's a rifle range on the island, isn't there, Adam?" she asked.

"Yes. And there's an indoor pistol gallery, too," he told her. "You can't practice with the Smith & Wesson, of course, but if you'd like, I can reserve a time for us tomorrow. You can use one of the resort's target pistols and blast away to your heart's content."

He had taken a hard line against her carrying a weapon, but clearly he understood how much this new bit of information about herself meant to her. Shooting at an inanimate target wasn't the same as shooting at a man, but if it meant saving her life or Adam's, she knew she could make that transition with ease.

Tomorrow, she would find out exactly what it meant to be an expert marksman.

And as long as Adam was the one with custody of the gun, she decided she'd better find out how good he was, too.

CHAPTER NINE

THE MAN WAS DYING in her arms. His blood was everywhere, and he was whispering to her. She knew his words were important, but she couldn't hear them. Images flew at her out of the darkness, and then she was running, leaving the blood behind. Running, with the sound of a hundred voices shrieking at her, blaming her for the blood. Blaming her for the lifeless body she'd left behind.

And then the voices caught her. Their dark, faceless shapes pinned her into a suffocating space as they congealed into one shape, a giant shadow that spread its dark, evil wings and streaked toward her. The black wings enfolded her, the demon screamed again, and this time the woman screamed, too, as she fought against the trap she had fallen into.

"Maddy, wake up! Damn it, Maddy! Wake up!"

Finally words that made sense. Words the woman could understand and respond to. She fought her way toward the familiar voice, desperately hoping she would find safety there, but something was holding her and she couldn't break free, no matter how hard she struggled.

"Damn it, Maddy! Stop fighting me! I don't want to hurt you! Freeze, damn it!"

She froze. The harsh command pierced through the black veil of her nightmare and brought her into the present. What she discovered, though, wasn't vastly different from the dream. She was sitting on an unfamiliar bed in a dark room with only a sliver of light falling across her, barely illuminating the man who had her pinioned against his chest.

"Adam?"

Maddy saw the relief that flooded the handsome face only inches from hers. "That's right, Maddy. Are you awake?"

"I think so," she replied thickly, still trying to make sense of her surroundings and the strange predicament she found herself in. She was experiencing a moderate amount of discomfort, particularly because Adam had her left arm stapled behind her back, and her right wrist was pinned between her chest and his in an unbreakable vise grip.

It was a threatening tableau, but Maddy had regained her senses enough to realize what had happened. She'd had the nightmare again, and some of the screaming she'd heard had probably been her own this time. Adam had rushed in here to awaken her, she'd fought him, and this had been his way of defending himself.

But she wasn't fighting anymore. "I'm okay," she said. "You can let me go now."

Adam didn't move. "I'll be happy to let you go, darling, just as soon as *you* let go of that... thing."

Maddy's right wrist was beginning to ache and her clenched fingers felt numb. "What thing?" she snapped. She started to squirm, but Adam gave a hard tug on her left arm, holding her still.

"That sharp, pointy thing you have pressed to my jugular vein, darling," he replied calmly. "If you release that, I'll be happy to let you go."

Maddy lowered her gaze a few inches to the dark, shadowed area below Adam's chin. The reason her fingers felt numb was because she was holding her nail file in a white-knuckled death grip, with the stiletto point pressing into Adam's throat.

"Oh, my God," Maddy breathed, relaxing her fingers at once. The nail file fell out of her hand and Adam relaxed, too, gentling his hold, but not quite letting her go until he was certain she was supporting herself. When she was sitting upright in bed of her own accord, Adam leaned over and turned on the light.

The part of her mind that was growing more rational immediately registered two things. One was the gun on the nightstand, which Adam had obviously grabbed after he heard her scream; the other was that her husband didn't sleep in pajamas. He was naked except for a pair of plain white briefs.

He didn't seem to notice, so Maddy tried not to, either.

"Adam, I'm so sorry," she said, gently brushing at the reddening scratch on his throat. "It's a miracle it didn't break the skin."

"It's a miracle you didn't kill me," he corrected her. "Maddy, what the hell was that and where did you get it?"

She ran her hands over the rumpled bedclothes until she relocated her weapon. "It's a nail file I found in my cosmetic bag."

Adam took it and studied the sharply honed blade. "You were filing your nails in your sleep?"

"Don't be ridiculous," she snapped. She was still trembling from the nightmare, she was embarrassed about having attacked him, and she was keenly aware of Adam's state of undress. All three combined to put her on the defensive. "I've been keeping the file with me all the time for more than a week now."

He looked at her sharply. "You even sleep with it?" he asked incredulously.

"Yes."

"My God, Maddy, do you have any idea how dangerous that is? You could've hurt yourself!"

"I need something for protection!" she argued.

"Why? I had guards at your door in the hospital. Here, you've got—"

"Those are *your* precautions, Adam, not mine!"

He looked surprised. "You don't trust me to protect you?"

"I don't even know you! Why the hell should I trust you?"

The words flew out of her mouth before she could censor them, and it was too late to call them back. The damage was done. Adam's face went absolutely blank, then turned as cold and hard as stone.

"Oh, Adam, I'm sorry..." she began, but he rose abruptly, snatched the gun off the nightstand and left without a word.

Cursing her short temper and sharp tongue, Maddy climbed off the bed and slipped into her robe. The dressing room was dark, but there was a light coming from Adam's room and she followed it.

"Adam?"

He wasn't in the bedroom, but the French doors were wide open. A cool breeze stirred the curtains and filled the air with the scent of magnolia and roses. Tightening the belt of her robe, Maddy padded across the thick carpet to the balcony and found Adam standing at the railing, his face turned toward the perfect half-moon that hung above the western horizon.

He had stopped in his room long enough to don a pair of trousers, but he was still bare-chested, which highlighted the fact that his back was ramrod straight and the well-defined muscles in his shoulders were bunched with tension.

Maddy moved to the railing, mirroring his position. "Adam, please, I'm really sorry."

"For what?" he asked without looking at her. "You were just telling the truth—your husband is a complete stranger."

"Truth or not, I know it hurts you and I'm sorry for that."

"Are you?" Adam looked at her finally, but Maddy almost wished he hadn't because the coldness in his face was frightening. "If you're so sorry, why do you keep bludgeoning me over the head with it?"

Maddy frowned in confusion. "What do you mean?"

"You refuse to trust me, Maddy. If you were keeping me any farther away *emotionally* we'd be in separate time zones! Why? Why are you doing this to us?"

"I'm not doing anything to us! I'm just trying to survive!"

"By keeping me at arm's length?"

"Yes!"

"For God's sake, why?"

"I don't know! It just feels safer!" she flung back at him, her fists clenched in frustration.

"Physically safer or emotionally?" Adam asked, his voice hushed and hard.

Maddy felt tears of frustration welling up. "I don't know. I don't know anything anymore! Twelve days ago I woke up weak, confused and alone, surrounded by a world full of strangers—one of whom wants me dead! I'm scared, Adam! Don't you get it? I'm so scared I can't see straight!''

A huge knot of emotions exploded inside her, stealing her breath and bringing the tears flooding to her eyes. No matter how hard she tried, she couldn't stop them from spilling over. The tears she'd never allowed herself to shed in the hospital coursed down her cheeks, and a sob caught in her throat.

When Adam reached for her, she didn't pull away. She went into his arms and let him pull her close, let him wrap her in a loving cocoon that promised warmth and safety and a dozen other things that were so foreign Maddy couldn't even put a name to them.

She cried until there were no tears left, until the fear she'd been living with didn't seem quite so overwhelming, until her confusion and frustration began to take a back seat to a number of imminently pleasurable sensations.

As the black emotions ebbed away, they made room for other feelings. Feelings that Maddy had been suppressing since the day Adam walked into her hospital room—because she'd known even then that once she opened the door to him she'd have to let him in all the way.

And she'd been right. The warmth she'd always felt low in her abdomen when he looked at her was increasing now from warmth to heat. Her pulse was quickening the way it often did when he flashed his devilish, dimpled smile. Her feminine senses were growing a hundred times sharper than they had when he'd brushed her lips with a chaste good-night kiss or when his hand had accidentally touched hers.

But of course he wasn't just touching her now; he was holding her. Maddy's body was pressed against the full length of his and she could feel the corded sinews of his arms, the sculpted musculature of his torso and the supple strength of his thighs. A wonderfully pleasurable ache was beginning to throb between her thighs, and amnesia or no amnesia, she knew exactly what it would take to make that ache go away.

That thought—that feeling—was so intense it frightened Maddy, but this was a fear she wasn't sure she wanted to run from. The man who was generating these intense feelings of desire was her husband, after all. If he could make her feel this way with just a simple embrace, how much more could he do with a kiss or a caress? What other sensations would she experience if Adam touched her intimately, with a hand on her breast or his lips on her throat?

Maddy wanted desperately to find out.

She raised her face from Adam's chest, and he gently cupped her cheek in one hand, brushing at her tears with his thumb. "Better now? Maddy, you're..." Adam looked into her eyes then, and what he saw made whatever he'd been about to say fly right out of his mind. Maddy's gray eyes were usually guarded and reserved, even when she was at play or at rest. Now they were dark with a sensuality so potent it robbed Adam of thought.

For over a week, he'd been keeping his thoughts and his feelings under tight rein, doing everything in his power to keep Maddy from seeing what torture it was to be near her and not be able to touch her.

The way she felt in his arms and that totally unexpected look of hunger in her eyes nearly undid him. Senses that had already been aroused by having her in his arms escaped his control, and a hunger matching hers coursed through his veins.

This wasn't the result he'd had in mind when he deliberately pushed her into getting her emotions out in the open. He'd wanted to break down the wall she'd built between them, get her to admit she was afraid and hopefully lead her a step closer to trusting him.

Opening *this* door hadn't been part of his agenda today.

But that didn't mean much when Maddy arched against him, stretching up to bring her lips to his. The temptation was just too great. Adam gathered her even closer, placed his lips on hers, deepened the kiss and let all the hunger he'd been suppressing surge to the surface.

The intensity of the kiss was stunning. Like a fire that kindled, flared and burned out of control, the kiss created its own fuel, generating more hunger and more heat, robbing them both of breath and thought.

And it wasn't nearly enough to satisfy the needs that were taking on a life of their own. Adam wanted more, and everything Maddy poured into that kiss told him she wanted more, too. At that moment there was nothing standing between them. There was nothing to stop him from sweeping her off her feet, carrying her into his bedroom and allowing the fire to run its course.

Nothing to stop him except his own conscience. A voice that had been silent for longer than he cared to remember spoke up from the dark, murky pool of his soul and reminded him of all the reasons he'd hate himself if he didn't stop. It was one of the hardest things he'd ever done, but he reached inside himself, found a scrap of the integrity he thought he'd used up long ago and commanded his mind to take control of his body.

"Maddy, no..." He tore his mouth away from hers, slid his hands up to her shoulders and pulled back to put a little distance between them. Her body was still touching his in all the places that counted, but his gesture gave them a little breathing room. "We can't do this," he told her, still fighting for air. "I don't think you're ready."

Maddy looked up at him, her eyes smoky with confusion and desire. "I'm not ready? Oh, Adam, you couldn't be more wrong." She arched up to kiss him again, but he wouldn't allow it.

"I'm not talking about being ready physically, Maddy."

Her brow furrowed as her confusion turned to irritation. "Aren't you the one who just complained because I've been keeping you at arm's length?"

"But I wasn't talking about *this*. I was talking about trust and an emotional commitment that I was hoping would bring you closer to regaining your memory."

Maddy was beginning to feel foolish and more than a little embarrassed. She slipped out of Adam's arms, her hands clenching into fists as she tried to control the passion-induced adrenaline coursing through her. "You don't think going to bed with my husband might bring back memories?" she asked sharply.

"It might," he conceded. "But if it doesn't, you're going to hate me for letting something happen you weren't ready for. You're vulnerable and confused right now, Maddy. I won't take advantage of that."

Maddy was too stunned to acknowledge the logic of his argument. All she could see was that she'd thrown herself at him, and he was rejecting her!

The desire that had engulfed her began ebbing away as quickly as it had come. "I don't believe this," she said, stepping back to put even more room between them. "What's really going on, Adam? I'm your wife, remember? It's obvious to me that a strong sexual attraction was very much a part of our relationship. So what's the *real* reason you're putting the brakes on something you obviously want as much as I do?"

Adam took a step toward her, his dark eyes glittering with a mixture of emotions Maddy couldn't begin to identify. "Because I want more than a quickie with a woman who thinks of me as a stranger," he told her bluntly. "When you give in to whatever you feel for me, I want you making love to your husband! I want you to remember all the things that we've shared!" He paused a moment, gentling his voice. "I want you to remember loving me, Maddy. I can't settle for less."

Maddy was suddenly breathless again, but not from passion this time. His declaration made her want to cry, and in that instant, she finally understood the depths of the love she and Adam had shared. The thought that she might never get it back was almost more than she could bear. "What if I don't ever remember, Adam?" she asked softly as a new kind of fear began gnawing at her. "Will I lose you?"

Adam reached for her and brought her into his arms again. "No. Of course not. We'll just...start all over. If that's what you want."

He was giving her an option, but of course there wasn't really any decision to be made. Two weeks ago Maddy had awakened in the hospital knowing what it meant to be lonely to the very core of her soul. Now she had no doubts that for the ten years of their marriage, Adam had made that loneliness go away. She might not remember being happy with him, but she was sure that nothing could have been more precious to her than being with him, loving him and having him love her in return.

Making peace with that truth enabled her to say, "Of course I want that, Adam. I want that so much it scares me. I think that's the real reason I built a wall between us."

"Is the wall gone now?" he asked.

"Yes."

"Thank God. Now maybe we can get things back on track." He smiled. "I'm not giving up on the old Maddy, you know. You'll remember everything soon. I know it." He brushed his lips against hers lightly, and then stroked her hair when Maddy buried her face in his shoulder.

"I guess I should be grateful to you for being so noble and saving me from myself," she murmured.

"Oh, there's nothing noble about me, Maddy," Adam assured her as his lips grazed her forehead. "Nothing noble at all."

If she'd been looking into his eyes at that moment, Maddy would have known those were probably the most truthful words he'd spoken to her since the day he'd walked into her hospital room.

CHAPTER TEN

WHEN MADDY AWOKE the next day she wasn't at all surprised to discover she'd slept until nearly noon. After all she'd gone through yesterday she wouldn't have been alarmed if she'd slept *all* day, instead of just half of it. It was early afternoon before she was actually dressed and ready to start her day.

Adam teased her through lunch about being a lady of leisure. Neither of them mentioned what had happened—or what *hadn't* happened—on the balcony, but it seemed clear that their relationship had entered a new phase. They were more at ease with each other and Maddy's level of anxiety had lowered considerably.

In fact, she felt freer than ever as she and Adam headed for the combination outdoor rifle range and indoor shooting gallery. They spent several hours there, and Maddy discovered she was every bit as good as Adam had claimed—and Adam was even better. When they returned to the hotel, they spent the rest of the afternoon sitting around the pool visiting with other guests and catching up on island gossip.

There were rumors about romances among certain guests and hints of scandal were circulating about a well-known actress who was spending a few days at the resort "in hiding," as the woman circulating the rumor had put it. Another woman said she'd seen one of the housekeepers crying this morning, and someone suggested she might have been upset over the death of an employee named Roger who had been rushed to the hospital after suffering a crippling stroke.

There was also a great deal of comment about the impending visit of the President, which led to a heated debate about politics in general and, more specifically, the President's arms-reduction bill. From what Maddy could glean, the issue had been a hotly contested topic in the U.S. for a year or more.

Maddy soaked up all the information like a sponge, taking in every detail of every discussion in the hope that something would trigger a memory. All she succeeded in doing, though, was exhausting herself mentally, as well as physically. When Adam suggested they return to their room, she was too tired to even think of arguing with him. They collected their belongings and went upstairs.

"Would you like to have dinner on the balcony tonight?" Adam asked her as he opened the door to their room and stepped back so that she could precede him.

"What? Give up dinner and dancing till dawn? Surely you jest."

He chuckled. "I'll take that as an affirmative and call room service."

"Thank you." She dropped onto the sitting-room couch, slipped out of her sandals and put her feet up, with her ankles crossed in front of her. She closed her eyes and threw one arm over her head, allowing it to dangle off the headrest of the divan.

"My, my, such wanton abandon," Adam couldn't resist saying. "All you need is a barge and a suitable large body of water, and you could pass for the queen of the Nile.''

Maddy snapped her fingers insistently without bothering to open her eyes. "Grapes, slave! And be quick about it, or it's off with your head."

"Don't look now, darling, but that is definitely a mixed metaphor. You seem to be confusing Cleopatra with Marie Antoinette."

Maddy turned her head and looked at him drolly. "Are you insinuating there's something wrong with my memory?"

Adam laughed as he crossed the room and sat on the divan facing her. "Have I told you lately what an amazing woman you are?" he asked.

"I'm not amazing, Adam. Merely astonishing, occasionally remarkable and usually extraordinary."

"Don't forget modest."

"And modest," she added.

"Would you consider adding honest to the list, too?" he asked.

His inquiry was so lightly spoken Maddy almost missed the subtle signs that their playful exchange had just turned serious. She met his gaze with all the honesty she had at her disposal. "I'm trying to be as truthful with you as I'm being with myself, Adam. What else can I do?"

"Be a little more honest with yourself," he suggested.

Maddy straightened and tried not to let his insinuation pull the trigger on her temper. She couldn't keep a small element of terseness out of her voice, though, when she asked, "What, exactly, do you think I've been lying about?"

"Last night, right before you went back to sleep, I asked you what your nightmare had been about. Do you remember me asking the question?"

Oh, boy, Maddy thought miserably. The moment he was referring to wasn't exactly her finest. "Yes. I remember."

"And do you recall telling me that you couldn't remember anything about the dream?"

"Yes."

"That was a lie, wasn't it?"

Maddy didn't want to answer him, but it had nothing to do with the fragile, newfound trust she was beginning to have in him. A psychologist would have called it classic avoidance; Maddy wanted to pretend the dream didn't exist.

But despite her mounting agitation, she admitted, "Yes, it was a lie."

"You remember the dream?"

She clenched, then unclenched her fist over and over again as she answered. "Now I do. Yes. At first, I couldn't remember anything, then I started retaining fragments, and now it seems to get more vivid each time."

"Each time? Maddy, how often do you have this dream?"

Maddy squelched an urge to scream. "How often do I sleep?"

"My God, Maddy. That's horrible," he said, his voice filled with concern. "You have the same dream every night?"

"Yes."

"Why didn't you tell me that last night?"

"Because I wanted to avoid this conversation! I don't like thinking about the dream, and I like talking about it even less."

Adam's frown deepened. "Who have you been talking about it with?"

That sounded a lot like jealousy, but Maddy didn't call him on it. Instead, she answered, "No one."

He seemed to relax a bit. "Then how do you know that talking won't help?"

Maddy couldn't ignore her instinct to escape any longer. Though she had nowhere to go, she sprang to her feet as she told him, "The same way I know that the sun will rise tomorrow, gravity will make things fall down, instead of up, and Adam Hopewell will continue to be a pain in his wife's posterior!"

"Darling, if wanting you to be safe and well makes me a pain in the you-know-what, I stand guilty as charged," he said. "Now, tell me about your nightmare."

"Do I have to?" she asked as she started pacing in front of the French doors.

"I think you should," he replied calmly.

"Why?"

"Because I have no intention of giving up until you tell me everything you remember about the dream."

He meant it. She could be as stubborn as she wanted, but short of hiding in her room until her memory returned, there was no way to avoid this conversation. She had no choice but to describe the whole hellish nightmare to him. She crisscrossed the room again and again as the details unfolded, and Adam listened without comment.

Even in her agitated state, Maddy was impressed by the intensity of Adam's concentration. When she finished her narration at the point where she generally awakened, he started asking questions, forcing her to examine even the most insignificant details of the dream. After a time her head started to ache.

She'd stopped pacing and was sitting beside him on the couch, massaging her temples, when he started on yet another tack. "You said you heard screaming," he commented. " 'Like the cawing of crows,' I think you described it."

Maddy pinched the bridge of her nose, but it didn't lessen the ache behind her eyes. "That's what it sounds like, yes."

"Focus on the voices, Maddy. Listen to them and see if you can hear what they're saying."

"They're not *saying* anything, Adam. They're just making that horrible noise."

"And it frightens you."

"Yes."

"You perceive the voices as a threat?"

"Yes. Absolutely. There's a definite threat involved, but I can't identify the source."

Her obvious discomfort didn't seem to faze him. "What about the man in the dream?" he asked. "What does he look like? Tall, short? Fat, thin?"

Maddy tried to pull up his image, but it was associated with so much blood and so much fear that her mind rebelled. It took a lot of discipline to bring him into focus. "He's lying on a floor—a dirty tile floor—so I can't really tell how tall he is, but he's..." She struggled to find the right word and finally came up with, "Plump. Not obese, just slightly rounded everywhere."

"How had he been killed?"

A little shudder snaked down her spine. "I don't know. All I remember is the blood. A lot of it."

"Could he have been the man who was killed at the airport when he distracted your attacker?"

She paused to think. "No. For one thing, I never saw the man at the airport. The man in the dream is someone I know and he's someone I saw die. I'm certain he's real, not symbolic."

She didn't tell Adam about the incredible guilt she associated with the blood or the certainty that those cawing voices were blaming her for the man's death. Instead, she told him, "And besides that, Detective Hogan said the man who saved my life at the airport was African-American."

"But the man in your dream is white?" Adam asked.

Maddy frowned in concentration. "Well, he's swarthy. Looks...Arabic."

"Good. Now we're getting somewhere," Adam praised her. "What about his words? Concentrate on what he was trying to tell you."

Something in Adam's tone struck Maddy. He suddenly sounded like a teacher who already knew the answers to the questions and was just trying to elicit the correct response from his pupil. "What are you trying to get me to say, Adam?" she asked, betraying a suspicion she was ashamed of feeling.

Adam looked surprised. "Whatever you remember. Whatever you can bring into focus."

"But you're behaving as though you're fishing for something specific."

He seemed genuinely mystified by her accusation. "Maddy, I just want you to remember as many details of the dream as you can. If you're having this dream every night it's obviously very important—it may even be the key to regaining your memory. At the very least it might help us figure out what happened to you during those days you were missing."

"Only if the parts of the dream that seem real happened recently and not a dozen years ago," she countered.

Adam shook his head emphatically. "No, it's recent, Maddy. It has to be. You've never been plagued with nightmares before, and if you'd ever had a man die in your arms, you would've told me."

"Are you sure?"

"I'm positive." His certainty was so complete it didn't leave any room for her to doubt him. "Finding the key to your dream is just a matter of separating remembered images from the symbolic ones."

He dove back into his questioning and Maddy tried to be as cooperative as possible, but no matter how many times Adam asked, she couldn't bring the dying man's words into focus, nor could she ascribe meaning to the black wings that enfolded her or any of the other metaphorical images. It was all just mumbo jumbo.

"Adam, that's all I remember, I swear. Please, can we stop now?" she pleaded, massaging her temples again.

"All right." He slipped his arm around her and pulled her close. "I'm sorry I pressed you so hard. I just want so much for you to remember."

"I know. And I should have told you before." She looked at him. "It just scares me so badly, Adam."

Adam pressed a kiss to her forehead. "Don't be scared, darling. Don't be scared," he crooned softly. "I won't let anything hurt you. I promise."

God, how she wanted to believe that.

CHAPTER ELEVEN

ON THEIR THIRD FULL DAY at the resort, Adam rented a small sailboat and they spent most of the day on the water, until a little squall blew up and forced them back to the island—exactly as it had on their honeymoon, Adam told her. Maddy discovered that she was a fair deckhand, but the only memories that stirred were those regarding which line to pull to trim the jib and how to tack into the wind. Though she was utterly captivated by Adam's wit, charm and tenderness, Maddy couldn't scrape up even one tiny memory of their honeymoon—or anything else about their ten years of marriage.

She could see how hard Adam was trying to keep his disappointment from showing, but it leaked through occasionally, particularly when he went back to discussing her nightmare—something he did more often than Maddy would have liked. For some reason, he seemed certain it was the key to unlocking her memory, and the pressure he applied when they were discussing the dream was disconcerting.

It did have one benefit, though—talking about the dream in broad daylight had apparently acted as some sort of escape valve, because Maddy had two consecutive nights of blissfully dreamless sleep. When she awoke on the morning of the fourth day, she felt fabulous—no hint of a headache, no dizziness, and not one of the muscles in her left leg screamed at her. Time had healed the contusion and exercise had strengthened the damaged muscle tissue. For the first time since she'd awakened in the hospital, Maddy felt as though she was in control of her own body, rather than having pain and incipient exhaustion controlling her.

Feeling energized, she showered and dressed for the day in a pair of lemon-colored shorts and a white tank top, over which she wore an unbuttoned yellow-and-white-striped camp shirt tied at the waist. She gathered her hair into a loosely constructed knot that kept most of it off her neck but allowed a few stray tendrils to waft around her face, and she even applied a bit of makeup.

As she'd come to expect, Adam was at the table on the balcony reading the morning newspaper, still dressed in the hotel's white terry robe. He was sipping from a cup of coffee, but other than that the breakfast he'd ordered from room service was untouched.

"Good morning, coach," she said. "What's on the agenda for today?"

Adam glanced up from the paper and grinned as he assessed her mood and corresponding clothing. "Good morning, sunshine. What's gotten into you today?"

"Two full nights of undisturbed slumber." She applied a swift kiss to his cheek and sailed around to her side of the table. "I feel wonderful."

"It shows." He folded the paper and laid it aside while Maddy poured herself some coffee.

"What are we going to do to take advantage of it?"

Adam sighed. "I hate to dampen all that enthusiasm, darling, but I have to make some phone calls this morning. I've neglected our business interests for nearly two weeks now."

Maddy was intrigued. "What kind of calls? Anything I can help with?"

"No, it's just routine. I have to follow up on a transfer of funds from our bank in Paris to our new bank in New York. And I have several calls to make regarding the shipment of Pere Ruben's pre-Columbian artifacts."

That sounded so deadly dull that Maddy was grateful he had rejected her offer of assistance. "Are you sure you can't put them off until later?" she asked. "I was looking forward to tennis or horseback riding."

"No, no," Adam said quickly. "You haven't been cleared for anything that strenuous, no matter how good you're feeling today. If Dr. Manion says it's okay after your checkup tomorrow, then I'll be happy to beat the socks off you on the tennis court, but until then we'll find something a little less strenuous to help you burn off all that energy."

"Adam—"

"This is not negotiable, Madeline," he said in the dictatorial tone that grated on Maddy like fingernails on a chalkboard. "Remember what happened when you insisted on climbing the lighthouse tower. Just because you're feeling wonderful today doesn't mean you get to go overboard. Why don't you go down to the beach and read that book I bought for you in the village? As soon as I finish my calls, I'll join you."

"Sunbathing? What a lovely suggestion," she said with a touch of sarcasm. She didn't know which was worse, having physical limitations or a husband who was always right. In a burst of sheer frustration she picked up the serrated fruit knife beside her plate and vigorously applied it to her grapefruit, sending juice flying everywhere. ''Why, that was just the sort of healthy, aerobic activity I was looking for!''

Adam wiped a sticky splatter of juice off his cheek, then unfolded his napkin with a flick of his wrist and held it up by two corners in front of his face. ''Why, thank you, darling. I'm glad you like the idea.''

Maddy looked at the blank white square where Adam's face had been, and her irritation disappeared. ''All right. It's safe to come out now,'' she said. How could she possibly stay mad at someone who responded to her churlishness with such good humor?

Adam peeked cautiously around the left side of the napkin. ''Are you sure about that?''

''I'm sure.''

He lowered the napkin, and Maddy couldn't resist the temptation. Without missing a beat she flicked a perfectly aimed grapefruit seed with her finger and hit him smack in the center of the open vee of his robe.

Adam looked down at the seed nestled in the dark curls of hair on his chest. ''I hate walking into an ambush. I just hate it,'' he deadpanned.

Maddy laughed merrily as she said, ''I'm sorry. I couldn't help myself.'' She leaned across the table with her fingers extended toward the seed, but Adam grabbed her wrist and pinned her with a stern glare.

''Just the seed, Maddy,'' he warned her.

She widened her eyes in mock disbelief. ''Why, Adam, are you suggesting that I might pluck something other than that seed off your chest?''

''Yes.''

''Oh! What a horrible insinuation. Would I hurt you like that?''

"Absolutely." He met her gaze steadily, but the twinkle in his eyes told Maddy he was enjoying their game as much as she was. "If it meant getting the last word or the last laugh, you'd do *anything*."

"You have my word of honor," she swore raising her free hand. "I'll get the seed and nothing but the seed, so help me God."

"Well . . . all right." He still looked dubious, but he released her wrist so that Maddy could dig her fingers into the curly matt of hair and pick out the seed. As she'd promised, it was a painless procedure—for Adam, at least. For Maddy, the contrast of hard muscle, warm skin and soft hair against her fingers brought instant and torturous images of exploring that enticing region more fully.

Unfortunately Adam had disallowed any such intimacy, and though Maddy occasionally saw signs that he was having difficulty living up to his own rules, neither of them had ventured across the imaginary line he'd drawn between them. Part of her appreciated his restraint; their relationship was complex enough without adding sex to the jumbled-up alphabet soup that passed for her life right now. But another part of Maddy wanted very much to know what making love with Adam Hopewell felt like.

Adam must have read the direction her thoughts were taking, because as soon as she settled back into her seat he tugged on the lapels of his robe, closing the vee. "Thank you, Maddy," he said, making it sound like the decree of a benevolent monarch. "Since you've just proved yourself to be so trustworthy, I propose a compromise."

"Oh? What's that?"

"A compromise? It's a settlement of differences by mutual concessions," he said with a devilish grin, clearly pleased with his own joke. "You know—give and take. You get something you want and I get something I—"

"I get it! I get it!" she said, laughing. "I know what a compromise is, Adam. Just state the terms."

"All right. You take your book down to the beach—"

She glared at him. "So far I'm not hearing any compromise."

"—and as soon as I finish my calls, I'll bring a picnic lunch down and we'll walk down to the south shore," he said as though she hadn't interrupted him. "We can explore the beach and have lunch on the catwalk of the lighthouse. How does that sound?"

"Sensible." *And wonderfully romantic,* she added mentally, thinking of Adam's description of the way the lighthouse had figured into their honeymoon. Considering the line they couldn't cross, Maddy would have preferred activity to romance, and she didn't want to be sensible today, either, but she knew Adam was right about not overexerting herself. "Is that your best offer?"

"Yep."

She shrugged. "Then I guess I'll have to accept it, won't I? Although, I must say I'm a little surprised you're willing to entrust me to Frick and Frack."

Adam frowned. "Frick and Frack?"

"My bodyguards," she explained.

He chuckled. "They go by the names Ed and Bobby, I believe. And actually I've been very impressed with them so far. I've never once seen their attention wander, and whenever there's any type of

potential threat they're always right there, ready to
intervene. I think I can trust them to take care of you
on the beach—so long as you make sure they're behind you when you leave the lobby."

"Aye, aye, coach," she said, digging into her
grapefruit.

They finished breakfast, and while Adam was
showering, Maddy tossed all her beach paraphernalia
into the striped bag Adam had bought for her in the
village. She yelled goodbye to him, though she
doubted he could hear her over the roar of the shower,
and left the suite, wishing she was off to do something more exciting than curl up with a book.

In the hall she waved to the security camera in the
far corner and began toying with the idea of defying
Adam's latest edict. If she tried she could probably
scrape up a tennis opponent without too much trouble, and watching Adam hit the roof because she'd
disobeyed him had a certain appeal. Sooner or later
she was going to assert her independence and force
Adam to stop treating her like a fragile porcelain antique. When she did, it was a sure bet that the resulting fireworks would put any Fourth of July display to
shame.

But rebelling just for the opportunity to watch
Adam explode seemed foolish—even though butting
heads and matching wits with him had proved to be
the most enjoyable part of her "second honeymoon." As much as she hated to admit it, he was
right: it would be stupid of her to overdo things today
just because she felt ready to take on the world.

She hit the stairs prepared to have to ferret out her
bodyguards, but they weren't loitering unobtrusively

this morning. Instead, they were standing large as life at the foot of the stairs, waiting for her.

Shaking her head in exasperation, she galloped down to the bottom step, stopped and looked from one guard to the other. "He called you, didn't he?"

"Sort of," the sandy-haired one replied. "The security office patched his call through to us." He pulled a cellular flip phone out of his pocket to show her the method of communication.

Maddy nodded. "I'll bet he told you to stay close, didn't he?"

"Yes, ma'am."

"Did he threaten to tear you both limb from limb if you let anything happen to me?"

The guards exchanged a quick glance and Maddy could tell they were trying not to laugh. "Something like that," Sandy replied.

"Then you'd better stick close. One thing I've learned about my husband is that he generally keeps his promises," she told them. "Well, if we're going to get chummy today, we might as well get acquainted. Which one of you is Bobby?"

"I am, ma'am," the shorter, dark-haired one answered.

She looked at "Sandy." "Then you must be Ed. I'm pleased to meet you both."

She led the way across the lobby, chatting casually with both her bodyguards, but once they reached the stairs off the veranda she noticed that Bobby lagged behind, placing some distance between them. They stayed in that formation throughout the long stroll to the beach and down several hundred yards to the Cabaña, a beach center that offered changing rooms, lockers, refreshments and beach paraphernalia rang-

ing from blankets to balls, to padded chaise lounges.
There was even a boutique called Everything Under
the Sun.

While Bobby surveyed the area, Ed escorted her to
a relatively uncrowded stretch of sand and helped her
set up her chaise. Maddy spread her own beach towel
over the chair pad, thanked Ed as he moved off and
settled in with *The Lazarus Prophecy*.

Thirty minutes later, Maddy closed the book, took
off her sunglasses and turned her face to the sun,
leaning her head back against the chaise. Adam was
wrong. She didn't care at all for the spy thriller, even
if the author *was* one of her favorites. Apparently,
along with all the other modifications it had made in
her life, the bump on her head had apparently changed
her taste in reading material, too.

She relaxed then, soaking up the sun, and nearly
drifted off, until a rustle of movement next to her
brought her wide awake. Everything inside her in-
stinctively tensed. She glanced to her left and found a
small thin man lugging a chaise lounge a little closer
to hers than was appropriate, considering how empty
the beach was.

Maddy put her glasses on so that she could observe
her new neighbor without being obvious, and she decided that there was something disquieting about him;
he was handling the chair so clumsily it almost seemed
as though he was trying to call attention to himself.
She looked behind her to make sure Ed and Bobby
were taking note and saw them moving purposefully
closer. That didn't stop her from deciding that this
would be a good time to file her nails, though.

Eventually the little man, who was dressed in plaid
Bermuda shorts, a blinding floral-print shirt and a

Panama hat that dwarfed his face, stopped fussing with his chaise, but he didn't sit.

"Excuse me, miss, are you planning to use that beach umbrella?" he asked her.

Maddy glanced over her shoulder at the detachable umbrella attached to the back of the chaise. She had been working so hard to get rid of her hospital pallor that she hadn't even considered opening it. "No, I hadn't planned to."

He took a step toward her and Maddy's heart leapt into her throat. "Would you mind if—"

"Of course not," she said hastily, rolling to her feet on the right side of the lounge so that she could reach the umbrella—and prevent her neighbor from getting too close.

As she moved, he protested, "Oh, that's not necessary. I can do it," but he was too late. Maddy had the umbrella out of its socket before he'd come two steps closer. She handed him the umbrella and he responded with an apologetic smile.

"Thank you, miss. You're very kind. I certainly didn't mean to inconvenience you."

"You haven't at all," Maddy assured him.

"They were all out of umbrellas at the Cabaña when I got my chaise," he told her as he stumbled and fumbled back to his own lounge. "Frankly, it seems like very poor planning—there should be an umbrella for every chair, don't you agree?"

"I suppose so," she said politely, though alarm bells were ringing in her head and her nerve endings were dancing a jig. Bobby and Ed were right behind her, which gave her the confidence to resume her seat, but she didn't relax. There was something wrong with her new neighbor; she just couldn't pinpoint it.

She went back to filing her nails, watching him covertly as he grappled with the umbrella. It took two attempts for him to fit it into the socket, and several more to get it to stay up. Maddy would have felt sorry for him if she hadn't been convinced that his bumbling was all an act, but it did give her an opportunity to make a few pertinent observations—like the fact that despite his short stature and ill-matched, ill-fitting clothes—was he deliberately trying to look like a tourist?—he was no ninety-pound weakling. The calves of his legs were lightly tanned and as keenly muscled as a runner's, and the same was true of his arms. He was small and wiry, not puny and uncoordinated, though that seemed to be exactly the impression he was trying to convey.

The question was why?

And equally important, why had he chosen Maddy to witness his performance?

It wasn't a coincidence. She was sure of it.

So she continued to file her nails, pretending to ignore him, until he finally settled into the circle of shade he had created. "There now. That's ever so much better than the blinding sun."

Maddy flashed him a reserved smile, certain that she didn't have to encourage him. He was going to talk to her whether she welcomed his companionship or not. "I'm glad you could make use of it," she said politely.

"Have you been here long?" he asked her. "At Bride's Bay, I mean."

"Four days," she answered.

"Then that gives you seniority, I suppose," he told her. "I'm only on my third. It's a lovely place, isn't it?"

"It certainly is, Mr....?"

"Oh, forgive me. I should have introduced myself straight off. I'm Arthur Rumbaugh," he said, removing his hat.

"Madeline Hopewell," she responded.

He smiled at her. "It's a pleasure to meet you, Ms. Hopewell."

CHAPTER TWELVE

MADDY WAS RIGHT about Rumbaugh. Getting him to talk took no effort at all. He conversed on so many subjects with so little prompting, in fact, that Maddy began to wonder if she had misjudged him. It was possible that he'd put his chaise so close to hers for no other reason than loneliness and a desire for companionship.

Though Maddy allowed for the possibility that he was harmless, she never relaxed her guard completely, and she was relieved when she finally saw Adam coming down the beach with the picnic basket he'd promised. In fact, she was more than relieved. Even at a distance, her husband had the power to quicken her pulse and heighten her senses.

She waved to him and he waved back, but it was a halfhearted gesture at best. Maddy had learned Adam's moods well enough to tell from his body language that he was displeased about something.

Arthur seemed a bit confused—or perhaps perturbed—that she was no longer paying attention to him, and he glanced over his shoulder just as Adam returned her greeting. "Someone you know, Madeline?" he inquired.

"My husband," she told him, and then stiffened her jaw to hold back a laugh when Arthur's face fell like a jostled soufflé. *Poor guy*. He'd obviously thought she was single and had been flirting with her.

He sat upright in his chaise, muttering, "Perhaps it would be best—"

"Oh, I don't think you need to leave because of Adam," Maddy said quickly.

"Certainly not," Arthur replied huffily, settling his straw hat on his head as he dropped his feet into the sand. "But I do think it's time I went back in. I have been in the sun a bit too long this morning."

Actually he hadn't been in the sun at all thanks to Maddy's umbrella, but she didn't challenge him. "Well, it was very nice meeting you, Arthur. But I do wish you'd stay and meet my husband."

"Yes, Arthur, stay and meet Madeline's husband," Adam said as he stepped between the two chaises.

Arthur visibly gulped as he looked up at the towering form. "Oh, well ... Hello, there."

"Hello," Adam replied, moving toward Maddy's lounge. He dropped a proprietory kiss onto her forehead, placed the wicker picnic basket on the foot of the chaise, then sat with his body angled so that he could converse with his wife and her neighbor.

"Adam, this is Arthur Rumbaugh," Maddy told him, trying to get a fix on his mood. He didn't look as irritated as he had appeared coming down the beach, but he certainly didn't seem like his normal charming self, either. "Arthur, this is my husband, Adam Hopewell."

"Nice to meet you, Mr. Hopewell," Arthur said as he came to his feet, "but I was just leaving. Perhaps you'd like to use my lounge."

"Don't run off on my account," Adam said, but Arthur was already moving, and doing so with a great deal more agility than he'd displayed earlier.

"Bye, Arthur," Maddy called after him, and wasn't surprised when he didn't respond.

"What the hell did you think you were doing?" Adam demanded once Arthur was out of earshot.

His tone brought out the fighter in Maddy. "I was having a conversation with a computer salesman from Connecticut, if you must know."

"Did you approach him or vice versa?"

"He approached me," she replied.

"Then why didn't you leave immediately?"

"Because I assessed the possible threat he posed and decided the risk was minimal," she said, bristling with anger.

"Minimal," he repeated, his jaw clenched. "You don't take even minimal risks, Madeline!"

"And you don't order me around!" Maddy began throwing her things into her beach bag as she shifted to the edge of the lounge opposite him. "In case you hadn't noticed, Adam, there are other people on this planet with whom we might have to converse on occasion. Poor little Arthur Rumbaugh is one of them, and he was perfectly harmless—unless you count boring me to death as a murder attempt."

"All right, all right," Adam said crossly. "Calm down."

"I will not," she snapped, coming to her feet and circling the lounge. "I have two bodyguards and a very finely honed instinct for self-preservation. I don't need a husband who turns into Attila the Hun every time I leave his side for five minutes. When will you get it through your thick head that I am not going to do anything stupid?''

Maddy fully expected his reply to be "When you stop doing stupid things!" but he restrained himself.

"You're right, Maddy," he said as he rose. I overreacted. But I got scared when I saw that Ed and Bobby had moved in closer than usual. I took that to mean there was some kind of threat."

Maddy regarded him suspiciously. "Are you sure you weren't just jealous?"

"Jealous? Of that pipsqueak? Don't be ridiculous."

"Pip...?" Maddy suddenly felt as though she'd been poleaxed between the eyes, and she completely forgot about her argument with Adam.

There was something there, right on the edge of her consciousness; some memory that wanted to break out of the black hole.

A memory that was in some way associated with Arthur Rumbaugh!

"Pip...pipe...pep? Pepper?" she murmured, frowning in concentration.

"Maddy? What's wrong?" Adam asked, reaching out to her. "Are you remembering something?"

She whirled around, searching frantically for Rumbaugh, but he was nowhere to be seen. "Damn it, where is he? How could he have gotten off the beach so fast?" she muttered scanning the beach for a glimpse of his shirt.

"Maddy!" Adam grabbed her shoulders to hold her still. "What the hell is going on? Did you remember something?"

"Yes!" she shouted at him, then frowned in frustration. "No. I don't know. When you called Arthur a pipsqueak I got a flash of something. A name...like Pippin or Pepper... It was just a flash and then it was gone. But it was somehow associated with Arthur Rumbaugh. I think,'' she added, because now that the image had evaporated she wasn't sure of anything.

"All right,'' Adam said, guiding her back to the chaise and urging her to sit. "Let's calm down and analyze this. When he first approached you, did Rumbaugh show any sign that he recognized you?''

Maddy thought back. "No, but he did act as though he was trying to draw attention to himself.'' She went on to explain how he'd initiated their conversation, and she even confessed the suspicions she'd had about the incongruities she'd spotted.

"You thought he was putting on an act?''

"At first, yes.''

"Did he say anything that indicated he knew about your amnesia?''

"No. Nothing.''

"Think back, Maddy,'' he commanded. "Could he have been posing for you?''

"Posing?''

"Making sure you got a good look at him so that he could find out whether or not you recognized him?''

Maddy felt like an idiot for not having considered the possibility herself. "Of course. That could have been exactly what he was doing.''

"And you did recognize him, didn't you?''

"No! At least not until you said what you did. Then it was as if someone held up a picture in front of me and snatched it away before I could get a good look. It could be that Arthur just *reminded* me of someone I once knew.''

"Or he could have been the man who attacked you at the airport."

A shiver ran down her spine and she nodded. "It's possible."

Adam carried it one step further. "And if he somehow learned that you have amnesia—by hanging around the hospital, maybe—then it's logical to assume he'd want to know if you'd regained your memory before..."

"Before he tries to kill me again."

"Yeah." Adam came to his feet, grabbing Maddy's arm and bringing her with him, but when he started pulling her across the sand, she yanked away.

"Wait a minute! My bag! Our lunch!" she protested, reaching toward the lounge.

"Forget about them!" Adam got hold of her again. "I'm getting you to someplace safe, and you're going to stay there until we know everything there is to know about Arthur Rumbaugh or Arthur Pippin or Pepper, or whatever the hell his name is. Now move!"

"Oh, what the hell," Maddy muttered, letting Adam hustle her toward the Cabaña. "I didn't like that book, anyway."

ADAM'S URGENCY was hard to miss and Maddy's bodyguards responded accordingly by closing in. With Ed and Bobby flanking them, Adam dragged Maddy into the alcove entrance between the men's and women's changing rooms.

"What's wrong, Mr. Hopewell?" Ed asked him.

"That man who sat down next to my wife. What do you know about him?"

"His name's Arthur Rumbaugh. He's a computer salesman from Hartford, Connecticut, who checked in three days ago," Ed replied. "When I heard him introduce himself to Mrs. Hopewell I phoned the office and found out he'd cleared a stage-one security check."

"What does that entail?" Maddy asked him.

"It's a general background search conducted by computer."

"Does it validate that he is who he claims to be? Could he be an impostor?" she asked.

Ed thought it over. "I suppose it's possible. Our search proves that there is an Arthur Rumbaugh, but it would take a stage-two security check—maybe even a stage-three—to prove that someone is impersonating him."

"Then get on it. Now," Adam commanded. "Call Tom Graves and have him send a vehicle down here— something enclosed—so I can get my wife back to the hotel, and tell him I want to see him as soon as we get there."

"Yes, sir!" Ed pulled out his cellular phone and set the wheels in motion.

TWO HOURS LATER Maddy's head felt worse than it had the day Adam walked into her hospital room and introduced himself as her husband. Once he had her safely back in their hotel room he'd bombarded her with more questions about the vague memory flash she'd had, then the Bride's Bay security chief, Tom Graves, had arrived to ask her even more questions.

She explained what had happened with Rumbaugh from beginning to end, and it sounded so innocuous that she didn't blame Tom for looking at her as though she was nuts for raising such a fuss. To placate Adam, Tom put out a security alert to determine where Arthur had gone after he left the beach, and word came back that Rumbaugh was at the pool sitting in the shade of a beach umbrella. Not exactly suspicious behavior, Tom noted, flatly refusing Adam's request that he question Arthur directly.

"Flirting isn't a crime at Bride's Bay," the chief told Adam. "I won't harass a guest without good reason."

"But you don't understand," Adam argued. "Maddy remembered him after he left, and she associated a different name with him."

"Begging your pardon, Mr. Hopewell, but that's not what I heard your wife say. She said he *reminded* her of someone. And she can't even recall who that someone is."

"He's right, Adam," Maddy said, inserting herself into the conversation in the hope of calming her husband down. "Arthur didn't do anything wrong. I overreacted to a perfectly harmless stranger."

"But what about your memory flash?" Adam asked.

"What about it? I remembered part of a name. Big deal. When I can remember my *own* name, then we'll get excited."

Tom Graves folded the notebook he'd been scribbling in and stood, looking down at Maddy. "I don't blame you for being frustrated, Mrs. Hopewell," he said sympathetically. "If I were in your situation, I'd probably... Hell, I don't have a clue what I'd do, but I guarantee you I wouldn't be handling it half as well as you are."

Maddy looked up at him with her lips pursed thoughtfully. "You know, for a security guy you've got a pretty nifty bedside manner. I'll bet you say that to all your cranky guests."

He smiled at her. "Nope. Only the ones who have a right to be cranky." He glanced at Adam and back to Maddy. "Look, I don't want either of you to think I'm dismissing your concerns. As soon as I get downstairs I'm going to initiate a full security sweep on Mr. Rumbaugh and I'll ask Luther if he can make some additional inquiries. By the time we finish with him, we'll know what brand of after-shave he uses and whether or not his mother wore dentures."

"I'd settle for knowing that he is who he claims to be," Adam replied tersely, though Maddy could tell that he was somewhat mollified by Tom's promise.

"I think I can assure you of an answer on that by this time tomorrow," Tom replied, moving toward the door. "And in the meantime I'll have my people keep an eye on him."

Adam escorted Tom across the room. "Please let us know if he does anything suspicious."

"You can count on it." He stopped just short of the door. "This hasn't changed your plan to go into Charleston tomorrow, has it?"

Maddy could tell from the way Adam hesitated that he hadn't thought that far ahead yet, so she took the high ground. "No, it hasn't," she said, coming to her feet. "We'll need Ed and Bobby to accompany us to the hospital at eight-thirty in the morning, and you can expect us to be gone most of the day. Once Dr. Manion finishes examining me, I have some shopping to do."

Adam turned to her. "Now, wait a minute. We're not—"

"Oh, yes we are," she argued. "The only clothes I have are the ones you bought for me while I was in the hospital and the odds and ends I picked up in the boutique downstairs. Would you like me to recite my shopping list in front of Mr. Graves?" She smiled sweetly at the security chief. "I'm in desperate need of a number of toiletry items, as well as—"

"All right! All right!" Adam looked at Tom. "We'll need Ed and Bobby all day tomorrow."

"No problem," Tom said, doing his best to restrain a smile. "We'll keep Mr. Rumbaugh under surveillance and notify Ed on the cellular if he leaves the island."

"Fine."

They confirmed the flight arrangements Adam had already made with Duke Masterson, and then Tom left.

"Maddy, are you sure about tomorrow?" Adam asked as he came toward her. "We could postpone or maybe even get Dr. Manion to come out here."

"No, Adam. I am not going to let one little blown-out-of-proportion incident send me into hiding."

"Who says it was blown out of proportion?" Adam asked, frowning.

"I do," she replied. "We let our paranoia get out of control today, but it won't happen again. I am not going to keep crying wolf and find that no one will come when I really do need help."

Adam closed the scant distance between them and gently pulled her into his arms. "I will *always* come, Maddy," he swore. "Don't ever doubt that."

Maddy was moved by his sincerity. "I don't doubt it, Adam. But I should remind you that you were the one who took a flying leap off the deep end today. I was just along for the ride, remember?"

"I won't apologize for doing everything I can to protect you."

"I don't expect you to, Adam," she said, resting her head on his chest. "Truth be told, I'd rather be embarrassed than dead any day of the week."

His arms tightened around her as though he was trying to pull her inside him where she'd be even safer. "You are not going to die, Maddy. I don't want to hear you say that, even in jest."

An overwhelming warmth engulfed her that had nothing to do with the intense attraction she felt whenever Adam took her in his arms. This feeling went so much deeper than desire; it was as though all the separate emotions she'd felt for him these past weeks had congealed into one wave of warmth, tenderness and something Maddy was ready to put a name to.

"Thank you, Adam."

"For overreacting?" he asked lightly.

But Maddy wasn't in the mood to joke. She wanted to tell Adam how much she loved him, and that wasn't a laughing matter. "Thank you for taking care of me. For always being just what I need, whenever I need it."

She raised her head and looked into his eyes, trying to find just the right words. Suddenly Adam pressed a brief but fervent kiss to her lips, then released her.

"You're welcome, darling. Now, if you're absolutely intent on going shopping tomorrow, I have a few more phone calls I need to make," he told her as he moved toward the bedroom. "I think a limo will be safer than depending on taxis, and I want our own private investigator doing some checking on Arthur Rumbaugh.''

''What? Adam . . .''

''This won't take long, I promise.''

He ducked out of the room, leaving Maddy feeling as though someone had just fast-forwarded her life, cutting out the most important part. One second she'd been about to tell Adam she loved him. The next she was alone.

Maddy couldn't help but feel shaken. For two weeks now, Adam had been the perfect husband, sensitive to her every mood, saying all the right things at exactly the right time. It wasn't fair of her to expect him to be perfect twenty-four hours a day, but he'd picked a helluva time to shut off his sensitivity meter.

Or had he? Maybe he hadn't totally misread her mood. Maybe he was just trying to avoid a repeat of their encounter on the balcony several nights ago when she'd thrown herself at him.

Or even worse, maybe he'd seen what was in her eyes and hadn't wanted to hear her say ''I love you,'' because he couldn't say the same thing in return.

But, no. That couldn't be true, not after everything that had happened, not after all the things he'd said to her, all the tenderness and loving concern he'd shown.

Or had she taken too much for granted? Just because Adam had been protective and supportive of the *shell* his wife had once inhabited didn't mean he loved the woman she'd become—the woman who argued with him at the drop of a hat, who challenged his judgment every time she got the chance, and then clung to him for dear life whenever she got scared or felt insecure.

"I'm a different woman, aren't I, Adam?" she murmured to the empty room. "Have I changed into someone you can't love?"

Maddy sank onto the sofa, curled her legs beneath her and fought the urge to cry. "What's going to happen if you don't get *your* Maddy back?" she whispered. "What if I never remember *us?*"

She'd asked that question once and Adam had told her they'd start over. Now it appeared he might have changed his mind.

Maddy wasn't even close to being emotionally ready to ask the question again.

ADAM CLOSED the bedroom door and fought the urge to smash his fist through it. "Damn, damn, damn, damn," he muttered.

That sweet, loving, trusting look in Maddy's eyes had undone him, and he didn't know how much more he could take. Fury at himself and this whole miserable situation swept through him, and he moved quickly to the nightstand, snatched up the cordless phone from its base and hurried into the bathroom. He locked the door, turned on the water and punched in a ten-digit phone number and four-digit code.

When a man answered after only one ring, Adam made his position crystal clear.

"I want out," he said harshly. "And I want out *now.*"

CHAPTER THIRTEEN

"I NEED A CLONE," Tom Graves muttered as he hurried out of the Fortress. He'd spent the whole day trying to be in two places at once, and the pressure didn't show any sign of letting up. He'd been so busy he hadn't even had time for lunch, and his body was telling him that if it didn't get some nourishment soon he wasn't going to make it through the strenuous staff seminar in self-defense he was supposed to conduct in thirty minutes.

Like it or not, he had to take a few minutes and run downstairs to the staff dining room, throw himself onto the tender mercies of head chef Columbia Hanes and beg for an afternoon snack. *If* he could make it through the lobby and past the main dining room without running into someone who needed a question answered or a problem solved.

"Thomas! What perfect timing!"

Halfway across the lobby, Tom stopped in his tracks, mentally kissed a snack goodbye and turned toward the husband of the hotel's owner. "Good afternoon, Judge Bradshaw. What can I do for you? Has the Secret Service been mauling your hedge maze again?"

The silver-haired man shook his head. "No, there's no major garden crisis today, Thomas. I just learned at the front desk that Mr. and Mrs. Hopewell went into the city for the day. Do you have any idea when they'll return?"

"No, I'm sorry. Bobby DiVesta called just after lunch to say it had taken the entire morning for Mrs. Hopewell's doctor to give her a clean bill of health, and he had no idea when they'd be getting in. I suspect it won't be until later this evening."

"Oh, I see." The Judge seemed disappointed.

"Is something wrong?"

"Oh, no. It's nothing urgent. I have an invitation I want to tender, that's all. Elizabeth and I have been racking our brains all week trying to think of something special to do for them," the Judge said chattily, falling into step beside Tom when he began moving toward the dining room. "I wanted to throw them a big anniversary bash, but Elizabeth didn't think something that personal was appropriate for a couple who are essentially strangers to us—no matter how nice they are."

Emily Post wasn't Tom's strong suit, and the Hopewells' anniversary was the least of his worries about the couple, but he wouldn't have been rude to Cameron Bradshaw no matter how busy—or how hungry—he was. "Your wife has a point, I suppose. And it's very likely that Adam Hopewell will have plans of his own."

"Yes, that's what Elizabeth said. So, instead, we're inviting them to the President's reception next Tuesday, the day before their anniversary. Don't you think that's a lovely idea?"

Tom was a little taken aback. "Well, yes. I suppose they'll be thrilled, but . . ."

"But you're worried about the guest-list clearance, aren't you?"

"Actually, yes."

"Well, don't. I've already cleared it with Agent Luther. He didn't see any problem with inviting them."

"Oh. Good," Tom said, though he was a bit surprised. If he'd been in charge of presidential security he wasn't sure he'd have wanted a woman with a bull's-eye on her back at a party for the Chief Executive. But he wasn't in charge. "I'm sure the Hopewells will be thrilled with the invitation."

"I certainly hope so," Cameron replied. "I believe that a couple celebrating their tenth anniversary at the hotel where they spent their honeymoon deserves some special acknowledgment by the management."

"The Hopewells spent their honeymoon here?" Tom asked with some surprise.

"Oh, yes. Ten years ago," the Judge confirmed. "Of course, the assault on Madeline has certainly changed the complexion of their anniversary, but I don't think that should make a difference to the resort, do you? They had made reservations to celebrate the occasion here long before the attack, and I think that deserves some recognition on our part."

Tom went from surprise to disbelief in the space of a heartbeat. "Wait a minute, Judge. You must be mistaken. There was never another reservation on file for the Hopewell couple."

Cameron's silver brows drew together in a frown. "I'm quite sure you're wrong, Thomas. I had a long talk with Madeline the day after she arrived, and she told me that she and her husband had reservations here for their anniversary, and that he simply moved their arrival date forward a week. I'm certain that's what she said." He shook his head definitively. "Yes,

I'm positive. We were talking about the attempt on her life and she said that her husband's theory on what she was doing in Charleston had something to do with the possibility that she was planning on coming to Bride's Bay early."

Tom was positive the old man was wrong. Unless… "Tell me, Judge, where did Mrs. Hopewell get her information about having reservations here?"

"Why, from her husband, of course. Until she regains her memory, he's the only source of information she has," Cameron replied.

"Excuse me, Judge," Tom said, turning in another direction. "There's something I need to look into." And with that he hurried toward the front desk where Shane Foster was on duty by himself. "Is Ms. Jermain in her office?" he asked the young man as he moved into the reception alcove.

"I think so, sir. I could buzz if you like."

"Not necessary," he said, knowing that he could cross the alcove and knock in a lot less time than it would take the rookie to figure out how to use the hotel intercom system. Foster had been working at the resort for more than a week now, but he wasn't catching on to the computer and communications system as quickly as he should have. According to his résumé he should have been able to run the hotel database computer program in his sleep.

Investigating that inconsistency was just one of the many things on Tom's extensive to-do list, but right now the Hopewells had moved to the top of that list.

"Liz? You got a minute?" he asked, sticking his head into her office.

When Liz looked up it was clear he was distracting her. It seemed to take her a second to bring him into focus. "Of course, Tom," she said, motioning him toward a chair. "What's up?"

"Something puzzling," he said as he settled into his seat. "Tell me, Liz, have you noticed any problems with Judge Bradshaw recently?"

The question clearly surprised her. "No, of course not. What kind of problems are you referring to?"

"Memory lapses or getting his facts mixed up. Anything like that?"

"Absolutely not. Cameron sometimes lays on his kindly old Southern gentleman routine a little thick, but he's still as sharp as a tack. Why would you even suspect that—"

"Something he just told me," Tom said, cutting her off because he could see that his question had upset her. "And if he's right, it doesn't make any sense. According to the Judge, the Hopewell couple already had reservations here before the attack on the wife. They were supposed to check in sometime this week to celebrate their anniversary."

Liz shook her head. "No, the Judge is mistaken. I dealt with Adam Hopewell personally every time he called. I know for a fact that there was no reservation on file before his wife went into the hospital."

"That's what I understood when you first told me about them. You even commented on how lucky they were to get one of the high-security suites."

"Right. If Senator Luccacio hadn't changed his mind about vacationing with the President, we wouldn't have been able to accommodate them. Adam Hopewell called just an hour or two after the senator's secretary phoned to cancel his room."

"So there was never a reservation on the Hopewells before that call?"

"Absolutely not."

Tom leaned forward in his chair. "Then why did Adam Hopewell tell his wife there was?"

Liz shook her head helplessly. "Are you sure he did?"

"Unless the Judge is confused," Tom replied. "Has Hopewell ever said anything to you about having spent his honeymoon here ten years ago?"

Liz leaned over to her computer and called up the file in question as she replied, "He didn't, but Duke Masterson mentioned it. He wanted to make sure we did the champagne-and-flowers treatment for their anniversary."

"Did you verify that they really did spend their honeymoon here?"

Liz looked at him, confused. "Why would I do that?"

Tom grinned sheepishly. "You're right. You wouldn't have any reason to. But I'm the suspicious sort, so humor me. Is there any way to verify it?"

She shook her head. "No, sorry. We lost all our back records about six years ago when our old mainframe crashed." A bolt of inspiration lit her face. "However, you could always check Grandmother's guest register. She's got them going all the way back to the very first guest who ever stayed here. Of course, it's been nearly twenty years since signing in was compulsory, but most everyone does it for the sake of tradition."

"Where are the old registers?"

"Downstairs in the fire vault with the rest of the Jermain family papers."

"Can I get a peek?"

"Now?"

"If you don't mind."

"All right," Liz said, rising. As she led the way out, she asked, "Tell me, why is this so important, Tom?"

"It's probably not," he replied, falling into step with her. "But like I said before, I don't like loose ends. If Adam Hopewell lied to his wife about having reservations here, there's got to be a reason. I want to know what it is."

They passed the employee dining room on their way downstairs, and the luscious smells wafting out of Columbia's kitchen made Tom's stomach rumble. Supper preparations were well under way.

They went down a stairway, then moved through a warren of corridors past the laundry, linen storage and maintenance. Just when it seemed that they'd run out of corridor, Liz stopped at a door that led through a large storage room to a thoroughly modern walk-in fire vault.

Liz dialed in the appropriate combination and led Tom to the back of the vault. Elizabeth's papers were so well organized that it took only a few minutes to find the appropriate journal...

And even less time than that to determine that there was no entry in it for honeymooners Adam and Madeline Hopewell.

LIZ WAS QUICK to remind Tom that signing in wasn't mandatory, and that it made no sense for a man to lie about where he spent his honeymoon. His amnesiac wife was bound to ask questions about things they'd seen and done ten years ago, which meant that the husband would be required to concoct an extensive web of lies. And all for what?

Liz couldn't answer that and neither could Tom, but he was more determined than ever to find out. He escorted Liz back up to the first floor, thanked her for her help and hurried on upstairs to the room the Secret Service had commandeered as its command center.

Days ago, when Tom had told Dan Luther about the Hopewells, the agent had assured Tom that the Secret Service would investigate the couple and their situation fully. With resources like that focused on the couple, Tom hadn't seen any need to waste time and manpower conducting his own background investigation. He had spoken extensively with the Charleston police detective in charge of the attempted murder case, but beyond that Tom knew next to nothing about the Hopewells.

That was going to change.

The door to the room across from the Presidential Suite was ajar, and Tom poked his head in. The sitting room that would eventually be the nerve center of the Secret Service command post could have qualified for disaster-relief assistance. Most of the furniture had been removed and equipment was strewn everywhere, knots of disconnected cable of assorted sizes and colors snaked across the floor, and walking across the room was a risky proposition, at best. Tom knew that eventually order would be made from the chaos, but for now it was a nightmare. And Dan Luther, with his suit coat off and his shirtsleeves rolled up, was smack in the middle of it.

It was the first time Tom had seen the agent out of "uniform." "Dan? You got a minute?"

Luther looked up from the cables he was connecting to a console and nodded. "Yeah. Come on in. What's up?"

"I'd like to take a look at your background file on the Hopewell couple," Tom replied as he carefully picked his way across the obstacle course.

"Oh? Has something else happened?"

"Not exactly. At least, nothing like the Rumbaugh incident yesterday."

Dan Luther chuckled as he shunted two cables to a junction switch. "You mean no more hysterical accusations against harmless computer salesmen?"

"Not today," Tom replied as he made it safely to the console. "And I guess there's nothing new on Rumbaugh since we discussed him this morning?"

"Not a thing. The word I get from the investigators in D.C. is that he's exactly who he says he is. But we're still checking," the agent replied. "So what's up now?"

"I just found out something strange and it's made me curious."

Luther laid the cables aside and propped his hip on the tabletop. "Well, if you're curious, I am, too. Tell me."

"This is probably going to sound silly, but it appears that Adam Hopewell has been lying to his wife."

Luther looked at him blankly. "That has been known to happen on occasion, Tom. I don't think marital difficulties fall within our jurisdiction."

"Normally I would agree, but what he lied about doesn't make sense, and I like things to be nice and orderly," he replied, then went on to explain.

When he finished, Luther said, "So?"

Tom knew he didn't have much to go on, but he'd expected a little more reaction than that. "Don't you think it's odd? Why did Adam Hopewell tell his wife he had reservations here?"

"Probably because he really did."

Tom wondered if the agent had suddenly gone deaf. "No, Dan, I told you. I checked that out. There was nothing in the computer."

"Clerks have been known to make mistakes."

"True, but if his reservations were lost, why didn't he complain about it to Liz Jermain?"

"Perhaps because there was no reason to," the agent suggested. "His original reservation wasn't for a high-security suite, was it?"

"No, of course not."

"Well, if Hopewell was set on staying in a high-security suite from the time his wife left the hospital until the end of the month, it wouldn't have made any difference whether he had a reservation, would it? There wouldn't have been a room available if Senator Luccacio hadn't just canceled. Ms. Jermain probably put Hopewell into the suite automatically, and there was no need to make an issue out of a lost reservation. In fact, Hopewell might not even have known it."

"That's possible, I suppose," Tom said hesitantly. There was a slim chance that Luther was right, but Tom's gut instinct was telling him no. There was something strange going on. He could smell it. "Tell me, Dan, why did Senator Luccacio cancel his vacation with the President so suddenly?"

"Something to do with his recent appointment to the Appropriations Committee, I believe." A look of disbelief slowly evolved on the agent's face.

"Tom . . . surely you're not suggesting there's some connection between a United States senator and a slick, jet-setting antique dealer? That's ludicrous."

"So is lying to your amnesiac wife about where you spent your honeymoon," Tom said, his voice growing hard as alarm bells finally began pealing in his head. There was something a little too calculated about Luther's disbelief—and his answers. They were too pat, and they were coming a little too quickly. Tom finally realized that he was being "handled." He couldn't imagine why, but he didn't like it one bit.

"I want to see the background file you've compiled on the Hopewells," he told the Secret Service agent.

Luther clucked his tongue. "That's a little problematic, Tom. All our security checks are being conducted out of the office in D.C. I just get flash updates, not the full reports."

In a pig's eye, Tom thought. Agent Dan Luther was the Secret Service point man for a presidential visit, which meant that he was responsible for every aspect of the Chief Executive's stay at Bride's Bay. If anything happened to the President, Luther would be held accountable. His career, possibly even his own life, was on the line, and with stakes that high it was ludicrous to suggest that he didn't have immediate access to all security reports.

Tom would have bet his last dollar that Dan Luther had the security check on the Hopewells in his possession—possibly even in this very room.

So why was he lying?

It took everything Tom had to keep that opinion to himself and affect a look of mild puzzlement. "Really? That surprises me, Dan, because you had enough information on the couple to clear their attendance at the reception the Judge and Miz Elizabeth are giving the President.''

Luther's eyes narrowed just the tiniest bit. "My boss cleared that, Tom. I just passed the good word on to the Judge.''

Two lies in as many minutes. As point man, Luther had the final say on anything relating to the security clearances. This was getting curiouser and curiouser. ''Be that as it may, you can get the full report on the Hopewells down here, can't you?'' Tom asked casually.

The agent nodded. ''Absolutely, but it's not going to do you any good. You're wasting your time.''

Ah, the truth this time. If Dan was lying about not having immediate access to the Hopewell file, then it could only mean that he was stalling to give himself time to clean it up. Obviously there was something about the couple that the Secret Service wanted kept quiet, and that information would certainly be deleted from the file before it got to Tom.

But Tom was determined to find out what was going on. So he simply shrugged and told Luther, ''Hey, it's my time. I'd really like a look at that file.''

''Okay. I'll have the office courier it down here,'' the agent promised. ''In the meantime, maybe you can give me some help with something.''

''What?''

''It's a rumor one of my men heard this morning about Liz Jermain being involved in a secret love affair.''

Tom nodded. ''Yeah, that rumor has been circulating since before I started working here.''

Luther frowned. ''Is there any truth to it?''

"Probably," he admitted. "She's been known to leave the island on very short notice without telling anyone where she's going, or giving any explanation of where she's been when she gets back. She was behaving very much like a woman in love when I first got to the island, but her behavior lately suggests that there may be trouble in the relationship."

"But you haven't determined who she's involved with?"

"No," Tom had to admit.

"Why not?"

Despite their age difference, Tom felt as though he was being scolded by his father, and it put him on the defensive. There was no way that he was going to admit that he'd wanted to investigate but just hadn't had the time. "I haven't investigated because Liz Jermain's private life is none of my business," he replied tersely, then added, "And it's none of yours, either."

"I disagree," Luther argued. "It is imperative that we learn who Liz Jermain is involved with. Assassins have been known to use inside help to get close to their targets, and Ms. Jermain is just the sort of—"

"Assassins?" Tom said incredulously. "Are you telling me that you have knowledge of a specific threat against the President? Something that's supposed to happen while he's here at Bride's Bay?"

"Of course not," Luther said quickly. He waved his arms at the equipment cluttered around him. "But that's the purpose of all this gear. The President gets hundreds of death threats every year, and we have to be ready for every eventuality."

"No, Dan. That pat answer won't wash. You're concerned about something very specific, aren't you?"

Luther's usually implacable gaze went absolutely glacial. "Just give me what you've got on the Liz Jermain affair and let me worry about the President. If there's anything you need to know, I'll tell you."

Luther's tone was calculated to intimidate, but he was using his steely-eyed glare on the wrong man. "Are you telling me to butt out, Dan?"

"I'm asking you to do your job and let me do mine."

That was all the answer Tom needed to confirm his suspicions. Something deadly dangerous was going on that the Secret Service didn't think the lowly Bride's Bay security chief needed to know about.

But the security chief disagreed, and he wasn't going to stop until he knew exactly what was happening.

CHAPTER FOURTEEN

DR. MANION had been very pleased with Maddy's progress. After a thorough physical that morning, he'd told her she could do anything she felt up to, so long as she was sensible about it.

Adam had been right beside her when the doctor made the statement, and twenty-four hours earlier, he would've gotten a good laugh at the notion of Maddy being sensible. At the very least, he would have made some crack about how unlikely it was. Today, though, Manion's comment barely seemed to register on him.

For some reason Maddy couldn't fathom, Adam had changed. Oh, he was making all the right moves, saying the right things, just the way he always did, but now it seemed that he was just going through the motions. Where before Maddy had seen tenderness in his eyes, now she saw nothing. When he smiled, there was no humor. When he frowned, there was no anger.

When he looked at her, there was no love.

His eyes were a cold, blank slate. After he'd walked out of the room yesterday, Maddy had tried to convince herself that she was imagining things. She tried to pretend that she hadn't seen the transition on Adam's face that took him from warmth to withdrawal in that instant before she could say, "I love you."

But when he had finally come out of the bedroom a few minutes later, smiling and affable, he looked a cardboard caricature of himself; like an actor playing a role. Something was wrong, but Maddy couldn't work up the courage to ask Adam what it was because she didn't know if she could live with the answer if he said he didn't love her anymore.

Somehow she got through the afternoon of shopping, but she was glad they made it back to the resort before dark. Adam picked up several message slips at the front desk, and as soon as they got to their room, Maddy pleaded exhaustion and sought refuge in the rose bedroom, leaving Adam alone to handle his business calls.

Rather than resting, though, Maddy tinkered with the purchases she'd made, cutting off price tags, pairing up the separates and switching her wallet and other items from her old purse to her new one.

When she heard the soft chime announcing someone at the door to the suite, she assumed Adam had ordered a snack from room service, but a few moments later, he tapped on her door, then opened it and stuck his head in. "Maddy, we have a guest," he told her. "Do you feel up to a visitor?"

"Who is it?" she inquired, unable to imagine who would be coming to see them.

"Judge Bradshaw. He says he has something he wants to discuss with us."

"All right." Mystified, Maddy followed Adam back into the sitting room. She'd seen the Judge several times since their first encounter in the garden, and she'd even made a point of introducing him to Adam. She never would have expected a visit, though. "Judge Bradshaw! This is a welcome surprise."

The silver-haired magistrate was all smiles. "It's kind of you to say so," he replied, accepting the hand she extended to him. "But I'm sure you must be exhausted after your long day in the city. I won't keep you but a moment, I swear."

"Don't be silly," Maddy said, gesturing toward the sofa. "Please have a seat. Would you care for something to drink?"

"No, no. I'll just make my presentation and be on my way."

"Presentation?"

He handed her an envelope. "This. It's an anniversary gift from Elizabeth and me."

Maddy glanced nervously at Adam as she said, "Oh, Judge Bradshaw... this wasn't necessary. We specifically asked that the hotel not make any fuss."

"It's no fuss," he assured her. "At least not one that's directed straight at you. You may have heard that my wife and I are hosting a little reception for the President in the courtyard next Tuesday. Since it just so happens that his arrival coincides almost precisely with your anniversary, we thought you might enjoy a little treat on your special day."

"Oh, Judge..." Maddy didn't know how to respond. She opened the flap on the envelope and removed the engraved invitation.

"You'll need that to get past the Secret Service of course."

"Of course."

"They've approved your attendance—everyone had to be cleared naturally. And I do hope you'll come. It should be a memorable occasion."

She looked at Adam again, asking for confirmation as she said, "We'd love to attend, wouldn't we?"

"Absolutely," he replied amiably. "If we're still here, we'd be very honored by the opportunity to meet the President."

"There's a chance you'll be leaving?" Cameron asked, but he wasn't half as surprised as Maddy was.

"It's a possibility," Adam replied.

Cameron was too polite to question his guests about something that was none of his business. He expressed his hope that they would be able to attend, chatted with them for a few minutes more, then left, saying he didn't want to overstay his welcome.

As soon as he was gone, Maddy pounced on her husband. "Why didn't you tell me we might be leaving?"

"Because I'm not positive we are," he replied. "Detective Hogan has been getting nowhere with the investigation into the assault on you, and I've been playing with the thought that we might move on to New York if Dr. Manion gave you a good report. I hadn't mentioned it because I knew it would get your hopes up, but now it appears I'm going to have to go to New York regardless. Most of those phone messages that were waiting for me when we got back were from Anthony Vernandas and Pere Ruben."

Maddy knew that Ruben was one of Adam's clients, but she'd never heard of the other one. "Who's Anthony Vernandas?"

"He's one of the four buyers I lined up for Ruben's pre-Columbian artifacts. Apparently the deal is about to fall through. The men are furious with each other and with me for not being handy to mediate the sale and handle the transfer. I think the only way to salvage the situation is for me to meet with them in person. They've agreed to come to New York day after tomorrow and see if we can hammer out a new agreement."

Maddy didn't have any idea what Adam was talking about as far as the business was concerned, but she was thrilled at the thought of going New York. Bride's Bay hadn't stirred any memories. Maybe New York would. "That's wonderful, Adam. I can be packed and ready to go in half an hour!" she said, starting for her room.

"Stop! Slow down a minute," Adam said, stepping in front of her. "That's not the way it's going to work, Maddy. I'm leaving for New York in the morning—"

"And you're taking me with you," she said firmly.

He shook his head. "No, you'll be safer here, and a few more days' recuperation will be good for you. I've got business to conduct, and it won't be easy to find a security suite on a moment's notice in New York City. I'll find us a room, confer with our private detective to see if he can provide bodyguards for when we're out of the hotel, and once everything is in place, I'll come back here, and then the two of us will go to New York."

His proposal shocked her. Less than a week ago, this man had sworn that anyone who wanted to get at her would have to go through him to do it. Now he was considering leaving her alone. Was it just coincidence, or did his timing have something to do with what had happened yesterday?

She wanted to ask him that. Her first impulse, in fact, was to remind him that he'd sworn to protect her, but that was just fear and insecurity talking. He'd offered her his protection; she hadn't asked for it. She wasn't about to beg him not to leave her.

Besides, his plan made perfect sense. According to Tom Graves and the Secret Service, the flap about Arthur Rumbaugh had turned out to be nothing. He was exactly who he said he was—a computer salesman from Connecticut—and there was no reason to believe that Maddy was in any immediate danger here at the resort.

Even without Adam at her side, she would be well protected and safer than just about anywhere else in the world. It made sense for her to stay here while Adam arranged for her safety in New York. It was logical. It was sensible. It was the right course of action, and she knew it.

But that still didn't keep her from feeling as though Adam was deserting her.

CHAPTER FIFTEEN

UNABLE TO ESCAPE that feeling of abandonment, Maddy saw Adam off the next morning. It was obvious that his concern about leaving her was real—they'd had a long meeting with Tom Graves about the dire consequences of letting anything happen to her—but Maddy also had the distinct impression that Adam couldn't wait to get off Jermain Island. Or, more accurately, couldn't wait to get away from *her*. She went with him to the ferry, received a perfunctory kiss goodbye, watched the boat pull out and wondered if he would return.

Part of her mind said such thoughts were just maudlin claptrap. Adam loved her and she was foolishly imagining changes in him that weren't really there.

But there was no escaping the fact that she'd allowed herself to become too dependent on him. She'd been so frightened and felt so out of control that turning her life over to him had been easier than going it alone.

She saw now how much of a mistake that had been. She didn't like the woman she had become, so she decided to use the next few days without Adam to reinvent Madeline Hopewell.

She started with a confidence builder, heading for the rifle range as soon as Adam left. She spent most of the morning in target practice, and even participated in a lighthearted guerrilla warfare game being conducted by one of Tom's men.

Bobby and Ed tried to protest, reminding her that protecting her while she was skulking around in the wilderness area with two dozen other gun-toting guests wouldn't be easy. Their objections fell on deaf ears. Their only option was to join in and stay close to her, which they did.

Fortunately nothing happened that caused any of them the slightest alarm. Maddy's team won handily, and when the scores were recorded, it was discovered that Maddy had the most "kills." She wasn't surprised. Though no memories recurred, she knew from the way she handled herself that she'd played this type of game before.

After lunch with her fellow team members at the clubhouse, she began looking for an opponent for a game of tennis.

She found Loreen McKinley, a spritely sixty-seven-year-old widow from Duluth who claimed to have a touch of arthritis in her right hand and a trick knee.

Given her own limitations and the workout she'd already had this morning, Maddy figured that she and Loreen would be pretty evenly matched. However, Loreen trounced her handily in straight sets.

They shook hands as they walked off the court, and Maddy was about to demand a rematch tomorrow when she caught sight of a face she hadn't seen in more than a week. Detective Hogan was standing behind the long bench where she'd left her gym bag. He looked as rumpled and unfriendly as he had the first time she'd met him.

He did not look like a man delivering good news, but Maddy's heart felt a flutter of hope as she said goodbye to Loreen and hurried toward him.

"Detective Hogan! I hope you've come to tell me you caught the man who attacked me," she said as she snagged a towel out of her gym bag and applied it to her face.

"Not likely," he replied sourly.

"What do you mean by that? Have you given up looking for him?"

"Not voluntarily."

Hogan had never been verbose, but this was ridiculous. "Forgive me, Detective, but you're not making any sense. Why don't we start over? I'll say, 'Hi, Hogan. What brings you to Bride's Bay?' and you'll reply..." She held out her hand as though she was turning the floor over to him.

"You're in big trouble, Ms. Hopewell," he said.

Since Maddy already knew that, she made the logical assumption that the detective had learned something new—and obviously disturbing. "Why? What's happened? Has there been a break in the case?"

Hogan shook his head. "No. That's the problem. There is no case. My boss ordered me to stop investigating—that was the same conversation, by the way, in which he reminded me how close I am to retirement and how hard I've worked for my pension."

"You were threatened?" Maddy asked, aghast.

"That's what it sounded like to me."

"Why? Why would someone close my case? Why do they want you to stop investigating?"

"I suspect it's because they're afraid of what I'll find out."

Maddy stared at him. "And you have found out something, haven't you? You didn't stop investigating."

"Well ... we could probably split a few hairs about that," he answered. "It's not my fault if replies came in to inquiries I'd made before the case was closed."

Maddy's knees suddenly felt like rubber. She sat on the bench and Hogan came around to join her. "What have you learned?" she asked.

"I've got three things. One, you were probably damned lucky you got out of the hospital alive. The day before Adam Hopewell showed up, the name José Ruiz was placed into the hospital computer under janitorial staff. When no one picked up the paycheck the computer issued, it was discovered that no such employee ever existed at Charleston General. It was also discovered that the hours this Ruiz had worked corresponded to part of your hospital stay."

Maddy was glad she'd sat down. "You think it was the man who attacked me?"

"It's the only explanation I've been able to come up with. But it does suggest some disturbing possibilities."

"Such as?"

"Your assailant wasn't a garden-variety criminal, Ms. Hopewell. Even in this age of information there aren't a lot of people capable of manipulating a computer that effectively. And it takes a lot of moxie to successfully pull off an impersonation like that without arousing any suspicions. He did both. Very well. Which means that somehow you've gotten mixed up with some big-league players. I don't know what league they're in," he added quickly. "But there's someone with a lot of juice involved in this."

"Enough juice to get you thrown off the case?"

"Exactly."

"Like maybe the DEA?" she suggested, remembering the men who had talked to Hogan while she was still in the hospital.

Hogan shook his head. "I don't know. None of this makes any sense."

That was certainly true. "You said there were three things. What's number two?"

For the first time, Hogan looked truly uncomfortable. "Do you remember what your husband said about your arrival in New York?"

Maddy thought back. "Sure. He said that I came through customs on the nineteenth, thirty-six hours before I was attacked in Charleston."

Hogan's discomfort increased. "I'm afraid my information says otherwise."

"What information?"

"I had a friend of mine at the Charleston Port Authority call in a favor from a friend of his with U.S. Customs. I got a look at your complete file, Ms. Hopewell. You arrived in New York on the twentieth, and you made it through customs with just barely enough time to catch your flight to Charleston."

Maddy was astonished. "Are you sure about that?"

"Positive."

She shook her head. "Then Adam needs to have a long, serious talk with the private investigator who told him I arrived on the nineteenth. If he's that inept, it's no wonder he hasn't had any luck reconstructing what happened to me before I arrived."

"Ms. Hopewell..."

Maddy frowned at him. "What?"

"I wouldn't be too quick to blame the investigator, whoever he is. *If* he even exists."

Maddy stiffened. "Would you care to explain that?"

Hogan nodded. "Item number three—more information from your customs file." He paused again before he told her, "It's...about your name."

"What about it?"

"Lambert isn't your maiden name, and your parents weren't Paul and Irene. According to your birth certificate, you were born Madeline Renée *Hopewell* in Ogden, Utah, and your parents were Edgar and Francis Hopewell."

Maddy felt sick to her stomach.

"They're both alive and well, by the way," Hogan continued. "But they're pretty upset, because when I called to ask about their daughter Madeline I was told in no uncertain terms that they didn't appreciate cruel practical jokes. It seems that their daughter, Madeline, died at the age of two in a hospital in Salt Lake City. The bottom line, ma'am, is that you don't exist."

Maddy stopped breathing, stopped thinking. Her brain—her entire body—shut down for a fraction of a second, just long enough to let her feel what it was like to have the ground fall out from under her.

"That's...that's not possible."

Hogan looked sad when he told her, "It's more than possible, ma'am. It's the truth. Madeline Hopewell is an assumed identity. There's no other explanation."

"There has to be! Obviously there are two Madeline Hopewells—the one who died and me!"

Hogan shook his head. "That would mean there were two baby girls named Madeline born to the same parents in the same hospital in Ogden, Utah, on the fifth of February in nineteen-sixty—''

Maddy jumped to her feet. "No! There are two of us! Your information is wrong!"

"No, it's not," Hogan said. He came to his feet, too. "You're not Madeline Hopewell. And the man who's been claiming to be your husband isn't—''

"No!" Maddy screamed.

She turned and fled. She couldn't listen to him anymore. He was lying to her. This was a horrible joke, a prank, a mistake. It was a bad dream and she'd wake up in a minute. She *had* to wake up, because if she didn't it meant she didn't have a clue to her own identity—not even a name. And it meant that Adam—the sweet, kind, tender, sexy husband who'd made her feel safe, who'd made her trust him, who'd made her fall in love with him—was a liar and a fraud.

For all she knew, he might be a murderer, too.

"NO, NO, NO! Take him down!" Tom Graves shouted, moving quickly onto the workout mats where two of Bride's Bay's newest employees had taken center stage to grapple quite literally with self-defense techniques. Tom was starting to lose patience, but he held on to his temper because the problem was really his fault. As training partners these particular two students were a total mismatch.

Shane Foster was a bona fide preppie fresh out of grad school. He was trying—and failing—to take down Karl Olander, a wiry young scrapper who'd started work yesterday as a replacement for Roger Blaknee, who'd worked in the hotel laundry until last week when he'd suffered a stroke.

The exercise they were working on right now was a modified karate move that depended on balance. Tom stepped in to demonstrate the technique again and then stepped back to give Shane maneuvering room. Olander played his part, coming at Foster in full attack mode. Shane got set, grabbed Karl's arm and somehow ended up flat on his back with the wiry Swede standing over him.

Tom ran his hand through the rapidly thinning hairs on the top of his head. "Okay, guys, step aside." He moved to the center of the mat again and pointed at one of the three other students standing on the sidelines. "You. Over here. We'll start from—" He stopped talking when he caught a glimpse of Madeline Hopewell in tennis attire as she rushed by the floor-to-ceiling window of the health-club workout room. There was a man behind her, and Tom had a pretty good idea who it was.

It didn't surprise him when the door flew open and the Hopewell woman burst in, looking positively frantic. "Okay, guys, you're gonna get a break," Tom said to his students. "We're ending early today. Hit the shower and get back to work."

Mrs. Hopewell moved aside to let the students pass. They all looked at her curiously, but she barely gave them a glance. All of her attention was focused on Graves.

"I need your help and I don't know where else to turn," she said without preamble.

Tom nodded and looked at the man standing just behind her left shoulder. "You're Hogan?"

"That's right. It's nice to meet you finally."

"Same here," Tom replied. He had talked to Hogan about the Hopewell case several times before the couple had arrived, but the most intriguing conversation they'd had was the one this morning, when Hogan had called to ask if the Hopewells were still at the resort. That had been less than an hour after the husband left, and Hogan had seemed pleased by that news. Though he'd refused to tell Tom why, the detective stated his intent to come to the resort today to speak with Madeline Hopewell.

"Tell me what's going on and how I can help," Tom said.

"First, you have to promise that nothing I say to you will leave this room," Maddy demanded, her jaw clenched and her hands knotted into fists. She was clearly under intense stress. "If you're going to feel an obligation to report any of this to the man who calls himself Adam Hopewell, then say so now."

Her phrasing was not lost on Tom. He'd had suspicions about Hopewell yesterday, but nothing that bordered on the scope of what Madeline seemed to be suggesting. He glanced at Hogan, and the detective just nodded. "All right. Nothing leaves this room," Tom promised.

"You won't call Adam at the hotel in New York?"

"No. Now tell me what's going on."

It took everything Maddy had to control her voice as she related what Hogan had told her. She had fled from him at the tennis courts, but she hadn't been able to run from the truth. There was no reason for the detective to lie. She'd been forced to accept his information and to draw the logical conclusions from it.

But one thing had been clear. She needed more information—about herself and about Adam. Tom Graves was the only person she could think of who might be able to help her. If hotel security and the Secret Service had background files on all guests, that would include her and Adam.

She wanted to see those files, and once she'd finished telling Graves everything she knew—with Hogan filling in details from time to time—she made her intention clear.

"I'm going to find out what the hell is going on, Mr. Graves, and you're going to help me. I called Judge Bradshaw and told him I need help. He said you would give me anything I needed, and if you've got a problem with that, you're to call him."

"I don't have a problem with that, Mrs. Ho—" He stopped abruptly. "Jeez. I don't know what to call you now."

"Yeah, well, imagine how I feel," she said caustically. "Just call me Maddy for the time being."

"All right, Maddy. Anything you want that I can provide is yours." He shook his head to clear it. "I knew something strange was going on yesterday, but I never imagined anything like this."

"What made you suspicious?" Maddy asked him.

"I found out that no one named Hopewell had honeymooned here on the dates we have listed for your anniversary, and that Adam lied to you about having already had reservations here for those dates," he answered. "Tell me something, did your husband—"

"We're not exactly clear on the subject of whether or not he *is* my husband," Maddy said harshly. The pain that welled inside her was intense, but she fought it down. She had to think rationally if she was going to figure out why she'd been carrying phony ID and what kind of sick game Adam had been playing.

"Sorry," Tom apologized. "I don't know what to call him."

Hogan looked at Maddy. "Let's call him the husband for the time being, because it's always possible that you two really are married."

Maddy shook her head emphatically. "No. We're not. I know it. I *feel* it! I didn't believe Dr. Manion two weeks ago when he told me I had a husband, and I should have trusted my instincts! *Damn it!*" Maddy wrapped her arms around her waist, as if to hold in her pain.

Graves reached a sympathetic hand out to her as a gesture of comfort, but Maddy jerked away. She'd gotten into this mess because she'd allowed herself to depend on a total stranger for strength and solace. It was a mistake she'd never, ever make again. She had to find her own strength, and she sure as hell didn't want anyone's pity.

When she finally had control of her voice, she told them, "If Adam is really my husband, it means we both have to be using assumed identities. That suggests we were involved in something illegal, which could explain why he wouldn't give the police my real name. But why should he lie to me? Why weave this ridiculous story about our blissful honeymoon at Bride's Bay?" she asked bitterly.

Hogan and Graves just looked at each other, clearly at a loss for an explanation.

Since they didn't have answers, Maddy knew she was going to have to find them herself. "All right, here's what we're going to do," she said, taking charge the way she should have right at the beginning. "We're going back to the Fortress and put every scrap of information we've got into one pile. I want to see hotel security's background files on me and Adam. I want to know everything the police know about the attack on me at the airport. We're going to take this situation apart piece by bloody piece, *until I get some answers that make sense!*"

She whirled around and charged out. Hogan and Graves followed. It never occurred to either of them to dispute her right to order them around.

WHEN HE SAW the woman emerging from the health club, the Raven paused near the outer exit close to the golf pro shop. She had the police detective, the hotel security chief and two bodyguards following her in a miniature parade, and something was clearly wrong. The Raven had to find out if it had anything to do with him, so he pretended to be searching his pockets as though he'd forgotten or lost something.

It was risky, but he had to know. He was going to put himself into the woman's line of sight. He wanted to be looking into her face when she saw him so that he'd be able to determine whether or not she recognized him.

He lingered a moment longer, then timed his departure perfectly, closing in on the exit at just the right moment. She ran right into him.

"Oh, excuse me!" he exclaimed. "I'm so sorry. I wasn't watching where I was going. Are you all right?"

"I'm fine," the woman replied distractedly, hurrying on out the door.

Tom Graves paused a moment, though, and frowned at the uniformed man who had obstructed the door. "Shouldn't you be back at work?" he asked.

The Raven looked heartily chagrined. "I'm just on my way there now, sir."

"Good." Tom moved on out the door, caught up with the others in two giant steps and gestured toward a resort Land Rover in the parking enclave.

The Raven watched them for another moment, smiling. The woman had looked right at him without flinching. Something was clearly upsetting her, but so far she still hadn't regained any memories that included him.

Perfect. He was still safe. There was no reason to believe that his plan had been exposed, and no one had the slightest reason to question him or his right to be here. There were only four days remaining until the arrival of the President.

Everything was proceeding on schedule.

CHAPTER SIXTEEN

WHEN MADDY GOT BACK to the hotel the front desk had a message for her from Adam giving her a phone number to his room at the Regency Hotel in New York.

Graves and Hogan looked at her expectantly, but if they thought there was a snowball's chance in hell that she'd use that number they were in for a big disappointment. Maddy had no intention of talking to Adam until she'd figured out who she was and what kind of sick game he'd been playing with her. She'd turned the pain he'd caused her into a white-hot rage, but she knew she hadn't even begun to plumb the depths of the emotional anguish she was going to suffer because of the man who had made her fall in love with him.

Tom led them on to the Fortress, where they started pooling their intelligence resources, but his contribution was sketchy at best. He explained that he'd asked for the Secret Service file on her and Adam late yesterday afternoon, but it hadn't arrived yet and he hadn't had time to do much checking on his own.

He did have some credit information, which seemed pretty standard, but that was about as far as he'd gotten. Hogan went over the details surrounding the attack on Maddy and recounted his investigation step-by-step up to the point that he'd been told the case was closed.

Maddy tried to be as dispassionate as possible as she related some of the things Adam had told her about herself, hoping that Graves or Hogan might spot something in the lies that would lead to a clue. Nothing did.

In fact, nothing helped at all until Maddy remembered the phone calls Adam had made in the past few days. She asked to see a copy of the telephone bill for their suite—and that was when she struck pay dirt.

Instead of finding a lot of international calls on the bill—their bank in Paris, Pere Ruben in Austria, Anthony Vernandas in Buenos Aires and a half-dozen other overseas calls Adam had mentioned to her—she found all the calls were to numbers in the U.S., mostly the Washington, D.C., area. And all of those D.C. calls were to the same phone number.

She asked Hogan to check out the number, and within a few minutes he had determined that Adam's calls had been made to a phone belonging to one Jacob Carmichael at 469 Beech Street in Georgetown.

"Then that's where I'm going," Maddy announced.

"Whoa. Wait a minute!" Tom said, coming out from behind his desk. "We may not know what's going on here, but there's still the little matter of someone wanting to kill you. We've got no reason to believe that has changed."

"But Adam is in New York," Maddy argued. "We've got a phone call he made about two hours ago to prove it."

"Hold it," Hogan interjected. "Are you thinking that Adam is your assailant?"

Maddy wasn't taking anything for granted ever again where Adam was concerned, and it was becoming easy for her to believe the absolute worst about him. The first lie in this whole mess had been hers. For some reason she'd been using phony ID cards. But all the other things he'd told her—those were also lies, and they'd been told for a reason.

She swiveled her chair toward Hogan. "You're the one who first suggested that posing as my husband would be a good way for the killer to get close to me, remember?"

Hogan shook his head. "Yeah, but that theory doesn't hold water now. It's conceivable that he might be in league with your assailant, but if he wanted you dead, he's had ample opportunity to arrange an accident."

"Under the scrutiny of two bodyguards?" she asked archly.

"He's the one who requested those guards," Tom reminded her. He sat on the edge of his desk and looked down at Maddy. "He didn't have to do that. He could've played down the danger and told you that regular hotel security measures would be sufficient protection. Or when nothing happened after the first few days, he could have dismissed the guards."

"Oh, right," Maddy said sarcastically. "And the day after he dismisses them I have an accident, he plays the grieving spouse, and neither hotel security nor the Charleston police department suspects foul play? Yeah, that makes a lot of sense."

Hogan and Graves looked at each other. "She's right about that," Tom said. "He couldn't have dismissed the guards, but I still think he could've found a way around them if he really wanted her dead."

"Maybe he was just supposed to watch her to see if she got her memory back," Hogan suggested.

"Or to find out of she really had amnesia at all," Tom speculated. "Could be her assailant thought she was faking."

"I'm not," Maddy interjected. "And playing guessing games isn't getting us anywhere. I can't avoid the possibility that Adam is involved in a conspiracy to kill me. For what reason I don't know, but it's the only thing that makes any sense. He's not just some nut off the street who read about me in the newspaper and decided he wanted to play house. If that had been the case, he would have taken advantage of—"

Maddy stopped. She wasn't going to tell these two men about the night she'd all but begged Adam to make love to her. He'd claimed such noble reasons for saying no to her. Reasons so moving, in fact, that she had finally lowered all her barriers and placed her trust in him unreservedly.

Maddy realized that if she looked closely at the events of that night she would probably see a dozen tiny ways Adam had manipulated her, but she couldn't examine the details right now. They were too painful. They reminded her too sharply of what a fool she had been.

She would analyze what Adam had done to her later, when she could do it knowing she wasn't going to shatter into a thousand pieces. For the time being, all that mattered was getting to that address in Georgetown and seeing if a surprise visit to Mr. Jacob Carmichael could shed any light on the phone conversation he'd had with someone claiming to be Adam Hopewell.

"Look, gentlemen, here's the bottom line," she said in a voice that brooked no disagreement. "I'm willing to take my chances outside of Bride's Bay and risk going one-on-one with whoever tried to kill me, because as my life stands right now, it's not worth a whole lot. I'm leaving here and you're not stopping me. The only thing you can do is call Adam at his hotel in New York and tell him where I'm going, and if you do that you'll probably triple the risk. If someone has been waiting for an opening to kill me, my best chance of survival is to get off the island and hope no one notices I'm missing."

"Granted," Tom said. "But you're not leaving here alone, so we'll compromise. I'll send Ed and Bobby with you. If your husband calls, I'll cover for you—tell him you've joined in a volleyball tournament on the beach, or you're helping with Luau Night. He's eventually going to get suspicious when you don't call him back, though."

Maddy shook her head. "No. I can't call him. I should, but I can't." She rose and began pacing the room.

"That's all right," Tom said soothingly. "I'll cover for you as long as I can. Just stick close to Ed and Bobby and pray for the best."

THAT WAS EXACTLY what Maddy did for the next five hours as she and Tom made and executed plans to get her off the island and up to Washington. Hogan volunteered to go along, too, but Maddy vetoed his generous gesture. Considering the threats regarding his pension, going to D.C. to investigate a closed case would probably get him kicked off the force, and Maddy didn't want that on her conscience. Ultimately she convinced him that Ed and Bobby were sufficient muscle to keep her safe.

She packed her overnight bag with her toiletries and one change of clothes—the same drab brown outfit she'd arrived in Charleston with—and left quietly on the afternoon ferry. She caught a regularly scheduled shuttle to Washington, rented a car and let Bobby DiVesta do the driving to the Georgetown address while she sat in the back seat with Ed Raphaelson watching over her.

It was early evening and Saturday-night traffic was light. It didn't take long for them to reach Georgetown, and Maddy's heart began to race as they turned the final corner, inching forward to stop in front of 469 Beech.

Sitting very still, almost afraid to breathe, she studied the building with mounting anxiety and disappointment. This wasn't a residential neighborhood. The building was a stately old brownstone that looked like all the others on the quiet street. The building on its right, according to a hanging placard, was a law firm. The building to the left housed an accountant and an architect. This was undoubtedly some sort of office, as well. How likely was it that someone would be working this late on a Saturday?

She wouldn't know, though, until she walked up to the house and rang the bell.

She was utterly terrified.

"I don't suppose you gentlemen would consider lending me one of the guns that you took such pains to check through airport security. Would you?"

"Sorry, ma'am," Ed replied with genuine regret.

"I'm quite a good shot," she reminded him.

"I know, but I can't, ma'am."

Maddy took a deep breath. "If I do nothing else before I die, I'm going to break you of calling me ma'am."

"Yes, ma'am."

Maddy felt hysterical laughter bubble up in her throat. She tamped it down quickly and climbed out of the car.

Her bodyguards stayed right with her as she marched up the short flight of stairs. She rang the bell and waited. She rang the bell again, and this time she heard a distinct click. She almost jumped out of her skin when the door popped open automatically, and she wasn't the only one. Both her guards reached for their weapons and sprang into action. Bobby grabbed Maddy and pushed her behind him, and Ed seized the initiative, slamming his shoulder against the door to open it wide.

What they found inside wasn't the least bit threatening. A very pleasant-faced woman in her mid-fifties was sitting behind a reception desk in what looked to be a perfectly normal office reception room.

The only thing wrong with the entire scene was the fact that the woman didn't seem the slightest bit alarmed by the sight of two armed men.

Her smile encompassed all three of them. "You don't need the guns, gentlemen. We've been expecting you."

It took some doing, but Maddy navigated around her bodyguards. "Expecting us?"

"Yes." The receptionist rose and gestured for Maddy to accompany her. With Ed and Bobby following, they went across the cozy lobby, past an elegant polished wooden staircase, down a corridor past a half-dozen doors until they reached one marked Jacob A. Carmichael, Deputy Director of Internal Investigations.

Maddy's heart was hammering so hard she couldn't hear herself think—not that she had any thoughts worth listening to. All she had were questions and the knowledge that two possibilities lay behind that door: one was a man who might be able to answer all her questions; the other was a bullet meant for her.

Maddy reached for the handle, heard it squeak as it turned and pushed the door open to find herself facing a man sitting behind a desk. A little rectangular placard bore the name Jacob A. Carmichael.

But Maddy knew the tall, handsome, dark-eyed man behind the desk as Adam Hopewell.

CHAPTER SEVENTEEN

ODDLY ENOUGH, Maddy wasn't at all afraid. Her anger and confusion were too strong to leave room for something as mundane as fear. She wanted answers now. She wanted to know why this man had lied to her and betrayed her.

Her rage had boiled over into hatred. She used the force of that emotion to keep the tremor in her limbs under control as she stepped into the room.

Ed and Bobby came with her, but the man behind the desk rose and told them, "It's all right, guys. You can wait outside. She's safe here."

Neither man had let his guard down for a moment. "If you don't mind, we'll stay with the lady," Bobby replied tersely.

Adam seemed exasperated by their obvious suspicion. "If I'd wanted her dead, boys, I could've killed her while she was still in the hospital and been long gone before anyone realized she wasn't just sleeping."

"He's right," Maddy said without looking at them. "Leave us alone."

She could feel their hesitation, but she didn't take her eyes off the man behind the desk. A moment later she realized Ed was holding his hand out to her. She glanced down and saw the butt end of a Colt .38 Special.

"You might need this."

Maddy accepted the gun. "Thanks."

The man behind the desk raised one eyebrow, as though questioning what she was going to do with the gun, and Maddy very deliberately reached behind her and shoved it into the waistband of her slacks.

She met his gaze evenly, controlling her voice, but making no effort to keep her hatred from showing. "If I used it to kill you, would I get out of here alive?"

"Probably not."

"Will I get out of here alive even if I don't kill you?"

"Absolutely." He looked at the woman just outside the door. "Marta, will you take Mr. Raphaelson and Mr. DiVesta down the hall and get them something to drink?"

"Yes, sir. This way, gentlemen."

Maddy's bodyguards backed out of the room and she heard the door close behind her.

"I know you have a million and one questions," he told her, resuming his seat. "Where do you want to start?"

Maddy moved slowly but purposefully toward his desk, picked up the rectangular name plaque that read Jacob A. Carmichael and turned it to face him. "Is this you?"

He nodded. "Yes."

"Does the *A* stand for Adam?" she asked sarcastically.

"Yes. It does."

"Well, good. At least we know there was *one* thing you haven't lied to me about."

"Believe it or not, there are actually quite a number of things I didn't lie about," he replied.

"Are we married?" she asked skeptically, knowing what the answer would be.

"No. We're not."

"Is my name Madeline Hopewell?"

"No."

"Well, I'm glad you didn't lie to me about anything *important!*" Her rage finally erupted, and she slammed her hands onto his desk. *"Who the hell are you, and what kind of sick game have you been playing with me?"*

"A dangerous one. With very high stakes," he said as he leaned back in his chair. "Now, do you want to scream at me some more, or do you want to know what's going on?"

He was looking at her with a kind of resigned stoicism, and Maddy realized there was emotion in his eyes again. If she'd had to put a name to it, she might have called it sadness. She might even have decided it was laced with some pain and a lot of guilt. But she was beyond caring about his emotions. If he was feeling guilt it was richly deserved.

"Tell me," she said, straightening. "And make it good. What's my real name?"

"Jennifer Lambert. Most of your friends call you Jenn."

She stiffened when she recognized the name. "Lambert? Does that make me any kin to Paul and Irene?"

"They were your real parents, and as I told you in the hospital that first day, they were killed in a plane crash while you were a teenager in boarding school. In fact, everything I've told you about them has been the truth."

She frowned. "If you could tell me the truth about that, why did you have to lie about everything else? Why didn't you tell me my real name?"

"Because we didn't know where or why you'd picked up your Madeline Hopewell alias. We were trying to buy time until we could figure out what kind of game you were playing with us."

"We?"

"My superiors and myself."

"Who just so happen to be...?"

He hesitated for a moment. "Affiliated with a major U.S. intelligence-gathering organization."

Maddy didn't pause to let that information digest. "Why was my alias any concern of yours to begin with?"

"Because you're one of us."

Maddy's breath hitched in her throat and it was a moment before she could ask, "I'm a spy?"

"Yes."

Her mind flashed back to their first evening in the resort's dining room. He had told her the truth then, too, only he'd wrapped it in a package so playfully comical that considering the possibility seriously had been out of the question.

"Why? Why the elaborate charade?" she asked. "If I'm one of you, why did you trick me? Why did you lie to me?"

Jacob Adam Carmichael stood and walked around the desk. Maddy moved quickly away from him, but he clearly hadn't been headed for her in the first place. There was a credenza on the back wall, and he moved to it as he told her, "When a woman bearing your fingerprints and the identity of a dead girl from Utah appeared unexpectedly at a Charleston hospital claiming to have amnesia, it created a lot of confusion around here. Madeline Hopewell was not an Agency-sanctioned cover identity, and using an unsanctioned cover is against Agency policy. Given the prevailing circumstances, we had to be cautious."

"What circumstances?"

He poured a clear liquid from a carafe into a glass and held it out to her. "Here, drink this. It's only water," he said. When she just glared at him he took a sip himself. "See? No poison."

"Go to hell," she muttered. "What circumstances?"

He moved back to the desk, set the glass on the side closest to Maddy, then returned to his chair. "I'll have to go back a ways to explain. You might as well take a seat."

"I'll stand, thank you. Now talk, damn it! Make some sense out of this!"

Adam sighed deeply. "All right. For the past nine years, you've been an intelligence operative working back and forth between the European sector and the Middle East. Your specialty is collecting information on terrorists, and for a large part of the past eighteen months your work focused almost exclusively on an independent contractor—a hit man known only as the Raven."

Maddy sank onto the leather chair opposite his desk. "My nightmare," she murmured. "The black wings."

Adam nodded. "That was my interpretation, but try as I might, I never could get you to make the connection between the Raven and the dream."

"But it did happen to me, didn't it?" she asked, feeling a flutter of excitement because finally she was about to learn the truth about herself. And unlike the moment Dr. Manion had told her she was married, she didn't feel disconnected from the information. She knew this was the truth.

Jenn Lambert was her name. It *felt* like her name. She had spent most of her adult life trusting no one but herself and pretending to be someone she wasn't. She didn't actually *remember* living the solitary, schizophrenic existence of Jenn Lambert, but she knew she had. It was an exhilarating, liberating sensation.

Adam was nodding in answer to her question. "It seems very likely that your dream is about something that really happened. It fits the facts as we know them, anyway."

"What facts? Who was the man in my dream?"

"Majhid Al'Enaza, a shopkeeper in Al'Khatar, Turuq. He was one of a network of informants you cultivated a few years ago when you were working the Mediterranean sector of the Middle East."

The face of the man in her nightmare flashed in front of her, and with it came the memory of the crowded streets of the port city of Al'Khatar, in the tiny principality of Turuq. The images were so vivid that she could even see the exterior of Majhid's shop in the bazaar. She tried to carry the vision to the inside of the tiny store, but her mind rebelled because she knew that's where the blood would be.

The memory fragment left as quickly as it had come. "Is Majhid really dead?"

"Yes."

Jenn felt her stomach clench. "Did I kill him?"

Adam hesitated. "The Turuq military police think so, as do your station chief in Paris and my boss at the Pentagon."

"Do *you* think I killed him?" Despite her hatred for this man, she needed to know that he didn't believe she was responsible for the murder.

"No. I've never believed that you killed Majhid. Frankly, that's why I volunteered for this job," he told her. "I know you don't remember this, but I've been out of undercover work for quite some time. When you disa—"

"Wait a minute. You mean we actually do know each other? I wasn't a total stranger to you when you told Dr. Manion we were married?" she asked, a little glimmer of hope stirring in her at the possibility that Adam's betrayal hadn't been as total as she'd believed.

But as quickly as the hope rose, Jenn pushed it away. It didn't matter whether he'd betrayed her a little or a lot. What he'd done to her was unforgivable, no matter what his reasons. All she wanted from Jacob Adam Carmichael were explanations. Rationalizations didn't matter.

"Yes, Jenn, we did—"

She came to her feet abruptly. "I don't care. Forget I asked," she snapped. "Just tell me about Majhid Al'Enaza. Why does everyone think I killed him?"

Adam looked disappointed that she hadn't let him explain how he'd come to know her, but he controlled it quickly. "Because two women came into the shop while you were kneeling beside the body. Your veil had come undone, and they swore you'd killed him and were robbing the dead."

"That's ridiculous!"

"Of course it is, but when they started shrieking—probably that cawing of crows sound you hear in your nightmare—you ran past them into the street. You disappeared into the crowd and vanished off the face of the earth. No one saw or heard from you again until your fingerprints turned up three days later in the FBI computer under the name Madeline Hopewell."

"That doesn't make me a murderer."

"No, but it is suspicious. You see, you'd gone to Turuq because Majhid had gotten word to you in Paris that he had information about the Raven's next strike. You weren't working the Middle East anymore, and you'd been taken off the task force that was tracking the Raven, but—"

"Why?" she asked. "Why was I pulled off the assignment?"

Adam looked very uncomfortable. "Because you'd let the Raven slip through your fingers twice—once when he killed an industrialist in Germany, and again when he hit an American businessman who was traveling in Italy. The task force had solid leads on both those hits, but the Raven got away clean. The second time he had to move right past you at a train station in Rome, but you claimed you never saw him."

"What does the Raven look like?"

"No one knows for sure. He's a genius at disguises."

Jenn frowned. "How could I be blamed for not spotting him if I didn't know what he looked like?"

"Apparently you had a good description of the disguise he was using."

"He could have ditched it," she said irritably.

"That was the assumption at the time," Adam replied. "No one suspected that you had deliberately let the Raven escape, but you don't get many second chances in this business, Jenn. When you struck out in Rome, you were taken off the Raven task force and reassigned."

"To what?"

But Adam just shook his head. "Sorry. I can't give you any information on your caseload until you regain your memory or are cleared of the charges against you."

"You mean the murder of Majhid Al'Enaza?"

Adam hesitated a moment. "And treason."

"What?"

"Jenn, there's been a rumor flying for the past few months that someone has hired the Raven to kill the President of the United States. No one could get any hint of where or when the assassination was supposed to take place, but you were thrust right back into the middle of the task-force action when Majhid contacted you with the message that he had information about the Raven's next hit. He would only talk to you, so you were back on the case."

"Which began to seem a little too convenient when Majhid was murdered and I disappeared. You couldn't help wondering whether I had reinserted myself into the case so that I could feed information to the Raven."

"That was what everyone feared," Adam confirmed. "You'd let him get past you twice. It was possible he was paying you for inside information. And that seemed even more likely after we searched your Paris apartment and found a number for a Swiss bank account."

She felt no outrage at the invasion of privacy. "How much was in the account?"

"Nearly a million dollars."

She sprang to her feet and began pacing. "Where did I get that kind of money?"

"No one knows. Your parents left you modestly wealthy, but the Agency is supposed to have a record of all your assets. That kind of hidden wealth makes the Agency very nervous."

"All right, I understand why everyone was suspicious. Majhid was dead. I had taken whatever information he'd given me and disappeared with it. You found hidden assets, and when I finally surfaced, I was using an unauthorized alias that probably made it seem as though I was trying to evade detection."

"Exactly."

Jenn turned on him, unable to keep the venom out of her voice. "But that still doesn't explain why you pretended to be my husband or concocted the elaborate Bride's Bay honeymoon charade. Why the hell didn't you just pull me in and tell me the truth?"

"And say what?" Adam asked her. "Excuse me, Miss . . . you don't remember me, but your name is Jennifer Lambert and you're a spy under suspicion of murder and treason?" He shook his head. "Our doctors said it was the worst thing we could possibly do if your amnesia was genuine."

"You thought I was faking?"

"We had to consider the possibility. That's one of the reasons we came up with the Bride's Bay scenario. After we found the microdot and decoded Majhid's message—"

Jenn moved toward the desk. "Wait a minute. What microdot? What message? Where did you find it?"

"In your purse," he replied. "When your finger-prints appeared in the FBI computer, we sent two men down to Charleston to find out what was going on."

"The DEA agents!"

"That's right. We knew that you had specially de-signed cosmetics containers with hidden compart-ments and that it was unlikely the police would've found them. Since we needed to know if you were transporting any encrypted messages, we invented the story about your description matching that of a drug courier so that our men could search your belongings without arousing too many suspicions. When they checked your compact, they found a microdot en-crypted with Majhid's code."

"What was the message?"

"Just two words—Bride's Bay," Adam replied. "Since that's where the President was vacationing, we knew it couldn't be a coincidence. We concluded that if the Raven was, indeed, going to attempt a hit, he would do it at the resort."

"And you still thought I might be involved in his plan?"

"Yes."

Jenn tried to put all the pieces together. "Did you ever consider the possibility that maybe the Raven discovered that Majhid Al'Enaza had learned of his plan and was going to tell? Maybe the Raven killed Majhid, and I came in right after—possibly in time to see the Raven leave the shop," she suggested. "In my nightmare, Majhid presses something into my hand and he babbles words I can't quite hear. Isn't it pos-sible I used what he told me to put the pieces together and that I set out to find the Raven?"

"We considered that possibility naturally," Adam replied. "Some of us even pushed that theory very hard."

If he was trying to curry favor with her, it was too little, too late. "Evidently you didn't push hard enough," she said coldly. "Do you have any theories on who tried to kill me at the airport?"

"Theories, but no facts," he replied. "The most obvious suspect would be the Raven."

"Then doesn't that prove I'm innocent?" Jenn cried, moving quickly toward the desk. "Why would he try to kill me if I was working for him?"

"If you'd outlived your usefulness, he'd have disposed of you in an instant," Adam answered. "We have reason to believe that over the years, the Raven has killed more so-called friends than enemies."

"That must make him a very lonely man."

"The right amount of money will buy just about anything," Adam replied. "Including new friends."

And the Agency believed that she was one of those friends—one who'd become a liability to the Raven for some reason.

Suddenly it all made sense. Jenn knew exactly why Adam had pretended to be her husband and why he'd taken her to Bride's Bay. "You son of a bitch," she murmured as fury mounted in her all over again. "You were using me as bait! You wanted to see if you could get the Raven to go after me and expose himself!"

"Yes," Adam admitted, his face an unreadable mask. "My boss wanted to see if leaving you in the real world would flush him out, and since the assassination is scheduled to take place at Bride's Bay, that was the most logical place to throw out the hook."

"You bastard! *I* didn't matter, did I?" Jenn said, coming around the desk toward him. "The possibility that I might be innocent never entered into it! You had to keep me occupied, keep me visible. It didn't matter how many lies you had to tell! It didn't matter what those lies did to me!"

He didn't flinch from her fury. "No. It didn't."

It was everything Jenn could do to keep from slapping him. She was towering over him. His face was turned up toward hers. She wanted to hit him and hit him and hit him until he felt at least a fraction of the pain he'd caused her.

But she didn't do it. She stepped away and returned to the front of the desk, trying to master her anger and figure out what to do next. Only one thing seemed clear. She couldn't bear to stay in the room with Jacob Adam Carmichael a moment longer.

But leaving wasn't as simple as walking out the door.

"I need to think," she told him when she was in control again. "I want to get away from you. How do I do that?"

Adam pressed a button. "I'll have you taken to a safe house. You can rest tonight, and we'll talk again tomorrow."

"Not you," Jenn said harshly, planting her hands on the desk and leaning forward to bring herself down to his level. "I'll talk to your boss, or my boss, or any damned boss in the Agency! I'll even talk to that gray-haired lady out front, but I won't talk to you," she swore. "Not ever again."

She straightened just as the door to the corridor opened and Marta, the receptionist, appeared. Without a backward glance at Adam, Jenn swept through the door.

Adam stood. "Take care of her, Marta. Transport her to location Red Three and see that she gets a copy of her dossier so that she can read about herself tonight."

"Yes, sir." Marta stepped out, closing the door behind her.

The room was too quiet now. Adam came out from behind his desk, moved to the credenza and began pouring scotch whiskey into the largest glass he could find. Behind him, he heard a distinctive click as the door to the adjoining office opened and closed, but he didn't stop pouring until the tumbler was full.

"Why don't you just drink it from the bottle?"

Adam took a long swallow of the scotch and relished the fire it created in his belly. "Before the night is over, I'll probably do just that." He turned to face his boss, Tony Vernandas, and very deliberately took another drink.

The tall, lean director of Internal Investigations calmly moved to one of the leather chairs and sat. "If you think getting drunk is going to spite me, think again. I'm not the one who'll have to cope with the hangover tomorrow."

"Go to hell."

"Haven't you heard? That's where all Internal Investigation officials end up."

"Good. It's the very least we deserve." Adam took another drink—a sip this time—and moved back to the chair behind his desk. He knew that Vernandas had been listening to his conversation with Jenn, and he was keenly aware that his boss was studying him now, trying to assess the damage. Adam didn't give a damn what he thought. The operation was over. He'd come to D.C. to do battle with Vernandas, trying to convince him that it was time to pull the plug and tell Jenn the truth. Thanks to Hogan and Graves, things hadn't worked out exactly as Adam had hoped, but essentially he'd gotten what he wanted. He didn't have to lie to Jenn anymore, and that was all that mattered.

"Tell me something, Jake."

Adam hadn't become reaccustomed to that other name yet. He'd grown up with his family calling him Adam to avoid confusion with his father, Jake, and these past two weeks it had seemed so natural to have Jenn call him Adam. He'd even begun to think of himself that way again. Now he was going to have to recondition himself to the name everyone at the Agency used. It wouldn't be easy, because Adam had come to hate Jacob Carmichael, Jacob Carmichael's job and everything that Jacob Carmichael stood for. Adam Hopewell had been a much simpler man.

For a time he'd also been a much happier man, too.

"Jake?"

Adam pulled himself into the present and forced his attention onto his boss. That wasn't easy, either, because he was beginning to feel the effects of the scotch. "What is it, Tony?" he asked irritably. "I know you're still pissed because I didn't follow the scenario to the end, but it would have been over today even if I'd agreed to go back to Bride's Bay. Graves was so suspicious he was ready to go head-to-head with the Secret Service, and Hogan had the Madeline Hopewell customs file. Between the two of them, they had enough information to bury me. I couldn't have kept

Jenn in the dark any longer even if I'd stayed at the resort. It's better than she knows the truth."

"As I recall, that's what you said from the very beginning."

"It's what I've said every day for the past two weeks! If you'd listened to me, instead of the damned doctors—"

"Well, we didn't," Tony said. "We made a judgment call based on what we thought would be best for her."

"That's a load of bull," Adam said. "You wanted to use her as bait, and you wanted to play with her head."

"We thought she was faking," Tony countered. "Throwing you at her in the guise of her husband was a thoroughly brilliant way to smoke her out. She couldn't have possibly fooled you in that scenario for more than a few days."

"Except she wasn't faking," Adam reminded him.

Vernandas nodded. "Which you contended from the very beginning, as well."

Adam took another swig of whiskey. "For all the good it did." He wasn't drunk enough yet to dull the pain, but he was getting there.

Vernandas let the small silence grow into a larger one as he studied his deputy director. "Why didn't you tell her all of it?" he finally asked.

Adam leaned his head back and closed his eyes. "All of what? We covered the salient points. She knows I lied to her, manipulated her and set her up to be bait for a terrorist. What more does she need to know?"

"You could have told her why you did it."

"I did it because it was my job," Adam replied bitterly, not bothering to open his eyes.

"You did it because somebody had to, and you wanted it to be someone who believed in her—someone whose first priority would be keeping her alive, not advancing his career by capturing the Raven."

"So what?"

"So you should have told her that," Vernandas answered.

Adam gave a snort of laughter. "Yeah, right. 'Yes, I lied to you, Jennifer, darling, but my motives were pure of heart.' Bullshit."

"Oh, for God's sake," Vernandas said, coming to his feet in frustration. "Jump off that self-pity bandwagon, why don't you? In case you've forgotten, your protégée, Jennifer Lambert, was using unsanctioned ID and she's got a Swiss bank account—"

Adam finally opened his eyes and came upright in his chair. "Which was probably part of her father's estate, or something she's accrued from his investments. *You've* forgotten that he left her so well-off she wouldn't have had any reason to take money from the Raven."

"Greed doesn't—"

"Jenn Lambert is not greedy! She is not a traitor! And as for that so-called unsanctioned ID, I don't know an operative in the Agency who doesn't have a half-dozen of them tucked away for emergencies. I know mine came in handy more than once when I was still working in the field. That doesn't make her a traitor!"

"Well, we won't know that until we capture the Raven, or Jennifer regains her memory and can provide us with some pretty damned good explanation of her behavior.''

''Now that she knows the truth, maybe that'll happen soon.''

''And in the meantime?''

''In the meantime, I'm out of it.'' Adam leaned back in his chair again, took another sip of whiskey and closed his eyes.

''Jake, you're not out of it until I say so.''

''Then you'd better get the firing squad ready, because you've got a full-scale mutiny on your hands. I've done as much damage to that woman as I intend to do.''

''She's not damaged, Jake,'' Vernandas argued. ''She's just in love.''

The statement hung in the air for a long time. ''I know.''

''Women in love tend to be very forgiving.''

''Who's she gonna forgive, Tony? Adam Hopewell, the man she fell in love with, or Jake Carmichael, the man who betrayed her?''

''What's the difference?'' Vernandas asked. ''They're both in love with *her.*''

''Yeah.'' Adam slowly swiveled his chair, turning his back on Tony Vernandas, signaling the end of their discussion.

The director stood and moved to his door. ''Don't get too drunk, Jake,'' he advised. ''There's still an assassin out there who wants to kill the President—and Jennifer Lambert. I need you sharp and sober first thing tomorrow morning.''

Vernandas glanced at the back of Adam's chair, but it didn't move. With a heavy sigh and a shake of his head, he left the office.

CHAPTER EIGHTEEN

WHAT LITTLE SLEEP Jenn Lambert got that night in a safe house in Arlington, Virginia, was riddled with nightmare images of Majhid Al'Enaza and haunting scenes of the brief but blissful marriage of Madeline and Adam Hopewell. The combination was too disturbing, and she finally gave up trying to sleep altogether. Instead, she alternated between pacing the bedroom floor and rereading the dossier she'd studied before going to bed.

The information contained in the background file on Jennifer Lambert felt comfortable, like an old pair of shoes. What's more, it stirred up fragments of memories—some vivid, some vague. When she read about her parents she could almost call up their faces. She could see the vague outline of a building on a large manicured lawn and knew it was the house where she'd grown up. When she read a brief section about a horse named Toby that her father had given her as a child, she saw a flash of herself jumping a fence.

When she read that her father had been an upper-level diplomat in foreign service, she had a flash of the first embassy party she'd ever attended. When she read how her parents had died in a fiery plane crash caused by a terrorist's bomb, she felt the pain, and understood why, if not how, her life had taken a path into espionage.

The dossier was like reading an episodic novel that was all narrative and no dialogue. It started with an extensive background on her parents, then her own birth, and then it jumped from one event to another throughout her childhood. All the information Adam had given her in broad strokes was in the dossier in great detail, right up to the time she'd dropped out of college and began playing on the Riviera when she wasn't working on archaeological digs in Egypt and Turkey.

The information stopped abruptly just after her twenty-third birthday, which made sense if she'd been an agent for more than nine years. Everything that had happened since then was probably classified, and she wasn't exactly the best security risk on the block right now.

Sometime around dawn, Jenn stopped pacing. She found a measure of calm and steeled herself for what she knew would be a grueling day. She showered and dressed. She fixed juice and toast for breakfast. She sat down to wait.

She didn't think it would be a long wait, and she was right. It was still very early when a car pulled up in front of the house and a tall man with narrow shoulders and coal black hair climbed out of the back seat.

Since the arrival didn't generate any reaction from the unmarked van filled with the agents who'd spent the night guarding her, Jenn figured the man was from the Agency. He wasn't a particularly attractive man, but the way he carried himself seemed to demand a certain amount of respect.

Jenn was waiting by the door to admit him when he walked onto the porch, and she gave him credit for not offering her a phony smile as he came into the living room.

"I'm Anthony Vernandas," he said without preamble.

Jenn recognized the name and fought back a swell of anger. "Nice to meet you, Mr. Vernandas. You got Pere Ruben in your pocket?" she asked sarcastically.

Vernandas put his briefcase on the coffee table and turned to her placidly. "No. Perry Ruben is still in Paris. He's your station chief."

"That's just dandy. How many more familiar names did your friend Mr. Carmichael throw at me, instead of coming out and telling me the truth?"

"Quite a few actually. As soon as we made the decision to take you to Bride's Bay, we began salting the entire resort with Agency employees—all of whom you'd worked with before, I might add. We wanted our people around you at all times in case the Raven decided to strike, and it was hoped that using familiar faces might stir memories. You played tennis with one of our people yesterday morning."

"Loreen McKinley?"

Vernandas nodded. "About eight years ago she saved your life in Beirut."

"And Arthur Rumbaugh!" Jenn said.

"That's right. When you worked with him a few years ago he was going by the code name Sandpiper."

"Adam knew that?" she asked, incredulous.

"Yes."

Jenn thought back to her encounter with the strange little computer salesman and the way Adam had reacted when she'd remembered him. Adam's alarm had seemed so genuine, as though he really believed Rumbaugh was a threat, when he knew all along he was a plant.

Another wave of fury welled up in her and she fought it. Eventually she was going to have to deal with the pain of Adam's manipulations and betrayals, but this certainly wasn't the time.

"If Perry Ruben is my boss, are you Jacob Carmichael's boss?" she asked him.

"Yes. I'm the Director of Internal Investigations and Jake's my deputy."

"What does that mean precisely? Your job, that is."

"We follow up on allegations of misconduct and criminal activity within the Agency. Working undercover for months, even years, at a time, can take its toll on people. Idealism gets lost, and the dividing line between right and wrong sometimes gets a little blurry."

Jenn met his deceptively placid gaze without flinching. "You think I blurred that line by conspiring with the Raven, don't you?"

Vernandas gestured toward a chair, silently inviting Jenn to sit. When she didn't, the director lowered his lanky frame onto the sofa. "It's a plausible explanation for everything that's happened, Ms. Lambert, including two botched assignments in Rome and Berlin."

"Assignments that didn't put me under suspicion of any wrongdoing until you decided I killed that informant in Turuq."

"Give me a better explanation for the facts and you're off the hook," Vernandas told her.

Every one of her senses and every fragment of her consciousness reached out in search of the explanation he wanted, but the information that would clear her—or convict her—was just out of her reach. "I don't have an explanation. Yet."

"Then until you get your memory back, you're still under suspicion," he said without a hint of apology, and Jenn realized this was a man who didn't have the time, patience or inclination to varnish the truth.

That was good. Jenn didn't want any more lies, and she didn't want absolution unless she deserved it. Through her long night of trying to figure out who she was and how she'd gotten into this mess, she hadn't been able to escape the guilt that had always been associated with her nightmare.

Obviously she didn't want to believe that she was a murderer and a traitor, but she knew she had to be prepared for that possibility. "What happens to me now?" she asked Vernandas.

"What do you want to happen, Jennifer?"

"I want to go back to Bride's Bay."

He didn't seem surprised. "Why?"

"Because you still need bait. The President arrives day after tomorrow and there's a better than fifty-fifty chance I have information that could save his life." Jenn sat on the chair to bring herself closer to Vernandas's level. "I don't care what you believe about me, but *I* have to believe that something happened to me in Majhid Al'Enaza's shop in Turuq that put me on the trail of the Raven. At some point, he realized I was on his tail and he tried to kill me."

Vernandas shook his head. "It's a valid hypothesis, but it has one big flaw. Why didn't you check in with Perry Ruben? You were missing for three days. There had to have been some point when you could have gotten a message through to the station to let someone in the Agency know what was happening."

Oh, great! Carmichael hadn't mentioned that nasty little nail in her coffin. "I don't know why I didn't check in," she said shortly, coming to her feet again. "But you have to give me a chance to figure it all out—and to prove I'm not a traitor. You have to send me back to Bride's Bay."

"As I said before, why should I?"

Jenn faced him. "Because whether I'm innocent or guilty, I'm the only person on your side who knows what the Raven looks like. I can help you find him. He wants me dead for some reason, so let me flush him out."

Vernandas seemed to think it over. "We'd be taking a big chance. We might be putting an assassin's accomplice on the same island as the President."

"You were willing to take that chance when I was Madeline Hopewell and didn't have the slightest idea you were using me as bait," she reminded him.

"Only because Jake was completely convinced your amnesia was genuine. We figured as long as you couldn't remember being involved with the Raven, it wouldn't matter whether you were in league with him or not."

"It only mattered that he come after me," she concluded.

"That's right."

Jenn tilted her head to one side. "And what do you make of the fact that he didn't? Is it possible that the Raven changed his plan after he failed to kill me?"

"Possible but unlikely," Vernandas replied. "We have to assume he thinks he's safe as long as you can't remember why he tried to kill you."

"But I could regain my memory at any time. Why is he taking that risk?"

"He may not have had a choice. Killing you wouldn't serve any purpose if he couldn't do it and get away clean—and do it in such a way it wouldn't force the President to cancel his trip to Bride's Bay. He hasn't had the kind of opportunities he should have had, because you were given closer cover than I'd anticipated when I planned this op," Vernandas said.

"Closer cover?"

"Your bodyguards from hotel security," he explained. "Raphaelson and DiVesta were an unauthorized element that Jake took it upon himself to provide. Their constant presence would have made it nearly impossible for the Raven to arrange an 'accident' for you."

Jenn frowned. "Why did Jake do that? What's the good of throwing bait into the water if you're going to encase it in glass so that the fish can't reach it?"

Vernandas looked down at the floor, seeming a bit embarrassed. "That's my fault, I suppose," he replied with a sigh, then looked at her again. "When Jake volunteered to go undercover on this operation, I failed to realize he had a hidden agenda, one that would lead him to put his interests above those of the Agency and national security."

"What interests were those?" Jenn asked sarcastically, unable to keep herself from thinking of the hundreds of tiny, devastating ways he'd manipulated her into falling in love with him. Obviously he'd been on one gigantic ego trip.

But Vernandas didn't support her assessment. "I'm sorry to say that his primary concern was keeping you alive. That's not to say," the director rushed on, "that we're sorry you've survived. We would've preferred to have you alive *and* the Raven in custody. But despite my orders and the pressure I put on him, Jake refused to dismiss your bodyguards, and the die was cast. I'd sent him in to establish himself as your husband, and he knew damned good and well that I couldn't pull him out without exposing the whole setup."

He'd been trying to protect her despite opposition from his boss? Why? she wondered. What difference had it made to him whether she lived or died when he hadn't given a damn about the emotional damage he was doing? Jenn wanted to ask those questions and a dozen more that she hadn't let herself consider—such as why he'd volunteered for this assignment at all.

But asking the questions meant she'd have to process the answers, and Jenn didn't think she had enough strength to do that and clear her name at the same time. She needed her anger because it was keeping the pain from overwhelming her. No matter what his reasons, Jacob Adam Carmichael had betrayed her. He had preyed on her vulnerability and her fears, saying all the right things to make her trust him, believe in him... love him. He had seduced her—not physically, but emotionally—and as far as Jenn was concerned, that was far, far worse.

He was the enemy now. He was the very devil himself, and she hated him. Finding out that he had reasons, that he was human, might have lessened that hatred a little, but for the time being, hatred was the only defense she had. She wasn't letting go of it.

Anthony Vernandas had obviously guessed the direction her thoughts had taken. "You know, you're wrong to blame all of this on Carmichael," he told her.

"Oh? Who should I blame?"

"Me. I'm the one who planned the operation. Jake was only—"

"Following orders?" she snapped. "Well, let me tell you, he did a brilliant job. You should definitely give him a raise. He had me convinced he was the kindest, most loving and understanding husband on the face of this earth, and I was the luckiest woman alive."

"He was doing what he felt necessary to protect you."

"He was playing God and loving every minute of it," Jenn said.

Vernandas frowned at her. "Why don't you wait to make that decision until you know all the facts?"

"I know all I need to know. Now, are you going to send me back to Bride's Bay so that I can clear my name or not?"

Vernandas paused a moment as though debating the issue. "Yes. But I'm not sending you back alone."

"From what you've told me, Agency operatives already outnumber Bride's Bay guests, but you go ahead and do whatever you have to to convince yourself the President is safe. Just put me back on the island so that I can look for the Raven."

"All right." He stood and picked up his briefcase. "I'll have Jake pick you up in an hour or—"

"No!" Jenn protested. "You're not sending me back there with *him!*"

"Oh, yes I am," Vernandas said with all the blandness of someone who knew he'd already won the upcoming contest of wills. "Your cover is nicely established as Madeline and Adam Hopewell, so—"

"My cover is blown," she argued. "The chief of security—"

"Tom Graves is under control," Vernandas informed her. "Things have not remained static in the hours since you left Bride's Bay. When Arthur Rumbaugh saw Graves escorting you off the island, he notified us and we sent Secret Service agent Dan Luther in to talk to Graves."

Jenn remembered something Marta, the receptionist, had said yesterday. "That's how you knew to expect us."

"Yes. Agent Luther was briefed on this situation shortly after you arrived at Bride's Bay. He already knew about Graves's suspicions, but when he found out what Detective Hogan had learned, we authorized Luther to bring the security chief in on what was happening. As near as we can tell, your cover story is perfectly intact."

"That still doesn't mean I'm willing to go back to Bride's Bay and play house with Jacob Carmichael!" Jenn insisted.

"Then you're not going back to Bride's Bay." He shrugged. "It's your decision. What's it going to be?"

Jenn glared at him. The choice he'd given her wasn't any choice at all. "Damn you to hell," she muttered.

Vernandas nodded. "I'll have Jake here to pick you up as soon as the travel arrangements have been made."

THE BRIDE'S BAY high-security suite looked exactly as Jenn had left it almost twenty-four hours ago. The clothes Adam had bought for her were still in the rose-room closet. Most of his things were still in the tropical bedroom. Even the paperback spy novel, which Bobby had rescued from the beach for her, was on a side table in the parlor. The only thing missing from the suite was Jacob Carmichael, alias Adam Hopewell.

In fact, Mr. Carmichael had been noticeably absent all day. Despite Anthony Vernandas's edict, Adam hadn't arrived at the safe house to pick her up, and he hadn't been waiting for her on the private jet that whisked her from D.C. to Charleston. He wasn't at the airport with Duke Masterson, and he hadn't put in an appearance at the Bride's Bay heliport. Jenn had made it all the way to her suite without catching so much as a glimpse of him.

If his absence was a strategic ploy to fray her nerves, it was working. After Anthony Vernandas had left this morning, Jenn had steeled herself for seeing Adam, deploying her anger like chessmen arranged strategically to protect the queen. At every juncture of the trip, she'd rallied her defenses, but when no enemy had appeared the emotional roller-coaster ride had taken its toll.

By the time she reached Bride's Bay, Jenn was wondering how on earth she was going to survive the next week. She was already exhausted from doing battle with Jacob Carmichael—and she hadn't even seen him yet! How could she focus her energy on flushing out an assassin and clearing her name when she was so angry at Adam she couldn't see straight?

But the Raven was the enemy, she reminded herself. He wanted her dead. Carmichael was just someone who'd manipulated her emotions. If she survived the Raven, she could certainly survive what Adam had done to her. She was a professional, so she'd behave professionally toward him and the pain would go away eventually.

Moving restlessly through the empty suite, Jenn finally ended up on the balcony. The rose garden and the labyrinthine maze beyond it were crawling with Secret Service men who'd arrived en masse yesterday. The lobby had been the same; in fact, everywhere Jenn had looked on the ride from the helipad to the hotel she'd seen clean-shaven, short-haired men in dark suits, white shirts and sunglasses.

At the moment, the President's own personal security force seemed to be concentrating on preparations for the party in the garden. How many of them knew about her? she wondered. Had they all been given her photograph and told not to let her anywhere near the President? Did all those men in dark suits think she was a traitor? How could she possibly prove to them she wasn't?

"Damn it, Carmichael, where are you?" she cried in frustration. Before he'd left her this morning, Vernandas had made it very clear that Adam was in charge of this operation. If Jenn so much as breathed without his permission she would be yanked off the island immediately, robbing her of the chance to prove she wasn't a murderer and a traitor. And if she didn't prove that, she'd be arrested and spend the rest of her life in prison.

Which meant, of course, that as much as it galled her to stay put, she was stuck here in this room until Adam deigned to put in an appearance. That left her pacing anxiously when she would much rather have been using that energy downstairs, strolling the grounds and studying the faces. Memories seemed to be coming to her more easily now that she knew the truth about herself. It was possible that seeing the right sight—the right *face*—might bring everything flooding back.

But she couldn't test that theory until Adam arrived, and as he'd once told her, patience wasn't her strongest suit.

ADAM HAD NEVER DREADED anything in his life more than he dreaded climbing the elegant old staircase that would take him up to the room where Jenn was waiting for him. He'd just left a meeting in the Fortress with Tom Graves, who was still irate because he hadn't been told earlier about the potential threat the Raven posed. In his mind, the security chief felt that Adam had endangered the lives of two good men by putting them in the path of an international hit man and terrorist without any warning that they were up against a professional killer. He was furious with Adam, with Dan Luther and with the whole world in general.

But even as angry as the security man had been, Adam would rather have gone another two rounds with him than face Jenn. He hadn't wanted to come back here, but an hour of ranting, raving and threatening hadn't convinced Tony Vernandas to let him off the hook. The director had listened dispassionately, then pointed out that Jennifer Lambert had chosen to go back into the lion's den because she wanted to prove her innocence. Could Adam in good conscience let her face the Raven alone? After all he'd done to keep her safe, would he be able to live with himself if she died because he wasn't there to protect her?

Even as Vernandas had asked the questions, Adam had known he was being manipulated, but it hadn't mattered. He had to go back and see the job through.

He'd made a royal mess of things, letting his feelings for Jennifer color the decisions he'd made and the things he'd told her, but it was his mess and he had to clean it up.

So he'd made all of Jenn's travel arrangements and made separate ones for himself so that he could arrive ahead of her to see that everything was in order. Dan Luther had wanted to meet with him, and there'd been Tom Graves to face. But all of that was out of the way now, and he couldn't put off seeing Jenn any longer.

When he let himself into the suite, he found her pacing the area between the sofa and the French doors. She stopped and glared at him. Adam wondered if there would ever be a time when he didn't think she was the most beautiful woman he'd ever known.

"So glad you decided to put in an appearance," she said. "Where the hell have you been?"

"Meeting with the Secret Service and resort security," Adam replied, throwing his garment bag over the nearest chair.

Jenn planted her clenched fists on her hips. "Without me? How typical. Did you consider the fact that I might like to talk to the Secret Service? Or that I've been stuck here because I have orders not to blink without consulting you? Do you have a plan of action, Mr. Carmichael, or am I just supposed to stay locked in this room for the rest of my natural life?"

Typical Jenn Lambert—when in doubt, come out swinging. It was the first of many traits Adam had fallen in love with a decade ago; it was the one that had reeled him in this time around, too. He took her anger on the chin without flinching because it was the very least he deserved.

"Your schedule isn't too demanding," he told her, his voice calm and noncombative. "We've been invited to sit in on the Secret Service threat-assessment briefing at seven tonight. Beyond that, my plan is the same as it always was—to put you out among the guests and see if you recognize the Raven or he recognizes you."

"Then let's get to it," Jenn said, coming around the sofa. She was ready to take charge whether Jacob Carmichael liked it or not. "Thanks to you, I've spent over a week looking for memory cues in all the wrong places. Have I ever been to Bride's Bay before?"

"No."

She stopped in front of him. "Then tell me, what good was that delightful little trip to the lighthouse or our romantic sail around the island?"

"Because it wasn't our first sail or our first lighthouse," he said softly.

He was using the same voice on her that she'd heard a hundred times before, and his expression was achingly familiar—it was that sweet, sad, regretful, oh-Maddy-why-don't-you-remember look. But the game was over now, so why was he still trying to play with her head?

"The point is, I should've been looking at faces, not landmarks," she told him, trying her damnedest to ignore the way her heart wanted to open to him. She was striving for professionalism, and the only emotion she was willing to make the slightest bit of room for was anger. "Now, are you coming or not, Mr. Carmichael?" she asked as she moved on around him toward the door.

"Since I have no intention of letting you leave this room without me, I suppose I'm coming," he replied. "But there is one thing we should get straight."

Jenn stopped but didn't turn around. "What?"

"For the time being we have to maintain the cover we've already established, which means we should refer to each other as Adam and Maddy, even in private. When you're undercover, it's simpler than switching back and forth between real names and cover identities, and someone is bound to notice if you slip and call me Mr. Carmichael."

Jenn didn't want to go back to being Maddy Hopewell, the vulnerable, simpering little idiot who'd allowed herself to be emotionally seduced by a handsome, sweet-talking stranger. But she was the one who'd asked to come back to Bride's Bay, and she was the one who had accepted Anthony Vernandas's take-it-or-leave-it ultimatum.

"All right, *Adam.*" She turned to him and managed a sweetly venomous smile. "I'm going for a walk, *darling.* Would you like to come along?"

Adam knew that tone and that smile. Both were dangerous. "Don't push your luck, Jenn," he warned her sternly. "I don't blame you for hating my guts, but don't lose sight of the fact that there may be an assassin out there who wants you dead. You can blast me verbally all you want, but don't get cute and do something stupid just to spite me."

She glared up at him. "Oh, don't worry, Adam. Maddy Hopewell was the ninny with a gift for doing stupid things—like believing every word her loving hubby told her." She took a step toward him. "But Maddy Hopewell is gone. Oh, don't worry, I'll still answer to the name, but I'm Jenn Lambert now, and

I'm through being stupid. Just do your job, quit messing with my head, and we'll get along fine."

With that, she whirled on her heel and stalked out the door. Adam didn't have any choice but to follow her.

CHAPTER NINETEEN

"THESE ARE OUR PRIMARY targets. The first three are known to have made threats against the President, they have extensive paramilitary skills, and they are not currently under surveillance. They've gone underground, and they could be anywhere, including Bride's Bay. The next two..."

Dan Luther was using a remote control to advance the slide projector, so that the pictures flashing on the wall corresponded to his descriptions of potential presidential assassins. As he did so, another agent was passing out folders containing the same pictures to his sixty-five colleagues in the crowded meeting room. Jenn hadn't seen her picture up on the wall yet, but she fully expected to any second now.

She'd spent all afternoon at the resort studying faces, but none of them stirred any memories—not even the ones Adam pointed out as being agents she'd worked with before. It was frustrating, but at least she felt that she was finally exercising a measure of control over her life. As Maddy Hopewell, she'd been on the defensive—just a poor victim who was immobilized by fear and uncertainty.

Now she had knowledge and a purpose—to expose an assassin and clear her name. It didn't matter if the Secret Service splashed her photograph across the wall. She would prove her innocence eventually.

"I'm afraid you won't find a photo in your packets for the final threat of this briefing," Luther said, drawing Jenn's full attention. "Some of you may have heard that one of our intelligence-gathering networks overseas picked up the rumor that the international assassin known as the Raven has accepted a multi-million-dollar contract to kill the President. This is an unverified rumor, but an event here in South Carolina has led us to conclude that there may be a measure of validity to the threat."

At that point, he introduced Jenn Lambert and Jacob Carmichael as operatives from another government agency who were working undercover using the names of Maddy and Adam Hopewell. Their goal, he stated, was to flush out the Raven, and he went on to explain the circumstances surrounding the attack on Maddy and her resulting amnesia.

He told the story in broad strokes and made it clear that much of the information about the Raven's involvement in the attack was pure speculation. In fact, he placed no more emphasis on the Raven than he'd given the other six potential assassins, which surprised Jenn. Luther directed his men to look at two vastly different rough sketches purported to be the Raven, then went on to other business.

That's it? Jenn wondered as Luther began discussing employee clearances and the guest list for the reception in the garden. She glanced at Adam, who was sitting to her right, but when she caught his eye, he only shrugged as if to say, "What did you expect?"

It was another fifteen minutes before the briefing adjourned and she was able to ask the question aloud. As soon as the agents began filing out, Jenn pushed her way toward Dan Luther. "That's all?" she said to him. "An international terrorist plans to kill the President, and you make it sound like an inconsequential footnote!"

Luther began gathering up his notes. "Mrs. Hopewell, in the past ten years I've heard at least a hundred rumors about terrorist plots, and the Secret Service has taken every one of them seriously. In fact, I personally stood post over our past president when we heard that Carlos the Jackal had accepted a contract to kill him during a California political rally."

"I take it the assassination attempt never took place."

"No, it didn't. Now, that doesn't mean we dismiss threats like this one with the Raven, but frankly, I'm much more concerned about this man." Luther showed her the first photo he'd displayed on the wall. "He's a lunatic mercenary who blames the President's arms embargo on San Sebastian for the death of his wife. He's a dead-shot sniper, he's sworn to kill the President, and we don't have a clue where he might be. If there's going to be an assassination attempt during the President's vacation, I'd put my money on the embittered merc, not the professional hit man."

"Why?" Jenn challenged him. "Why would you think one more dangerous than the other?"

"Because in this day and age, anyone who wants to kill the President has to be willing to trade his life to do it. That doesn't fit the profile of an assassin like the Raven. I'll grant you he's versatile—he's claimed credit for just about every type of kill you can name— but he's never taken on a target as well protected as the President of the United States, and I don't believe he ever would. What's the point of a multimillion-dollar payoff if you know you'll never escape to enjoy it?"

He had a point, but Jenn still felt he wasn't taking the Raven seriously enough. "But what about remote-control devices, like a bomb?"

"A remote possibility at best." A smile played around his mouth as though he was pleased with his little pun. "I've spent most of the past month on this island with a team of dog handlers and demolition experts combing every inch of the golf course and every other location the President might visit. I'd stake my life on the fact that there's not an ounce of any type of explosive on Jermain Island, and there's not a prayer of smuggling any on at this point."

"So you're just going to dismiss the threat?"

"Not at all." He put the last folder into his briefcase and snapped the locks. "But I'm not going to ask the President to cancel his vacation because of it, either."

"You should," Adam said as he leaned his hip against the table that sat between him and the agent.

Luther shook his head. "We've covered this territory before, and the answer is still the same. The President will not cancel without a verifiable offer of proof. A rumor started by a shopkeeper in Turuq doesn't qualify as proof, even if the man did turn up dead."

"But what about the attack on me—and the microdot with Bride's Bay on it that was found in my purse?" she asked.

"You're in a very dangerous business," he countered. "That attack on you could have come from any number of sources, and as for the microdot, it could be something you invented to throw us off the track."

"Or it could be that the Raven killed a shopkeeper in Turuq and tried to kill me to prevent anyone from finding out how he plans to kill the President here at Bride's Bay," Jenn said.

Luther didn't argue with her. "That's absolutely right, which is why my men will take every possible precaution to prevent *anyone* from getting close to the Chief Executive. And that includes you."

Jenn wasn't offended. "Does that mean I've been *un*invited to the reception in the garden labyrinth?"

"No, your invitation stands, because I can't eliminate the possibility that you might recognize the Raven if he really is here." He clearly wasn't happy with what he was saying. "But like all the guests, you'll be searched and you'll be watched very closely," he said, glancing at Adam. "Now, if you'll excuse me, I've got work to do."

He picked up his briefcase and departed.

Jenn caught the last look that had passed between the men, and she took a guess as to its meaning. "Did you and Luther argue over whether I should be admitted to the reception?"

Adam nodded. "Several times."

"Who won?"

"I did. When Judge Bradshaw put our names on the guest list last week, Luther felt obligated to explain to me why he was going to reject us."

Jenn frowned. "He doesn't take the Raven threat seriously. So why did he think having me at the party was a problem?"

Adam came to his feet. "Luther takes everything seriously, and he doesn't believe in taking any more chances than absolutely necessary. That's why he threw a major fit when he learned that we had brought you here. He tried to put a stop to our operation, but when his boss went head-to-head with my boss, the Secret Service lost.''

Jenn still hadn't come to grips with the scope of the intricate scenario that had been playing out around her for the past two weeks. Knowing that she might well hold the life of the President of the United States in her hands was more than a little overwhelming, and there were still too many questions she didn't know the answers to. It was time she got her priorities straight.

She glanced at the door on the other side of the room. It was closed and all the agents were gone. She was alone with Adam, and there were some things she had to know.

She turned to him. "Why did you volunteer for this job, Adam?"

The question clearly caught him off guard. He registered surprise for a moment, then a cautious look came over his face. "Are you really ready to listen to the truth?"

"I'm ready to ask some questions and judge for myself whether or not they're the truth," she answered.

"Fair enough." He leaned against the table again, stretched his legs out in front of him and folded his arms across his chest. Jenn knew the pose wasn't nearly as casual as it seemed.

"I volunteered to play your husband because I was the only person in a position to do the job who believed you were innocent, and I didn't like the fact that they were throwing you out as bait. When I couldn't convince Tony Vernandas to bring you in and tell you the truth, I had two choices. Take you to Bride's Bay myself and play out the "second honeymoon" scenario, which was designed to give us an excuse to be on the island, or let the job go to someone who didn't know you, didn't believe in your innocence and who might be willing to sacrifice your life in order to make the biggest capture of his career."

"So you volunteered solely for my protection?"

"Yes."

Well, at the very least his answer coincided with what Vernandas had told her about Adam bringing in unauthorized bodyguards, but Jenn wasn't taking anything at face value ever again. "But why did you believe in me when no one else did?"

"Because I know that you could never collaborate with a terrorist. The death of your parents in that bombing shaped your life in ways you can't possibly imagine. You'd die before you'd let someone like the Raven use you."

He sounded so convincing, and he was saying exactly what Jenn needed to hear. Which made her even more suspicious of him. "What makes you think you know me so well? That night in the restaurant when you were teasing me about my occupation you said you recruited me into a life of espionage. Was that true?"

"Yes."

"Why would the Agency have chosen someone like me? A college dropout who was more interested in partying on the Riviera than doing anything of value with her life."

A restrained smile drew his lips into a tight line. "Don't take your dossier quite so literally, Jenn. I was ordered to recruit you because you didn't give us much choice. What's not outlined in the dossier is that after you left college you looked up some of your father's friends and colleagues in the diplomatic corps and asked them to put you in touch with intelligence sources. You hoped they'd lead you to the terrorists who murdered your parents and the seventy-eight other passengers on that plane.''

"I did?"

Adam nodded. ''Using your own finances and improvised resources, you were very methodically trying to infiltrate the terrorist cell—and what's remarkable is that you were getting close enough that you were about to get killed. That's when I was sent in to see if I could convince you to do things a little more conventionally.''

She tried to imagine doing something that audacious and couldn't quite bring it into focus. ''I was either very stupid back then or very brave,'' she said.

"You were never stupid, Jenn,'' he assured her. ''But you had a bad habit of not looking before you leapt. It's gotten you in trouble at the Agency more than once.''

She didn't want to hear the tenderness in his voice or see it on his face, but it was there nonetheless. She tried to rally her defenses against it. ''How did we really meet?'' she asked him.

"Exactly as I told you. The casino in Cannes during the week of the film festival. You were wearing that white drop-dead dress and I was totally blown away. You were the most incredibly beautiful—''

"Hold it. Don't lay it on too thick, Adam. I just had supper an hour ago,'' she said caustically.

"You asked me to tell you the truth,'' he reminded her. ''That's what I'm doing. Ten years ago you were the most beautiful woman I'd ever met, and that's still true today. I fell in love with—''

"That's enough," she snapped, starting for the door. "I asked for facts, not more emotional manipulation."

Adam wasn't ready to let her escape, though. He sprang away from the table and grabbed her arm before she was halfway across the room. "Oh, no, Ms. Lambert. You're not going anywhere yet. You wanted answers? Well, you're going to get them."

"I wanted the truth, not another phony love scene engineered to keep me under your thumb!"

"That was never my intention, Jenn," he replied hotly, his frustration finally getting the better of his temper. "You know, if you had your memory back, you'd understand where every word I said to you came from these past two weeks. If you had Jenn Lambert's memories, you'd remember the lighthouse on the coast of Malta where I asked you to marry me eight years ago. You'd remember how we fought like cats and dogs when we first met and you realized I was trying to put you out of the free-lance terrorist-hunting business. You'd remember how well we worked together in those early years after you finished your training. You'd remember how close we became—and how much I loved you."

His voice had grown soft, and though his hand was still on her arm, it wasn't what was keeping her close to him as he continued, "If you had your memory back, Jenn, you'd know that everything I said to you was something I'd said before or something I wanted to say but never got the chance."

Jenn was mesmerized, and she didn't want to be. "You asked me to marry you once?"

"I asked you several times, but you wouldn't do it. You were obsessed with doing everything in your power to eliminate terrorism in the world, and that took precedent over every other consideration. Even us.''

She finally yanked her arm away from his hand and freed herself. ''If I could remember all those things you just mentioned, would I forgive you for manipulating my emotions so brutally?''

Adam shook his head. ''I don't know. You might not forgive me, but I think you would understand that I was trying to tell you as much of the truth as I could without totally destroying the scenario Vernandas wanted me to follow.''

''Truth?'' she asked incredulously. ''You pretended we were married when the truth was I had rejected your marriage proposals. If you wanted to be truthful, why didn't you say we were separated, or our marriage was in trouble? Why didn't you give me a choice, instead of making me feel guilty at every turn because I couldn't remember a gloriously magnificent, utterly perfect marriage that didn't exist!''

''Jenn, you were already confused. If you think pretending we were happily married was cruel, try to imagine how much more confused you would have been if I'd added an element of marital strife. Since I couldn't have told you the real reason you wouldn't marry Jake Carmichael, I'd have been forced to invent reasons why our marriage was in trouble. That would have been totally counterproductive, because my first objective in this whole mess was to get you to trust me. And believe me, Jenn, trust doesn't come easy for you. It never has.''

He was right about that, but that didn't mean he'd been right about everything else. ''But you did more than try to get me to trust you, Adam. You played the perfect husband and worked overtime at getting me to fall in love with you!''

''That's not true,'' he protested, then took a deep breath to calm himself. ''Look, Jenn, I'm a long way from being perfect, and I will accept being accused of enjoying having you need me. And yes, I did manipulate your emotions once or twice, hoping it would help you to trust me, but I never, ever deliberately did anything designed to make you fall in love. And when I realized that you had, and that you were ready to tell me, that's when I bailed out. I knew if I let you say you loved me, you'd never forgive me.''

Jenn wanted to believe him. Part of her was crying out, begging to be allowed to believe, but after so many lies how could she possibly trust anything he said? How did she know that this wasn't just another layer of lies? ''Well, I'm sorry to burst your bubble, Mr. Carmichael, but if you were hoping for absolution, you bailed out a little too late,'' she told him. ''Maddy Hopewell may have been a weak little fool who fell for your sweet talk, but I'm not Maddy. But thanks, anyway, for the history lesson,'' she said as she turned for the door.

THE CENTER COURTYARD of the garden labyrinth had been transformed into a fantasyland. Hundreds of strings of softly twinkling lights had been woven into the seven-foot-tall shrubs that formed the perimeter of the enclosure, delicate paper lanterns lit from within hung overhead, and votive candles in white parchment luminaries lined the corridors of the maze that led the guests into the courtyard.

The Charleston Chamber Orchestra provided a musical background so soft and delicate that it didn't drown out conversations or the sweet tinkling of the central fountain. It was an exquisite setting for the small gathering, which was comprised mainly of the wealthy year-round island residents, a few friends from the mainland and a handful of hotel guests. As the evening progressed, the President seemed to grow increasingly at ease, like a man who was gradually shedding the weight of his work and assuming the new role of vacationing golf fanatic.

Liz Jermain was making a concerted effort to stay in the background. She was tucked away in the darkest corner of the courtyard, watching everything going on around her. It was such an impressive party that she was almost ready to admit that all the hard work and aggravation had been worthwhile.

"You're not mingling, dear. You should be rescuing the First Lady from Katherine Burkhoff."

Liz smiled as her grandmother approached, looking positively radiant. Even at eighty, Elizabeth Jermain Bradshaw was one of the most beautiful women Liz had ever seen. Tall and regal, with silver hair and pale blue eyes, she was the epitome of Old World elegance and breeding.

Liz slipped her hand into Elizabeth's and gave it a gentle squeeze. "I think the First Lady is holding her own for the time being. It's the President who needs rescuing from her husband. You know how furious General Burkhoff is about the San Sebastian arms embargo."

"Indeed he is. Men do love their wars," Elizabeth said. "That's why only women should run the world."

"Well, I won't argue that." Liz squeezed her grandmother's hand again. "This is a lovely party,

Nanna. I don't think the gardens have ever looked more beautiful.''

"Thank you, dear, but if it's such a marvelous party, why aren't you enjoying it?" Elizabeth asked. Her voice was mild, but when Liz looked into her eyes she went immediately on guard. She could always tell when her grandmother had something on her mind.

"I am enjoying it—from a distance. I've been in the thick of things for weeks, you know. I deserve a rest."

"You've been *miserable* for weeks," Elizabeth countered. "And it has nothing to do with all the preparations for the President's vacation. Would you care to tell me what's going on?"

Liz sighed with exasperation. "We have the President at Bride's Bay. Don't you think that's enough to distract anyone?"

"I didn't say you were distracted, dear. I said you were unhappy. There's a big difference."

"I'm fine, Grandmother," she said, praying for patience. This was vintage Elizabeth Jermain. She'd had any number of opportunities to question Liz in private, but she chose to do it in a public setting because she knew that the good manners she'd drilled into Liz would prevent her from storming off in a huff. "Not everyone handles stress as effortlessly as you do."

"Why thank you, dear, but it's the source of your stress that concerns me. I think it has little to do with the President, and a great deal to do with the young man you've been working so hard to keep hidden."

"The relationship wasn't hidden, Grandmother. It was private," she said quietly. "And it doesn't matter now, because it's over. I'm sorry, Nanna, but I have no intention of discussing this with you. If you'll excuse me—"

"There you are, Betsy! I couldn't imagine where you'd gotten to!" The Judge was bustling toward them, cutting off Liz's immediate avenue of escape. "What are you two lovely ladies gossiping about?"

"The Burkhoffs," Elizabeth replied promptly, letting Liz off the hook. "And I was just about to ask Liz for an update on that dustup with the Hopewells. I've never received a satisfactory explanation for why she was so upset the other day when she called and asked for your assistance."

"Neither have I," Liz said. "It's obvious that they're not what they seem, but every time I ask Tom Graves about them, he says it's nothing to worry about."

The Judge took his wife's hand and tucked it into the crook of his arm. "I have it on good authority that it's a matter of national security, which means that it's a little mystery for which we'll probably never see the solution.

"Come on, Betsy," he said, leading his wife out of the corner. "Let's go rescue the President from General Burkhoff. They can argue about San Sebastian during their golf game tomorrow."

CHAPTER TWENTY

JENN SIPPED her coffee and punched the "enter" key on the laptop computer in front of her on the balcony dining table. Another page with a photograph of a hotel guest she didn't recognize appeared on the screen, and she studied it for a long moment, trying to visualize the man with darker hair or a mustache, or no hair at all. She still didn't recognize him, and she yawned as she pressed the "enter" key again to clear the screen and bring up another photo.

Considering how little sleep she'd been getting lately it felt very early to her, but the gardens below were already buzzing with guests on their way to one facility or another, or searching for mementos from the President's dazzling but uneventful reception. The souvenir hunters were surely doomed to be disappointed, because the garden had been returned to normal yesterday, leaving no trace of the elegant party that had taken place thirty-six hours ago.

In a way, Jenn understood how the souvenir seekers felt. She would have given anything to have a keepsake from the event, but the memento she wanted was a concrete image of a face to associate with the Raven. Despite her diligence at the party, she hadn't seen anyone she recognized, and the same was true of the hours she and Adam had spent yesterday afternoon studying the faces of the spectators and guests who'd been cleared to watch the President play golf from a well-supervised distance.

The only thing that had stirred any memories at all was when Adam had invited Arthur Rumbaugh and Loreen McKinley up to the suite last night to talk about operations they had worked together. She'd had her first fully formed, concrete memory, one that was more than a fragmented collection of images. When Loreen had talked about how she'd saved Jenn's life in Beirut eight years ago, Jenn had remembered the whole thing—crawling through a bombed-out hotel, her cover as a reporter completely shredded. She remembered playing a life-and-death game of hide-and-seek with the terrorists, who were holding three British hostages, and how Loreen had smuggled her out of the country into Israel.

Most of all, she remembered how elated she'd been at the end of that long, exhausting journey when she'd seen Jake Carmichael's worried face waiting for her at the last checkpoint. She remembered throwing herself into his arms and feeling safe, as though nothing could harm her as long as he was holding her—feelings not terribly different from the ones she'd experienced a few days ago in his arms before she'd discovered the truth.

Jenn hadn't told Adam how complete the memory had been, but she was still haunted by the emotions it had evoked.

"Having any luck with the guest list?"

Jenn drew herself back into the present and advanced the screen to another photograph. "Not yet."

Adam was fresh out of the shower, clean-shaven and fully clothed. "I heard you pacing the floor between three and four o'clock this morning," he told her as he took his seat at the breakfast table. "Did your nightmare come back?"

Jenn refilled her coffee cup and slid the carafe across the table to him. She was beyond lying to him at this point. "Yes. It came back. Nothing new, though, just a few images that were a little more concrete than the last time. But I still can't bring Majhid's words into focus. I know he told me something, and I'm certain it's important, but I can't quite make it out."

"You will," he assured her.

They lapsed into silence as Adam ate his breakfast and glanced through the morning newspaper, which was heavily laced with photographs of the President playing golf. There were pictures of him teeing off, crouching on the green to line up a shot, driving a canopied golf cart, wiping his brow with his "lucky" towel and chipping out of a sand trap. There was even a photo taken after the game depicting him shaking hands with the winner—General Burkhoff.

Jenn had studied all the pictures first thing this morning, looking for anything that might stir a memory, but to no avail. She continued with her computer search while Adam read the paper. Silences like these seemed to be the hallmark of their new relationship. They were operating under a flag of truce, and Jenn was actually managing to be civil most of the time.

When the quiet of the morning was shattered by the sound of shouting below the balcony, Jenn's heart slammed into her ribs as Adam got to his feet and peered down at the garden entrance to the hotel.

"What is it?" Jenn asked, joining him at the rail.

"Just the press making a nuisance of itself as usual. Looks like the President is headed for the club-house."

Jenn relaxed and returned to her chair. "He probably wants to get an early start today because he found out that it's too hot to play golf in the afternoon around here, even with a stiff ocean breeze."

"No, he's probably getting an early start so that he can lose *two* rounds of golf today, instead of just one."

Jenn smiled at his joke, then caught herself and sobered. At times like these it was too easy to let her guard down. "Who's he playing golf with today?"

"He and the First Lady are taking on Senator Martin and his wife. Do you want to go out and work the crowd again?" he asked her.

"I suppose so. I'm almost through the guest files," she said, tapping the computer screen. "I want to take a shower, then look through the employee files before I go downstairs, though."

"I thought you studied the employee files yesterday."

"I did, but that doesn't mean anything. I never know when something is going to shake loose up here," she said, tapping her forehead.

"All right. I'm going down to the command post to check on the President's itinerary for this afternoon," he said as he folded the newspaper and tossed it onto the table. "Should I come back for you in about an hour?"

"That'll be fine."

"Okay. See you then."

He started for the parlor, and Jenn found she wasn't quite ready to let him go. "Adam . . ."

He stopped and turned expectantly. "Yes?"

There was something she had to know. "That incident in Beirut that Loreen and I were talking about last night..."

He seemed to tense a little as he nodded. "What about it?"

"You were the control on that operation, weren't you?"

"Yes," he replied. "Did you remember that or did Loreen tell you?"

"I remembered."

"That's wonderful," he said with a reserved smile. "Your memory flashes seem to be getting more substantial."

"Yes." She hesitated a moment, then plunged ahead. "Adam, you said you proposed to me eight years ago in Malta."

He tensed a lot this time. "That's right."

"And the incident in Beirut was eight years ago," she reminded him. "Which came first?"

"Beirut," he answered. "After you were almost killed, we rented a sailboat and took some time off together to explore the Maltese Islands."

"And that's when you asked me to marry you?"

He nodded. "I wanted us both to quit fieldwork and settle down in something sane stateside so that we could raise a family. Have a normal life. You said no."

"You mean you gave me an all-or-nothing ultimatum?"

"That's one way to look at it."

If he'd used that dictatorial tone he was so fond of, Jenn could easily imagine what her reaction had been. "Did we ever work together again?"

"No."

"Why not?"

"Because I took the Internal Investigations job right after that," he replied. "I knew that as long as you were working in the field you'd continue to take chances like the ones you'd taken in Beirut. I was the one who sent you in there and I didn't want to ever have to do that again."

She tilted her head to one side as she studied him. "Did you ever find your normal life?"

Adam shrugged. "Sort of, I guess. Working Internal Investigations doesn't make me the most popular guy in the Agency, but the hours are usually pretty regular and I still get to travel a lot. I even do some undercover work from time to time."

"Did you ever get married and take a crack at that family you wanted?"

"Almost. I was this close—" he held his thumb and forefinger an inch apart "—to the altar once."

"What went wrong?"

"I realized she was just a carbon copy of you. She deserved better than being used as a substitute, so I let her go."

Jenn didn't know what to say. He was tugging at her heartstrings, and part of her wanted to believe that he'd really loved her that much. Another part suspected that his portrait of himself was pure manipulation.

The part that wanted to believe must have allowed her sympathy for him to show, because he chuckled and moved a little closer to the table. "Don't feel sorry for me, Jenn. I haven't been pining my life away for the last eight years, gambling, drinking and keeping disreputable company to assuage my broken heart. In fact, I was pretty sure I'd gotten over you until this situation came up."

His wry smile faded. "Then I walked into that hospital room and saw you sitting there so pale, so vulnerable, almost too weak to move and more frightened than I'd ever imagined you could be..." He shook his head at the memory. "But you were still cracking wise, still using that sharp tongue as your first line of defense. In that first ten minutes every reason I'd fallen in love with you came flooding back, and I was hooked again."

Jenn's doubts slipped a little further away as trust kept trying to creep in. She decided she'd gotten enough answers for one day. "Thank you for your honesty," she said, giving him the benefit of the doubt. She started shutting down the computer. "I'm going to take my shower now. I'll see you in about an hour."

Adam recognized the dismissal, but he wasn't ready to let this moment pass. He'd been doing a lot of soul searching, and he'd realized a few things he wanted Jenn to know. "Can that wait just a minute?"

She hesitated. "I suppose so. Why?"

"Because I need to tell you you were right the other day in the briefing room," he answered. "I did manipulate you more than was necessary. And I did want to earn more than just your trust. I think deep down I think I wanted to see if I could make you fall in love with me.

"I wasn't trying to be cruel or pay you back," he added hastily. "I just wanted to see that look in your eyes again."

The tender look in *his* eyes was nearly Jenn's undoing. "What...look?" she managed to ask.

Adam reached out and gently brushed a wisp of hair off her cheek. "Believe it or not, Jenn, you did love me once." He withdrew his hand. "I'll come back in an hour or so and see if you're ready to hit the golf course again."

Jenn nodded and sat very still as he left the suite, fighting the urge to cry and trying to figure out why on earth she'd refused his proposal of marriage eight years ago. How could she not have loved him? How could she keep lying to herself now, pretending that what she felt for him was hatred?

She *had* to get her memory back. Because it was the only way she would ever be able to separate the Jacob Carmichael who'd asked her to marry him from the Adam Hopewell who'd made her fall in love with him. It was the only way she'd ever figure out what was real, and how much of what she was feeling she could trust.

She had to make herself remember.

FIFTEEN MINUTES LATER showered and dressed, Jenn had just finished drying her hair when she heard the door chime, followed almost immediately by a brisk knock. She hurried through the suite, checked the security peephole and was shocked to see Anthony Vernandas impatiently raising his hand to pound on the door again.

She opened the door quickly and stepped back to admit him. "Mr. Vernandas. This is quite a surprise. Adam didn't tell me you were coming."

"He doesn't know yet."

"Has something happened?" she asked, concerned.

"No. Well, nothing of consequence, anyway," he replied as he moved into the room. "Our colleagues in the Secret Service have gotten their knickers in a knot because they feel that we've got too many of our own operatives on site. They seem to believe we're attempting to trespass into areas of presidential security where we don't belong. I just came down to smooth a few ruffled feathers."

"I see. Please have a seat. I can offer you coffee . . . or juice?"

"Nothing, thank you. I won't be here long. This is a beautiful suite," he observed as he placed his briefcase on the divan. "Mine is nice, but not half as luxurious."

"You were able to get a room?" Jenn asked with a touch of disbelief. "From what I've heard, the resort was booked solid for this period *months* in advance. How on earth did you and all the rest of your people like Rumbaugh and McKinley get rooms?"

"Ms. Lambert, if we could persuade a U.S. senator like Sam Luccacio to vacate this suite, making it available for you, we can certainly find ways of altering the vacation plans of other guests. You'd be amazed at how many people are willing to change their plans because they've won a free week in Hawaii or Florida."

Jenn let her skepticism show. "You got a U.S. senator to give up this suite for a free trip to Disney World?"

"No. But the principle was the same. He got something he wanted, but it required a commitment of time that forced him to give up his vacation, so we got what we wanted."

Once again, Jenn found the scope of this operation mind-boggling. "I've put a lot of people to a great deal of trouble, haven't I?"

"You've no idea."

"When this is all over, will I still have a career?"

Vernandas waffled his hand in the air. "Who can say? A great deal depends on whether or not the Raven succeeds in his attempt to assassinate the President— and whether you can disprove any involvement naturally. I take it you haven't had any luck with your memory."

"Nothing worth writing home about."

"That's a shame." Vernandas bent and unsnapped the locks on his briefcase. "I've brought you something Jake asked for. He thought this might stir up some memories of your parents. It comes from your Paris apartment."

He handed her a thick photograph album, snapped his briefcase closed and started moving toward the door. Jenn moved with him.

"Thank you," she said.

"Save your gratitude for Jake," Vernandas advised her. "If he'd had his way, you'd have been given that album weeks ago while you were still in the hospital." He stopped at the door and turned to Jenn, irritation showing clearly on his face. "You know, Jennifer, if the Raven's assassination threat turns out to be genuine, and God forbid, he succeeds in even getting *close* to killing the President, you're not the only one who's going to be in hot water. When Jake made the decision to deviate from my plan for this operation, he did so knowing he was risking his career. By putting your protection ahead of the interests of national security, he may very well have traded your life for the President's, and believe me, if the President dies, neither one of you will walk away from this scot-free!''

He opened the door. ''Have a nice day, Ms. Lambert.'' He walked out and closed the door firmly behind him.

Jenn just stood there a moment, digesting the rebuke. If he thought she needed to be reminded that she was in big trouble, he was sadly mistaken, but she hadn't considered any of this from Adam's point of view. Twenty-four hours ago, she would've run after Vernandas and told him how little Adam's precarious position meant to her. Now she couldn't do that. For better or worse she was coming to accept that he wasn't the villain she wanted to believe he was.

Of course, accepting that meant more of the walls she'd erected to protect her tangled emotions would come tumbling down, and she was in no shape this morning to inspect the remaining walls too closely. Instead, she started for the balcony, flipping open the cover of the photo album as she moved.

The first picture nearly knocked her to her knees.

It was her parent's wedding photograph—her beautiful mother in a white satin gown was smiling up at her father. They looked so happy, so in love, so *alive*, that it brought tears to Jenn's eyes. She sank to the floor and sat cross-legged, studying every familiar detail of the picture. She flipped to another page and saw a studio portrait of her parents, but in this one her father was smiling lovingly at the swaddled-in-pink baby in his arms.

Another page, and a picture of her mother laughing at the antics of a toddler who'd stuck her hands in her birthday cake…then Jenn at age seven dressed in black jodhpurs and a red velvet coat, mounted on Toby... Jenn at eleven learning to shoot... Jenn posing with her parents and the first trophy she'd ever won...

Jenn turned page after page, absorbing her life—not just the static images of it, but the full, ripe, rich *memories* that were all she had left of her parents. They came at her so fast that the emotions they evoked overwhelmed her, but by the time she reached the last page she remembered being Jenn Lambert. She remembered the excitement of waiting for her parents to pick her up from the Wharton School for Girls so that they could spend Christmas vacation together; she remembered the hideous pain she'd felt when the somber headmistress had told her that her parents' plane had crashed with no survivors.

She remembered feeling numb as she'd watched television footage of the investigation into the cause of the crash; how she'd felt when she learned that terrorists were the cause of her pain... Jenn remembered everything, right up to the moment she'd made the decision to do something about the rage that had festered in her during the years after the bombing.

There were no more pictures to solidify her memories, but she remembered flashes of other things, too—grueling physical training in guerrilla warfare, linguistics lessons, survival skills, martial arts, weapons proficiency—everything the Agency had made her learn so that she could hunt down the monsters who had murdered her parents. She even remembered her moment of vindication when the terrorist who'd planned the bombing had been executed.

The only thing that didn't accompany the flood of memories was a sense of completion. She had sought revenge; she had gotten revenge. Justice had been done. But it hadn't brought her parents back. It hadn't filled the emptiness. It hadn't reduced the burning need to do more, so she'd kept going, believing that surely more revenge, more justice would eventually fill the void and make her whole.

It hadn't happened that way, though. Despite the huge gaps remaining in her memory, Jenn knew the void had still been there the day she lost her memory—and it had certainly been there the day she'd awakened in the hospital. In fact, the only time she couldn't remember feeling that awful, inescapable black hole of loneliness was when she'd allowed herself to trust Jake Carmichael; when she'd let him in, and found herself falling in love.

No matter what Jake's motives had been, he'd given Jenn something precious, something . . .

Motives.

The word hit Jenn like a ton of bricks. More memories came flooding back, too quickly to absorb all at once. She remembered the colors and the smells of the bazaar in Al'Khatar. She remembered a man brushing past her, nearly dislodging the veil of her *habbiah* as he hurried out of Majhid Al'Enaza's shop.

Jenn remembered entering the shop and seeing Majhid on the floor, blood pooling around him, then, exactly as she'd seen it in her dream, she saw herself kneeling beside Majhid, believing he was dead, but then finding a weak pulse. When his eyes had opened, they were glassy and he had known he was dying, but he used his last ounce of strength to remove one of the scarab rings from a chubby finger and press it into Jenn's hands. He murmured some words . . .

"Damn it!" Jenn exclaimed, coming to her feet. She still couldn't remember the words! Majhid had spoken to her in Arabic, his voice broken, the sounds garbled. Jenn knew that even at the time she'd heard them she hadn't really understood what he was trying to tell her, but now she couldn't remember the words at all.

But she could remember the face. Not Majhid's, but the face of the man who'd arrogantly brushed her aside as he'd left the shop. The face of the man who had killed Majhid Al'Enaza. The face of the Raven.

Jenn almost laughed at the irony, when she remembered how she'd felt at the time—as though she'd never forget that face. But she had forgotten it, though not until after she'd left Majhid's shop and began searching for him in the bazaar; not until after she'd found him and trailed him to a small house in the heart of Al'Khatar just off the marketplace.

What followed had been three grueling days without sleep, keeping the Raven under surveillance, not daring to let him out of her sight even long enough to make contact with her station chief. She still didn't remember how she'd gotten from Turuq to Charleston, but at least she knew now that she wasn't a traitor and that she hadn't killed Majhid Al'Enaza. More importantly, she had a clear memory of the Raven's face. If she ever saw him again...

"Oh, my God," she murmured. She *had* seen him! And recently, here at Bride's Bay.

But where? When? She'd done nothing but study faces for the past four days. Had he been in the crowd on the golf course yesterday? At the reception? In the dining room? On the beach?

What had he been wearing? Something blue? she thought.

No, it was his eyes that were blue now; not brown, the way they'd been in Turuq. But he'd been wearing brown...or tan...or...

"Think, Jennifer! Think!" she exclaimed, pacing furiously as she tried to put all the pieces together.

Brown or tan...or khaki. Like the uniforms worn by all of the resort's housekeeping and maintenance staff.

The Raven was working at the hotel!

Jenn dashed to the computer on the balcony. In less than a minute she had the employee file up and running. She confined the parameters of her search to men only in the two departments that wore khaki uniforms, and she started scrolling quickly, viewing one face after another until she found the one she needed.

"*Yes!*" she shouted as she ran through the sitting room, pausing only long enough to snatch her purse from the table by the door. "I've got you now, you son of a bitch!"

CHAPTER TWENTY-ONE

WHEN JENN BURST through the door of the Secret Service command post, every agent in the room jumped to his feet and three of them pulled out their guns.

Jenn paid no attention. "Where's Jake Carmichael?"

One of the agents moved toward her. "Mrs. Hopewell, if you'd kindly—"

"Jake Carmichael! Where is he? Or Adam Hopewell!" she said, reverting to the name they knew him by. "Where is he? Where's Dan Luther?"

"They're not here," the agent told her. "And I'm going to have to ask you to leave right now."

"But I know who the Raven is!" Jenn insisted, yanking away from him when he tried to take her by the arm to escort her out the door. "He's working downstairs in the laundry!"

The agent grabbed her arm more forcefully this time. "Please, Mrs. Hopewell. Return to your room and I'll have Agent Luther come talk to you as soon—"

"I am not returning to my room, and I'm not waiting on anyone!" Jenn said hotly. The agent tried to maneuver her toward the door, but he seriously underestimated her determination—and her skills. It was more instinct than planning that had Jenn jabbing the agent in the stomach with her elbow and reversing their positions so that in the blink of an eye she had his arm twisted behind him and his throat in a choke-hold.

The reaction of his confederates was swift and certain. Ten guns came up this time, cocked and ready to fire. Jenn immediately released the agent, and two more closed in and grabbed her.

"Damn it, why won't you listen to me? Get Luther up here! Didn't you hear the briefing? Don't you know about the Raven? He's here! I've seen him!"

"What the hell is going on?" Tom Graves demanded as he hurried into the room. He'd seen Jenn Lambert running down the corridor on his monitor and figured something important was up. He certainly hadn't expected to find weapons drawn, Jenn being forcibly subdued, or one agent massaging his throat and another one reaching for a pair of hand-cuffs.

"Tom, make them let me go," Jenn begged him. "I remembered the Raven! He's here. He's an employee!"

"That's impossible," Tom said. "All of our employees have been thoroughly screened."

"Even the new ones like Karl Olander?"

Tom looked at her in disbelief. Maybe the Secret Service agents had good reason to be holding on to her, after all. "Are you suggesting that Karl Olander is the Raven?"

"Yes!"

He shook his head. "Not possible. Olander applied for a job here three months ago. His background was thoroughly—"

"So what?" Jenn exclaimed. "Do you think the Raven started planning this operation yesterday? He's had months to establish a credible identity here in the U.S.!"

Tom's certainty began to waver just a bit. "But the man he replaced had a stroke," he said, realizing that his argument was ridiculous even as he said it. There were any number of difficult-to-detect poisons that could cause a heart attack or a stroke like the one fifty-nine-year-old Roger Blaknee had suffered.

Jenn didn't bother making the same argument Tom had just thought of. "Look, can we argue about *how* he accomplished this later? Find Olander now! Take him into custody. Put *him* in handcuffs and then start asking questions! Just get him up here before he goes after the President!"

Tom looked at the agent who was still rubbing his throat. "She's right. We've got nothing to lose by interrogating Olander. And if he's the Raven, he may not want to come quietly."

The agent nodded and moved to the nearest phone. "I'll track down Luther and mobilize Tac Team Three." He pointed at the two agents who were holding Jenn. "You can release her, but don't let her out of your sight."

Jenn breathed a sigh of relief when the agents let her go. Tom Graves ushered her to an out-of-the-way spot where they could watch and listen as Agent Pettigrew ordered a tactical strike force to move downstairs and take Karl Olander into custody as quickly and quietly as possible.

They waited nervously as the team moved into position, reporting their progress at every juncture. Jenn couldn't have said whether two minutes or twenty passed as she listened anxiously to Tac Team Three deploying their men around the laundry room, but they had just sent men inside when Dan Luther finally came into the command post with Jake Carmichael and Anthony Vernandas right behind.

Luther and Vernandas went immediately to the command console and Jake made a beeline for Jenn. "What's going on? What are you doing here? Luther got a call saying someone had spotted the Raven."

Jenn nodded. "I did. Last Saturday as I was coming out of the clubhouse. He stepped right in front of me and I ran into him. I guess he wanted to see if I recognized him."

It took a second for that to sink in. "You *remembered* him? Your memory is back?" Adam asked, excitement catching fire in his eyes.

Jenn nodded. "Some of it. Vernandas brought me a photo album you had sent over from my apartment in Paris. My brain feels a little like Swiss cheese right now, but things are coming back—"

She was interrupted by Luther, who was shouting into his transmitter microphone. "Then spread out and find him! Mobilize now! And get that supervisor up here immediately! I want to talk to him."

"What's going on?" Adam asked him.

The room was in chaos and the laser printer near the door was already spitting out reprints of Olander's employee photograph. "Olander wasn't in the laundry," Luther explained. "No one has seen him since he finished distributing linens to the housekeeping stations in this part of the hotel and then refurbished his carts to do the same in the south wing."

"When was that?"

"About forty minutes ago."

Jenn looked at Adam. "Isn't that about when the President left for the clubhouse?"

It was Luther who answered, "Pretty close. Yes." He shook his head. "Jeez," he muttered, reaching for his microphone again so that he could call the team of agents who were watching the President tee off. "Tac One, this is Command. Tighten the perimeter around the President! Repeat, tighten the perimeter! We have a missing employee who may be the assassin known as the Raven. I'll have photographs of him down to you in five minutes, but be on the lookout for..."

Jenn listened in astonishment as Luther rattled off a description of Olander. "You're not going to bring the President in?" she asked incredulously as soon as he signed off.

"Not until we have a better idea what's going on. Tac One will close in on the President very subtly. The size of his escort will double so quietly that no one will notice—not even the President."

Jenn shook her head. "This is nuts. I can't just stand here. I've got to do something."

Luther fixed her with his most intimidating glare. "You stay out of this," he commanded, then transferred his glare to Jake. "And that goes for you, too. This is our job, and we do it very well."

"But the Raven is out there somewhere. He's going after the President now! It's happening even as we speak," Jenn argued hotly, totally unintimidated. "I'm not going to stand here and do nothing!"

"What do you think you can do that seventy-five Secret Service agents, four fully manned Coast Guard cutters, and three missile-loaded air force Huey helicopters can't do?" Luther asked.

"I can work the crowd again," she snapped right back at him. "The Raven may have put on another disguise that would make it difficult—even impossible—for your men to recognize him."

Luther lost a little of his self-righteous steam. "But you think you could?"

"Yes! I've seen him disguised as an Arab merchant and a Swedish laundry man. I've got a better chance of recognizing him than anyone else. I'm not staying here!" She looked at the man beside her for support. "Jake?"

"She's right, Luther." Adam grabbed her hand and started for the door. "Come on, let's go. We'll work the crowd together," he said, snatching a handful of copies of Olander's face off the printer as they passed it.

"Carmichael!"

Adam stopped and turned to Anthony Vernandas, who tossed him a radio receiver that had been lying on the console. "Keep your head down and stay tuned to what's happening up here. Both of you."

"Yes, sir. Thanks."

Jenn and Adam dashed downstairs, where very tense resort-staff members were trying to pretend everything was normal when they knew otherwise. With the help of Shad Teach, Adam commandeered one of the resort's Land Rovers and totally ignored the island's thirty-five-mile-an-hour speed limit as they headed toward the clubhouse with Adam firing question after question at Jenn about what she remembered and what she didn't.

"Public telephones are scarcer than hen's teeth in Turuq, Jake," she said in answer to one particularly thorny question about why she hadn't checked in. "I couldn't abandon my surveillance just to go find one once I'd tracked the Raven to the house. As it was, I almost lost him early the next morning when a car came for him. He had two suitcases with him and he was wearing a business suit, so I took my best guess and hurried to the airport.

"Fortunately he was there," she went on. "But by then, the women who saw me in Majhid's shop had given my description to the police and I was afraid it was only a matter of time before they identified me. I did what I could to alter my appearance, switched to one of my backup IDs, and when I was sure I knew what plane the Raven was boarding, I bought a ticket under the name Madeline Hopewell. I spent the next forty-eight hours sleeping on airplanes and staying as close to the Raven as I dared without giving myself away."

"But forty-eight hours, Jenn? And you couldn't get even one call through to your station?" Adam asked, not because he doubted her, but because he knew that Tony Vernandas would be asking the same question sooner or later.

"We weren't flying first-class Air America, Jake," she replied. "None of the flights were equipped with cellular or satellite-uplink phones, and I was too busy trying to follow him without being detected to worry about telephones during our layover in London. I did learn a very valuable lesson out of the ordeal, though."

"What's that?"

"It's not possible to follow someone halfway around the world on three different airlines with only one change of clothes and no wigs without being spotted. I don't know whether he picked me up as we came through customs in New York or if it was on the plane to Charleston, but he definitely became aware of me somewhere along the line. He let me follow him as far as the parking garage, and then I lost him. By the time I realized I'd found him again, he was behind the wheel of a speeding car and I was flying through the air like a Ping-Pong ball.''

Adam took his eyes off the road long enough to look at her. "So you did have phony ID tucked away, then?''

Jenn met his gaze. "Of course. It's one of the first tricks of the trade you taught me. Or have you forgotten that?'' she asked softly with just a wisp of a smile, but it was enough to make Adam's heart leap into his throat.

"I haven't forgotten anything, Jenn,'' he said, reluctantly dragging his gaze back to the road. "The question is, what do you *remember?*''

"A lot.''

Adam wanted to know what that meant, but there was no time. They'd reached the small parking enclosure closest to the first hole of the golf course. They had an assassin to find now. There would be time later to find out if her wistful smile meant she understood why he'd taken this job and risked his career just to protect her. After the Raven was captured, he'd find out if she was ever going to forgive him.

As they jumped out of the car, a report came over Adam's one-way radio, and they paused to listen to Luther telling the leader of Tac One that Karl Olander had been last spotted leaving the hotel. Tac Team Two, a roving patrol, had been dispatched to look for Olander, and Tac One, the largest of the teams, had been advised to maintain their perimeter around the President.

Jenn and Adam started jogging toward the golf course. As they neared, they could see the long line of golf carts toddling toward the opposite end of the fairway. Because of the perimeter alert, the Secret Service was keeping the spectators behind a restrictive line near the first tee, not allowing them to follow the action from hole to hole as they had yesterday.

Adam shoved a handful of Olander photographs at the agent in charge of crowd control. He was the same one who'd been on duty yesterday when Jenn and Adam had circulated among the crowd, so he didn't challenge their right to be there. He didn't require an explanation of the photographs, either. Like most of the other Secret Service agents on the island, he was wired with a transmitter and receiver, so he knew exactly what was happening back at the hotel.

He distributed the photos among his men as Adam and Jenn moved into the crowd and began circulating. They separated briefly, then came back together only two or three minutes later. It was a small crowd.

"Anything?" Adam asked.

Jenn shook her head and kept looking around. "Nothing. Where could he be? What's he up to? How's he going to kill the President?"

"Surely he doesn't think he could get close enough to do it with a rifle," Adam replied. Like Jenn, he knew they had to analyze every angle. "There are motion sensors and security cameras covering ninety percent of the island—particularly this golf course. He couldn't possibly escape *after* the assassination. If he ~~nts~~ to get away cleanly he'll have to leave *before* it. ~~did~~ he even show up for work?"

"Obviously there was something he had to do this morning to set the assassination in motion," she said, following Adam's line of thought. It wasn't easy, though, because the whispering in her head was growing stronger. The sounds were guttural...Arabic...

And important. Jenn finally stopped trying to ignore the voice and focused on the memory that was trying to bubble up through another hole in her memory. The voice was Majhid Al'Enaza's. And his words were the ones he'd been muttering in Jenn's nightmare for weeks. Only now they were finally becoming clear.

"Maybe we should st—"

"*Germs.*"

Adam looked at her, wondering if she'd suddenly lost her mind. "What?"

"*He bought germs.*" She looked up at Adam, her excitement mounting as everything started to make sense. "That's what Majhid told me! The Raven bought germs."

Adam frowned. "What the hell does that mean?"

"Germ warfare! Get it? The Raven bought a designer virus! Genetics labs all over the world are playing with synthetic viral technology. And it's something that can be activated by remote control! That's why he had to go to work this morning. He needed to set his device before he could leave the island!"

"But set it where?" Adam asked. "In the hotel? That's the only place he had access to. But he couldn't have left something in the Presidential Suite—Luther doesn't let anyone near the place. They even bring their own housekeeping staff from the White House."

"Do they bring their own washing machines and dryers and—"

"No, of course not," Adam said, then grinned when he realized where Jenn's thoughts were headed. "And they don't bring their own linens, either. The Raven could have infected the sheets or towels—"

Jenn shook her head. "But only if he could guarantee that no one but the President would use the contaminated item," she argued, shooting down her own theory.

Adam took a deep breath and exhaled it in a frustrated huff. "You're right. His whole plan would fall apart if the First Lady took a nap on the infected sheets or used the wrong towel while the President was off sailing."

"Right. It has to be something more foolproof than that."

A flash of movement caught Jenn's eye and she glanced to her right. It was just a woman in a bright red straw hat fanning herself with this morning's newspaper. The newspaper that had all the pictures of the President Jenn had studied this morning. The pictures depicting him teeing off, lining up a shot on the green, driving a golf cart, chipping out of a sand trap...

...and wiping his brow with his lucky towel.

"Oh, my God," Jenn muttered as all the pieces fell into place. "It's the towel, Jake! The lucky towel! That's why the Raven got a job in the laundry—so he could have access to the President's famous lucky towel, which has to be washed every day! The Raven bought some kind of virus and infected the towel with it. It's probably activated by water, and either becomes airborne or is absorbed through the pores! When the President—''

''When he wipes the sweat off his face, it'll infect him and God knows how many other people. If it's a virulent plague virus, everyone on this island could be dead in a matter of hours!'' Adam concluded, whirling around to look down the fairway. The golf carts were parked in the rough just off the green. Secret Service agents were so thick that Adam could barely make out the President lining up a shot on the green.

''Go!'' Jenn said, slapping him on the back. ''The Secret Service will never let me near him. You have to get down there and warn him!''

Adam clearly didn't want to leave her unprotected. ''But the Raven—''

''He's beating a hasty retreat!'' Jenn countered. ''I'm the least of his worries. Now go!''

Adam hesitated a second longer, then yanked the automatic from his ankle holster and shoved it into the purse Jenn had slung over her shoulder. ''And they'll never let me near him as long as I'm carrying this,'' he said, though Jenn knew that the real reason he was giving up his weapon was that he didn't want to leave her with a flimsy nail file as her only protection.

''Thanks. Now go!'' She slapped him on the back again and he darted off. When he reached the crowd-control line and ducked under, one of the agents grabbed for him and Jenn saw them talking, both incredibly animated as Adam explained the situation. Then they both took off at a dead run for the green.

Jenn felt a little weak in the knees.

A towel laced with poison. Absolutely brilliant. It required no detonation, and on a scorching day like this one at the end of June it was only a matter of time until the President mopped his brow with the lucky towel he'd sent down to the laundry yesterday after his afternoon golf game. The moisture would activate the poison immediately.

It wasn't sane, but it was brilliant, and he would've gotten away with it if it hadn't been for a photo album.

Of course, he might still get away, Jenn realized, whether Adam saved the President or not. In fact, he was probably making his escape right now!

He obviously had a getaway planned, but what was it? How could he get off the island? The marina? Jenn speculated, turning to look across the bay, but it was too far. The marina didn't make sense, anyway. It was one of the most security-saturated points on the island, and it lay to the west of the hotel, not north, where the Raven had last been seen.

No, he wouldn't use the marina or any kind of public transportation—that would draw attention to himself. He had some quiet way of leaving the island.

A speedboat hidden in the marsh perhaps? The Coast Guard's constant patrols of the island made that sort of thing tricky but not impossible. Or scuba gear?

Much better! Jenn decided. That would have been her choice if she was planning an escape. She would have a boat waiting well away from the island and scuba gear hidden in some out-of-the-way location along the coastline.

When the image of the lighthouse on Sandy Point sprang into Jenn's head, she was sure she knew exactly where the Raven had been headed when he left the hotel. It was so remote that no full-time Secret Service contingent was stationed there, and the vacant keeper's cottage would be the perfect place to hide his scuba equipment.

The Raven had been on foot when spotted on his way to the staff quarters, which meant he was probably trying to reach the riding trails, which led to the lighthouse, through the woods. That meant several miles over rough terrain, and he had at least a fifty-minute head start on her.

But the Raven had done it the hard way. Jenn was going to do it the easy way.

She dashed for the Land Rover and drove like a bat out of hell toward the heliport.

"A BIRDIE! ONE UNDER PAR!" the President shouted, raising his putter over his head triumphantly.

"Congratulations, dear," the First Lady said, coming forward to line up her shot.

"This is a big improvement over yesterday, don't you agree?" he gloated, adjusting his soft leather gloves.

His wife smiled at him fondly. "You're three strokes ahead of your score at this point yesterday and it's only the first hole. I'd say that's a major improvement."

A trickle of sweat ran in a crooked little rivulet down the President's cheek, and he shrugged his jaw against his shoulder to wipe the droplet away as he moved toward the golf cart. His caddie was waiting to take the putter, but the President waved him off, sliding the club into the bag himself.

He bent to unzip the attached accessory pouch. His emerald green terry-cloth towel, which had arrived freshly laundered courtesy of housekeeping this morning, was right at the top of the pouch. As an extra little nicety, it had even been wrapped in a thin, parchmentlike paper that bore the words *Sanitized for your Protection.*

The embroidered appliqué of a colorful leprechaun in the middle of his back swing peeked out from beneath the wrapper, and the President smiled fondly at it. It was the leprechaun that made the towel so lucky, after all.

Another rivulet of sweat appeared on his cheek, and the President plucked the towel out of the pouch and tore off the paper.

CHAPTER TWENTY-TWO

"I WANT YOU to get this bird in the air right now! Fly, damn it!"

"Are you crazy?" Duke Masterson asked the woman who'd jumped into the front passenger seat of his chopper. He'd just returned from delivering a load of departing guests to the mainland, and the rotors hadn't even had time to stop when Madeline Hopewell had come running up and ordered him to take off.

"I'm not crazy," Jenn replied, pulling Adam's automatic from her purse. "Just very determined. Now fly."

Duke stared at her. "A hijacking? Where is it you want to go?"

"Down the island to Sandy Point."

Duke shook his head. "There's a no-fly zone for three miles around this island," he told her. "They've given me one flight path from here to the mainland straight over the bay and that's it. I deviate from that course, and I'll have three Hueys on my tail ready to blow me out of the sky."

"Yeah, but by that time, you'll be at Sandy Point. Now fly!"

"Give me one good reason," he said stubbornly. "Other than the gun."

"I think that the man who just tried to assassinate the President may be using the lighthouse as his point of escape, but so far I haven't had much luck in getting the Secret Service to listen to anything I've said. By the time they get around to checking it out, the Raven may have escaped." She didn't add that she had a personal stake in capturing the killer. It would have taken too long to explain to Duke that if the Raven escaped she might never be able to prove she hadn't conspired with him to kill the President.

Duke looked doubtful, but when Jenn reminded him of her gun, he revved up the engine of his chopper. Jenn reached for a headset and put it on, then hit a switch on the control panel that altered the radio frequency to the one the Secret Service was using. Unfortunately the chatter was so heavy on the channel that it was impossible for her to tell what was going on. Jenn thumbed the button of the microphone of her headset and tried to break in, but nothing happened.

"How the hell do I break through this chatter to let them know what's going on?" she shouted to the pilot as he put the chopper into the air.

"You can't. They've got that frequency locked out to all but their own communications," he shouted back over the roar of the engine. The chopper was going straight up, and Duke intended to keep it that way. His only chance of not being shot down was to cross the island at his optimum altitude. By the time the Coast Guard and the Air Force figured out that he wasn't going to be following his proscribed flight path and reacted to his defiance, he would be landing on the other side of the island.

"Then how can I let Luther know—"

"Call the resort." Keeping one hand on the stick, Duke slipped into his own headset and flipped the radio channel to another frequency. "Chopper One to Desk. Come in, Desk. I have an emergency situation."

"Duke? What's wrong?" The voice that came back over the headset was that of Liz Jermain.

"You're not going to believe this, Liz, but I've been hijacked, and I fully expect to be shot down in flames any second now."

"Don't get cute, Duke," she scolded him, her voice filled with panic. "Things have gone crazy here. What do you mean you've been hijacked?"

"Just what I said. I've got a guest with a gun and a crazy story about someone trying to assassinate the President."

"Someone did!" Liz told him. "Duke, what's going on out there? Are you all right?"

"He's fine," Jenn answered for him. "Ms. Jermain, this is Maddy Hopewell," she said. "Is the President all right?"

"I don't know. The Secret Service is crazy here! Something's happened but no one will tell us what!"

"I need to get a message through to Agent Luther immediately!" Jenn said. "Tell him I think the Raven is trying to leave the island from the lighthouse. Have him mobilize Tac Two and get them there immediately!" she demanded, then shut off the channel.

"The President is dead," Duke muttered.

"That's not what she said!" Jenn snapped, thinking of Jake trying to reach the President and remembering every horror story she'd ever heard about airborne viral contagions and how quickly they could spread—and how many they could kill.

Had Jake reached the President in time, or had he only gotten close enough to be caught by the deadly virus?

Jenn couldn't bear the thought. She shifted her mind away from the image just as Duke finally decided he was high enough and said, "Here goes nothin'." He veered sharply to the south, and within a matter of seconds was descending toward the lighthouse.

"Set down around the point!" Jenn instructed. "If he's really there, I'd rather he didn't see us coming."

"Bride's Bay Chopper One, this is Air Force Tactical! You are violating the no-fly zone. Halt your descent and immediately veer due east. Repeat, veer due east, away from the island. You will be intercepted and escorted back to your base."

"Look, Mrs. Hopewell—"

"My name's Jennifer Lambert, and I'm not letting you off the hook!" Jenn told him harshly. "Set us down, fast!"

"All right." He let the chopper fall straight down as fast as was aerodynamically possible, sending Jenn's stomach lurching and making her heart pound with a new infusion of adrenaline. The radio came to life again with more threats, but it no longer mattered to Jenn. The helicopter had landed near the road just around the bend from the lighthouse.

"Stay here!" Jenn commanded him as she flung off her headset and scrambled out the door.

"You can count on it!" Duke shouted after her, then flipped on his microphone so that he could start explaining his illegal actions to the irate air force officer who was ordering his missile-loaded Hueys into the air.

JENN PAUSED to catch her breath, crouching at the edge of the woods directly behind the keeper's cottage. She wasn't close enough now to see in any of the windows, and she knew from experience that all the access points were locked—with the possible exception of the one the Raven had used to enter the cottage.

The only open door she could count on was the one to the lighthouse itself. If she entered there, she'd have cover as she picked the lock of the door on the first-floor landing. Taking a deep breath, she sprinted across the narrow opening between the woods and the cottage, keeping low as she circled the tower.

As before, the door was ajar, and Jenn cautiously peered through. The tower well was deeply shadowed, but appeared empty. She moved through the door, her arms extended, with the Smith & Wesson in a steady two-handed grip.

Nothing but silence greeted her entrance.

She started for the stairs, stepping lightly so that her soft-soled shoes wouldn't create any noise that might echo in the well. She reached the steps and started up.

She was a quarter of the way up the first flight when she realized that the door that led into the second floor of the cottage was a few inches ajar.

She was halfway up the flight when the door opened completely and the Raven appeared on the landing wearing a pale blue wet suit and carrying tanks and flippers.

Jenn froze with her gun trained on him, and the shock on his face was so comical she wanted to laugh. She also wanted to shout out her joy at the victory she'd just won—after all, this was why she'd joined the

Agency. Moments like these were the ones she'd always counted on to fill the emptiness inside her.

But not knowing whether Jake was alive or dead only made that void yawn wider than it ever had before. For all the satisfaction that shocked look on the Raven's face brought her, she knew that capturing him—even killing him—wouldn't touch the emptiness inside her if Jake was dead.

"Well, well. Mrs. Hopewell. Or whatever your name is." The Raven's accent sounded slightly more European than he'd sounded that day in the health club. "I thought that you were a loose end I'd have to wait a while to tie up."

"Couldn't figure out a way to give me a stroke like poor Mr. Blaknee, huh?"

He gave her a disparaging look. "I never use any method of incapacitation twice on one job, and your bodyguards made it too difficult to arrange an accident."

"I guess it's lucky I ran into you today, then," Jenn said amiably, smiling up at him. "We'll get this over now, and I won't have to spend the rest of my life looking over my shoulder."

He nodded just as amiably. "And I can get on to other things," he said, taking a step toward her.

Jenn cocked the gun and the Raven froze. "If you would, please, very slowly and gently lower those tanks of compressed air to the floor, I'd be eternally grateful."

He didn't move. "Let me ask you something. Who, precisely, do you work for?"

Jenn shook her head. "Sorry. We're not going to play Twenty Questions here. Put down the tanks!" she commanded.

The Raven sighed heavily and slumped as though he was lowering the tanks to the floor, but the move was only a feint. He launched the air tanks at her and was flinging himself out of the way as Jenn clipped off one shot that was pure reflex. Before she could duck, the tanks hurtled into her, knocking her off her feet.

With no way to catch herself, she went tumbling down the stairs, her ribs taking a jolt against each step she hit. By the time she came to rest, there wasn't an ounce of air left in her lungs.

Gasping for breath, she tried to come to her feet and became aware of two things simultaneously. One was the roar of helicopter engines. The other was that the Raven had leapt to the bottom of the well and snatched up her gun before she'd even had a chance to start looking for it.

"Well, I see you've brought friends with you," he said mildly.

Jenn finally succeeded in catching enough breath to speak. "I don't know how *friendly* they are," she said between gasps of air as she straightened her purse, which had gone askew and slipped around to her back during her fall. "I had to hijack a helicopter and breach a no-fly zone to get here. They're probably out for my hide, so if you're thinking of using me as a hostage, I wouldn't count on getting any mileage out of their concern for my safety."

"It seems I have no choice but to take my chances," the Raven said, pointing Jenn's gun at her head. Since his hand was only about six inches away, she didn't think there was much chance he would miss.

"You said you hijacked a helicopter? Where is it?"

"Around the point."

"Let's go." He grabbed her arm and twisted her into position in front of him, the gun pressed into her temple.

Jenn figured that anything else she said about the unlikelihood of his chances for escape would sound like a cliché from a bad movie, so she kept her mouth shut and let the Raven use her as a shield. In tandem, they moved out the door and came face-to-face with the two gigantic, camouflage green-and-gray Huey helicopters that had landed only twenty yards down the beach. Soldiers with rifles trained on the door were lying on their bellies in the sand or were standing a perimeter; some were still running, fanning out to encircle the lighthouse. And behind them to the east, another Huey was landing.

Jenn took the risk of turning her head back toward him as far as the gun at her temple would allow. "You still think we're going to make it across the sand, through that perimeter with all those sharpshooters, to that little teeny tiny unarmed helicopter around the bend?"

"We're going to try," he replied. "Since I don't think I have anything to lose."

"Well, think again," Jenn muttered, giving her body a sharp twist downward, just as she stabbed her captor in the thigh with the stiletto-pointed nail file she'd managed to slip out of her purse when she'd straightened it across her shoulder.

The Raven howled in surprise and pain, and the gun discharged automatically, but Jenn's head was several inches below the muzzle by then. The blast hurt her eardrums, but nothing else, and she spun around, locking one leg around his to take him down. With his leg already injured, he didn't have a prayer of resisting her. He fell like a stone, and before he could do anything to compensate, Jenn had flipped him face-down with her knee pressing into his spine near the base of his neck.

The gun had fallen just out of her grasp, but she didn't need it. If he moved an inch in any direction, she could paralyze him for life just by pressing her knee a bit harder.

The Raven was captured!

THE LOBBY of the historic Bride's Bay hotel had turned into a zoo. With the media people, resort staff, hotel security, Secret Service, the air force officials who'd become involved, the Agency operatives who'd been working undercover and the Coast Guard commander who just didn't want to feel left out, there were enough clamoring people in the lobby to give a fire marshal apoplexy.

The President was alive and unharmed, but the media people had known immediately that something was wrong on the golf course when a half-dozen Secret Service men had tackled him, knocked his lucky towel out of his hands and spirited him to the bullet-proof van that hadn't been far away from him at any time during his vacation. The golf course had been cleared and virologists from the Center for Disease Control in Atlanta were already on the way to handle the analysis of the presumed murder weapon.

The President had been whisked off the island even before the Raven had been captured, but the assassin was gone now, too, though there'd been a lot of squabbling over who had jurisdiction. Dan Luther and Anthony Vernandas had been aboard the third helicopter that had landed, and while Luther quickly assumed control of the prisoner, he did so over the objections of the Air Force. Vernandas hadn't tried to take custody of the Raven, but within five minutes Luther had grown sick of being reminded that it was Jenn Lambert, an Agency operative, who had made the actual capture.

Now Luther was holding a press conference in the far corner of the lobby by the front desk. Jenn was sitting on the curving staircase about halfway up, so she had a good view of the show below, and Jake was in conference with Vernandas and Tom Graves near the door to the garden exit.

"Well, thank you very much, Ms. Hopewell, or Lambert, or whatever the hell your name is!"

Startled, Jenn looked down through the hand-lathed balusters and found the resort's helicopter pilot glaring up at her. "Mr. Masterson! Where have you been?"

"In custody, thanks to you!" he said, storming to the foot of the stairs and marching up. Jenn decided she'd better stand in case she needed to defend herself. The charming, devil-may-care pilot looked anything but charmed. "A very nasty air force colonel confiscated my chopper, put me under armed guard and forgot about me! Next time you want to stop an assassin, hijack somebody else, okay?"

Jenn gave up trying to keep a straight face. "I'm sorry I pulled a gun on you and got you in trouble with the Air Force, but we never would have captured the Raven without your help. In another five minutes, he'd have been swimming out to sea."

Duke looked moderately mollified. "Glad I could be of assistance."

"I'll have my boss make sure there are no charges against you. But I'd be more worried about your boss than the Air Force or the Secret Service if I were you," she said, looking down over his shoulder to the manager of the hotel, who was hurrying across the lobby. Jenn gestured toward her. "Ms. Jermain has been raising hell trying to find out what happened to you."

Duke turned and saw the woman he loved pushing her way through the crowd. Not knowing what to expect, he moved back down the stairs and was utterly stunned when Liz broke through the crowd and threw herself into his arms.

"Thank God you're all right!" she cried, running her hands across his shoulders, touching his face, making sure he was solid.

"I'm fine, Liz," he told her, then lowered his voice, a devilish twinkle in his eyes. "But you're not exactly being subtle, darling."

"I don't care."

"People will gossip," he warned her.

"I don't care about that, either. I'm just so relieved you're not hurt. I love you, Duke."

Jenn watched from above as the diamond-in-the-rough helicopter pilot gathered the aloof and elegant hotel manager into his arms and kissed her in front of an audience of resort-staff members. There was a moment of stunned silence followed by an outburst of applause.

Jenn was so intent on enjoying the show that she didn't realize Jake had joined her on the staircase until she heard, "Hmm. I didn't know those two were an item."

"Apparently nobody did," Jenn said, slanting a sidelong glance at the man beside her. "But he certainly knows how to treat a lady."

Jake looked at her, then did a double take as he tried to assess the sparkle in her eyes. "Miss Lambert, are you flirting with me?"

She put her hands on her hips in exasperation. "You mean you can't tell?"

Jake shook his head. "No. I can't. Two days ago I was a callous, manipulative bastard. Yesterday you were barely speaking to me. This morning, we graduated to communication with extreme suspicion. I'm not sure what to expect now."

"But all that was before I got my memory back," she replied. "You told me once that if I had Jenn Lambert's memories, I'd understand why you said the things you said, did the things you did. Well, you were right. I'm Jenn. I remember. And I do understand."

Jake was having a little trouble catching his breath. He'd seen that look in Jenn's eyes before. It was the look he'd seen once at a border crossing checkpoint in Israel eight years ago, and the same look she'd had in her eyes last week when he'd known she was about to tell him she loved him.

The first time he'd been so sure of the meaning of that look he'd asked her to marry him, and he'd ended up losing her because she said he was expecting too much from her. The second time he hadn't let her say the words. And this time...

This time he didn't know what to do. "Are you saying you forgive me, Jenn?" he asked.

She nodded slowly. "Yeah. I forgive you. In fact, one of these days I may even thank you for what you did to me."

"Why?"

"Because after all this time, you finally made me trust you. I had to lose my memory and become Maddy Hopewell to learn what I should have known eight years ago—that all the revenge in the world isn't going to fill the void in my life." Jenn slipped her hand into his and stepped closer to him. "You're the only thing that's ever done that, Jake. I want that feeling back."

Jake squeezed her hand gently and reached out to brush a smudge of dirt off her cheek. "If I take you to the lighthouse and ask you to marry me, will you say yes this time?"

She nodded. "Yeah. I will. I might even say yes if you asked me right here. In fact, I might even ask you myself. Will you marry me, Jacob Adam Hopewell Carmichael whatever-the-heck-your-name—"

Jake let out a joyful whoop, gathered her into his arms and silenced her with a long, gratifying, soul-stirring kiss that earned them the second standing ovation of the day at Bride's Bay Resort.

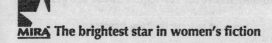

HARLEQUIN SUPERROMANCE®

WOMEN WHO *Dare*

They take chances, make changes and follow their hearts!

HOT & BOTHERED
by Ann Evans

Alexandria Sutton is hot on the trail of
Hunter Garrett. She needs to find him; he's
determined to avoid her. Join the chase in this
funny, touching, romantic story. It's a book you
won't want to put down.
Available in July.

Be sure to watch for upcoming titles in
Harlequin Superromance's exciting series,
WOMEN WHO DARE. Each story highlights our special
heroines—strong, caring, brave and passionate women who
know their own minds and dare anything...for love.

Available wherever Harlequin books are sold.

Look us up on-line at: http://www.romance.net

Bestselling authors

ELAINE COFFMAN
RUTH LANGAN
and
MARY McBRIDE

Together in one fabulous collection!

OUTLAW Brides

Available in June wherever Harlequin
books are sold.

HARLEQUIN ®

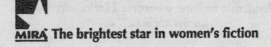